SWEET
for the
SUMMER

SARAH DELANY

Paperback ISBN: 978-0-6488144-6-7

Cover Design by: Amanda Walker

www.amandawalker.pa.com

Editing and Proofreading by: Rebecca Andrews

To everyone who said it's just for the summer.
You lied.
A little.

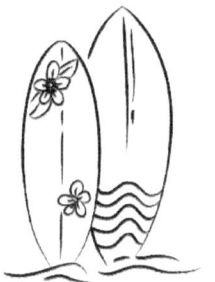

TABLE OF CONTENTS

PROLOGUE

Casey

Bright light pierces my vision as my lashes flicker to adjust. The sharp sting across my cheek registers as Colin's face comes into my view.

"Did you slap me?" My words slur as three blurry forms of Colin stare back at me. Before he can speak, the warm, foul contents of my stomach force their way out, drenching my shirt and pants.

"That is why I slapped you, you jackass. You were about to choke on your vomit while sleeping. You can thank me later." Even through my drunken haze, his anger mixed with sarcasm doesn't go amiss.

"Should have just let me choke," I mumble. The soft couch cushions my head as it flops backwards.

"I'll remember that for next time," he huffs, as he throws my legs to the floor so he can sit next to me. The dark room wraps around me as Colin turns off his phone light and slips it into his pocket. My eyes drift shut. "I can't keep doing this, Case." My brother's defeated voice catches my attention.

I welcome the numbness. It feels good amidst the chaos. With a resigned sigh, my head flops his way so he can see what little of my eyes are open. The heavy sadness wafts off him, penetrating through my drunken haze. My brain and heart no longer care. How do you explain to someone who loves you that you hold no value in your life anymore? You don't care whether you live or die. A bone deep tiredness sinks into you that nobody can understand, a tiredness you wish you could escape. And so, you do, with alcohol and any drug you can get your hands on to drag you into an oblivion you'd rather not wake from.

"Then don't," my scratchy voice whispers. Half hoping he heard it and half hoping he didn't. His deep inhale indicates he did. Colin is only eleven months younger than I. Irish twins are what they call us. I was born in January, and he came along in December of the same year. With our ages so close, we ended up doing everything together. Best friends are what we became, but complete opposites. Where he has his head on straight, mine is a constant mess. He handles stress well, whereas I don't. He's coped better with the lifestyle we were born into, whereas I've drowned in it.

Two people, similar in age and raised in the same home, ended up at opposite ends of the life scale. I believe I got the short straw in this situation.

The heaviness of my head pulls it forward, sizing up the room. People surround us, unaware and uncaring. In this room, you could disappear unnoticed. That's why I come here and hang out with them. Superficial, surface level friendships are what they are; they don't scratch the tiniest bit of anything deeper. I don't want them to either. If anyone scratched any deeper, they'd find the rotting wound of my soul that never heals.

All we have in common is our never ending need for an escape, and this is the place to find it.

A woman straddles a guy, grinding her hips while one of his hands claws at her naked back. His other hand wraps around her thick blonde hair, pulling her head back as his mouth attacks her neck.

The stench of cold vomit seeping through my clothes sobers me enough to clear my vision. More people dance on the side of the room. A few others take turns snorting white lines from the glass table in the corner.

"I'm leaving. Let me take you home?" Colin's words pull my attention back to him. I nod with a heavy head. He stands and offers a hand to pull me to my feet. I stumble into him, so he helps steady me. His arm around my waist leads me around the couch and through the unkempt house. People are everywhere, and my eyes close again as Colin drags me along.

"Shit." My eyes flutter open at the panic in his voice, and his arm releases me. The sight of him bent over a strange girl, lying on the ground, unconscious, jolts me. The foul whiff of vomit sprayed around her mouth, and the floor fill my nose. My attention focuses on Colin, who pushes down on her chest, his phone to his ear. His frantic words don't pierce through my brain fog as I stare at the lifeless body of the stranger.

My gaze travels back to Colin. Fear stares at me, hitting me in the chest. This could have been me if he hadn't come looking for me. With that final thought, my knees give, and the remaining contents of my stomach find their way out.

CHAPTER ONE

Dec 1st

Alexis

At dawn, crystal clear blue waves greet the first surfers of the day. Miles and miles of scorching white sand. Freedom for the summer, living my best life. What's not to adore about Wattle Downs, a tranquil Australian coastal town?

I've spent every summer here since I was eight years old, when my parents separated. Mum and I live a few hours away, because it's better for me to stay in the same place for school. With my final year of university approaching, I'm unsure if I should stay with Mum or explore the great unknown. Wattle Downs calls for me to move here, too. With my education soon finishing, it's perfect timing. But I have an entire year before I need to decide. It doesn't stop a restlessness racing through me, daring me for something. But what? I don't know.

My dad is a free spirit. Mum adored his spirited nature until it became a source of stress. It stopped being cute when she stressed about bills and her daughter. My dad, however, only cared about catching his next wave. So, they drifted apart and split.

You'd think I'd be mad, but I'm not. I get the best of both worlds. A stable year at school to focus on my studies and then a summer of amazing freedom, enjoying the sun, sand, and surf. A life others dream of.

I can't explain the persistent, irritating itch under my skin by not having my next stage in life planned out.

So here we are, after the four hour trip we endure at the beginning of every summer. She's hinted that a part of her misses the town she used to love and live in so she gives herself a small taste of her past for one day every year. My parents aren't spiteful, and they get along well. Neither has had a lasting relationship, so when she drops me off, Dad offers her the couch for a night. She always accepts. He doesn't want her driving the other four hours home after driving here, so it works out. Mum gets a good night's sleep, and it gives Dad peace of mind that she's not exhausted behind the wheel.

As we pull into the long, bumpy driveway to Dad's small beach house, the memories from past years wash over me. Peace fills my soul, like it knows it's home. The salty scent of the sea assaults my nose as I step out of the air conditioned car. The rays of the sun warm my skin as a sense of homecoming settles in me.

"Welcome back, my little love bug," Dad calls, as he walks down the rickety porch stairs. My feet push off the gravel as I rush him and leap. His open arms catch me, and he swings me around twice before squeezing me in a warm embrace. It's hard being apart for the other ten months, but this moment right here makes it all worth it.

"Hey Darcy, beautiful as always," Dad greets Mum, over my shoulder.

"You need a haircut, Corbin," Mum says, before leaning forward for Dad to kiss her cheek. They always greet each other this way, and Dad never listens; his hair keeps getting longer. It hangs halfway down his back now, and he usually sports it in a plait most days. Today, it's unruly and hangs wild against his bare back without restraint. It's rare to see Dad wearing a shirt during his free time. He's at the beach so much that he doesn't see a point in putting one on for him to have to remove it again.

"It's good to see you, too, Darce," he says, as he releases me. Without a word, he does his usual walk to the boot of the car, retrieving my bags for me. Mum and I wait for him before we follow him into the small two bedroom house. He walks down the familiar hallway and pushes the door to my room open. He hasn't changed it, even though I only spend the summer with him. I once asked him about it. He said it wasn't worth it since I come back every summer. He thought it was a waste of energy to do anything else with it for the rest of the year.

He drops my bags on the wooden floor before he walks back towards the kitchen. Mum and I both take seats at the small round table in the corner of the open space.

"Lemonade?" he asks the pair of us.

"Yes, please," we both reply. He grabs glasses and fills them with his homemade lemonade. He knows it's my favourite.

"I've got the couch made up for you already, too, Darce," he informs Mum, as he places our full glasses in front of us.

"Thanks," Mum replies before she sips the tart, refreshing liquid.

"So, what are the plans for today? The usual trip down to the boardwalk?" Dad asks, as his drink touches his lips hidden under his moustache.

"You know me too well," Mum laughs.

7

"You're in time for the markets this year, too. I heard they were setting up over the weekend."

"Really?" Mum squeals.

"Yeah, Mike mentioned they wanted to be set up before Christmas this year."

"How is Mike doing these days?" Mum asks.

Mike is Dad's business partner and best friend. Together, they run a surfboard shop. They make their boards in our garage, which Dad converted into a large workshop. On the main street, you will find their shop filled with surf supplies and swimsuits. Dad also works as a lifeguard. He usually leads in the summer when it's busiest. Then, another lifeguard takes over in the winter. This way, Dad can focus on his shop.

"He's good. He's still seeing Megan, who he was with last summer."

"That's good to hear. It's about time he settled down," Mum says, which makes Dad roll his eyes as these two haven't settled down either.

"I'm going to change Mum, and then we can go to the boardwalk if you're ready," I say, as I lift the glass and finish my drink.

"Sounds good."

I push my chair back, place my glass in the sink and kiss Dad on the cheek before I head to my room to change. I grab one of my many bikinis out of my bag and change into it, then pull a pair of jean shorts over the bright red bottom half. Releasing my dark brown hair from its ponytail, I braid it so it hangs down my back. A pair of thongs completes my outfit, then I'm ready to go.

We leave Dad to it as Mum and I spend the day together. We always head to the boardwalk when we arrive. It seems to be Mum's favourite place in the small town. She said before it's where she met Dad. I've often wondered if they'd get back

8

together, but they both seem happy, so I keep those thoughts to myself.

It doesn't take us long to reach the boardwalk as Dad's place is only a few streets away from the beach. There are a few shortcuts we take to get there faster. My first glimpse of the beach for the summer, and I smile so hard it hurts. It's always the same as I remember it. People are swimming in the water. A few surfers are further out but the waves aren't very good today. People spread out on the white sand. They lay on towels and soak up the sun under the clear sky. This is my idea of heaven, and I'm fortunate enough I get to spend every summer here.

"Do you want to get something for your dad from the markets for our Christmas dinner tonight?" Mum asks.

"Yeah. Last year, they had some wind chimes I thought would look great hanging above his door. The wind blows that way, so it would be perfect."

"Sounds great. Let's go have a look."

With one last glance at the ocean, I can't wait to swim in, I follow Mum. Sand flies up when I kick my thongs off and dangle them from my fingers. The hot sand burns, so I quicken my steps until we reach the concrete path leading to the boardwalk. The concrete isn't any cooler, so I drop my thongs and wriggle my feet back into them, finding some relief. You forget how hot the sand is when you haven't been around it for months.

The boardwalk comes into view, and we climb the wooden stairs to reach the top. Dad was right, the markets are on early this year, and as I glance at Mum, her eyes shine with glee. We scan stall after stall. Everyone else is checking out the markets early as well. It's always a popular place until about two weeks after New Year's, when they pack up and head off to their new location.

Mum grabs some sarongs and a new necklace she likes the look of. I finally find the stall with the wind chimes and pull Mum's arm for her to follow me.

"Ooh, these are pretty," she says, her fingers brushing against a purple one with glass baubles.

"Do you think Dad would like one?" I ask, as my eyes roam around in search of one that would suit his house.

"Your dad would like anything you get for him, honey."

"What about this one?" I ask, pointing to a wooden one. It has a couple of gold butterflies dangling from it, as well as some painted and carved into the wood.

"Ooh, that's nice. I'm gonna get myself one too," Mum informs me.

I point out the one with the butterflies to the young girl at the makeshift counter. The sign says not to pull them down yourself. She grabs a small stepladder and climbs up the steel steps and unhooks it.

"Could you get this one for me, too, sweetie?" Mum asks, while standing under a metal wind chime. The chime has leaves painted on its base and gold leaves hanging from the strings. The girl places mine on the counter, then collects Mum's. She wraps them for us in bubble wrap and white paper before Mum pays.

"Thank you," we both call out again, as we leave the stall.

I follow Mum while she shops. She picks up earrings and some organic skin care products. They promise to make her skin look younger, but I don't think she needs them.

She checks out all the stores that catch her eye then she promises me ice cream. We head to Pierre's, a staple on the main strip, near Dad's shop.

Tutti Frutti is my first choice while Mum gets her favourite of rum and raisin. We lick the delicious dairy treat as it drips from the heat on our way back to Dad's. After being gone for a few

10

hours, we walk back in to be greeted by the delicious scent of what I associate with Christmas. His glazed, cooked ham sits on the table with a salad ready and waiting for us.

"Looks great, Corbin," Mum greets him, as she hauls all her bags of shopping into the living room.

"Well, I thought you two might be hungry after all the shopping you were bound to do. I thought we could start our annual Christmas dinner early." He juggles plates and cutlery to the table with another pitcher of lemonade.

"It looks great, Dad. Thanks."

"It was nothing, love bug. Now let's dig in," he says, pulling a seat out. He carves up the ham, and by the size of it, I know we are going to be eating leftovers for a few days. We serve up ham and salad onto our plates, and Dad grabs some bread rolls he'd forgotten to get from the bench.

A silence falls over the table as we eat our fill. As we eat, Dad asks about school and how the year has gone. When we are all stuffed from the delicious food, we move into the living room for our usual present giving. Mum and I always get Dad something together, and he always gets us individual presents. Mum buys me enough throughout the year, so I told her not to worry about Christmas. The fact I receive less has never been an issue for me, considering I spend every summer in this heavenly place. It's a gift itself. An attitude of gratitude is how I like to see it.

Mum hands Dad the wrapped wind chime, and his eyes light up when he opens it.

"Aww, this is amazing, ladies. Where should we hang it, love bug?" he asks, his eyes shifting to me.

"I thought right over the side door would be a suitable spot." He nods in agreement.

"I'll put a hook up there tomorrow. Thank you both," he says.

"You're welcome," I reply.

"Now Merry Christmas," he says, handing Mum a medium sized box wrapped in festive paper while he gives me a gift bag. I dig through mine, finding new surfing supplies plus a new swimsuit.

"Thanks, Dad," I say, smiling at him, as I'm always in need of new surfing supplies when I come here.

"I also have a new board for you," he beams, causing my eyes to widen.

"Aww, Dad, you didn't have to do that," I tell him, as I know how much work goes into making one, and he could use the money from the sale.

"It was nothing for my favourite daughter," he says.

"I'm your only daughter."

"Well, it makes it easier to be my favourite, doesn't it?" he jokes, making me roll my eyes.

"Very funny," I laugh.

"Thank you, Corbin. It's lovely," Mum gushes, as she wraps her new fuchsia shawl around her shoulders. Luckily, she didn't buy herself one today at the market.

"I saw it and I thought it would be something you'd like," Dad says, making her smile widen. "Now, do you want to come out for your first surf of the season with your old man? We could test out the new board?"

"Yes. Let's go. I'm dying to get out there," I blurt out, before I jump from my seat.

"Darce, you want to come watch? You can relax on the beach? It'll be cooler around this time."

"Yeah, I will actually," Mum says, as she stands. She walks over to Dad's small bookshelf and plucks a book from the shelf to take with her. Dad heads out to the garage and comes back with my brand new board. It's plain white, with streaks of pink and purple paint splatters.

"It's awesome, Dad. Thanks," I say, as I lean in and wrap my arms around his waist to squeeze him.

"Glad you like it." He squeezes my shoulder in a side hug before releasing me and handing me the board. He picks up his own bigger board and chucks me one of my old wetsuits that I'll put on once we reach the beach.

The three of us follow the same path Mum and I took earlier. I can't help but think it's an amazing start to the summer holiday. I bet this summer is going to be the best one yet.

CHAPTER TWO

Dec 2nd

Alexis

Saying goodbye to Mum in the morning is always bittersweet because I wish she could stay with me. She has to return to work, which is a shame. Even though I'm sad at her leaving, I wouldn't give up my summers here because they are the one part of the year when I experience complete freedom.

"I'll be back to get you on the twenty seventh," Mum reminds me.

"Yes, Mum. I'll be counting down the days," I joke, which only makes her shake her head at me before pulling me in for another hug.

She kisses me on the cheek before whispering in my ear, "Be safe, honey. I'll see you soon."

"Love you, Mum."

"Love you too." She releases me, and Dad steps forward to pull her in for a hug as well. She laughs at something he whispers, which I can't hear. "Take care of her, you ratbag," she tells him.

"You know I will. Message us when you get back home safe," he tells her, as he loops his arm over my shoulders.

"I will. I'm expecting weekly check ins, Alexis."

"Yes, Mum, I know the drill," I mutter, as it's always the same spiel with her.

"Well, I think I've got everything. I'd better go now, so I miss the traffic," she says, before she pulls me in for one final hug.

I squeeze her back and wait for her to release me. She hops into the driver's seat and winds down her window to wave as she backs out of the driveway and out of view.

"How about I whip us up bacon and eggs for breakfast?" Dad asks as he leads me into the house.

"Sounds great, Dad." I walk into the kitchen, and together we pull the ingredients out. I put the bread in the toaster while Dad throws the bacon in the pan. In record time, we are sitting at the table with our cutlery clinking as we eat.

"What are your plans for today?" Dad asks between bites.

"I was gonna head over to Kara's house and see if she and Ruby are around," I tell him.

"Awesome. I've got to head into the shop, so if you're around the strip, pop in and say hi. Otherwise, I'll be back around five to get dinner started."

"Will do." I push my chair back and pick up both our empty plates. Squeezing the dishwashing liquid in the sink, I run the water to fill it halfway and scrub the plates clean. I place them to the side to dry after I rinse the bubbles off. Dad and I found it's easier if we wash our dishes after every meal instead of letting them pile up. Mum has a dishwasher, so we usually wait until it's full, but I don't mind hand washing dishes when I'm here. There's something cathartic about it. "I'm gonna change and head out, Dad," I call to him, as he wanders off to his room.

"See ya later, love bug," he says, as he pops his head into the hall. He smiles before his head disappears back into his room.

I walk to my room and put on a black one piece swimsuit with an open back. I tie one of my old navy blue sarongs around my waist. My sunnies slide on my face before I pull my favourite straw hat on. In the hall, I snatch a towel from the cupboard and toss it in my bag and head out the side door to collect my thongs.

Kara only lives a few streets away from Dad's. She's in the opposite direction of the beach, but it's a nice day out, with only a few white clouds in the sky. A light breeze blows the trees I pass, but the warm air does nothing to cool me. The closer I get to Kara's house, the louder the familiar laughter sounds. I see her and Ruby in the front yard. They run back and forth on the grass, battling with water guns. Their laughter and squeals cause me to smile.

"Got a spare water gun for me?" I yell.

They stop and turn their heads. Then, their high pitched squeals increase. They drop their weapons and run at me, forgetting them.

"Lexi!" they call, seconds before I'm squeezed between the two of their soaking wet frames.

"Gosh, I missed you two," I admit, emotion washing over me as I hug them back.

"We missed you, too," Ruby tells me, as they release me. Their dripping wet hair, plastered to their faces.

"You cut and coloured your hair," I tell Kara, noticing her light brown highlights. Her hair now sits at her shoulders, while it used to hang down past her backside.

"Yeah, I was over the headaches I was getting from the weight of it. Plus, I wanted something different. You like?"

"I love it," I tell her.

Her smile brightens at my compliment.

"When did you arrive?" Ruby asks, as they walk towards the porch to sit on the wooden steps. I sit on a lower step and turn to face them.

"Yesterday. Mum and I checked out the market. Then we had our early Christmas dinner together and Mum left this morning," I informed them. "So, what's been going on around here?"

"The same old stuff. Courtney and Marcus broke up again in July and then got back together in September, but you know how off and on they are. Apart from that, I've been completing my online course. Can't wait for this last year to be over and then freedom." Ruby screams freedom at the top of her lungs, making us laugh.

"You're pretty free already, doofus," I say.

"You know what I mean. We'll have big decisions to make about our futures soon."

"I'm not too keen on that. I'd rather stay a kid forever," I admit.

"Me too," Kara says, holding up her hand for a high five, which I deliver.

"Well, I can't wait to live life on my terms. Do what I want when I want," Ruby adds.

"You pretty much live the life you want already, Rubes," Kara tells her.

"Ugh, I give up. Let's go to the beach."

"Yeah, let's go," Kara says. She stands up from the porch and grabs the two towels hanging over the railing. Then, she throws one to Ruby.

She catches it, and we start our way down the path I followed to get to Kara's house. We pass my dad's on the way, but his car is missing from the driveway, so he must have left for the shop already. They tell me about all the hookups from the year. Some surprised me, but a few were easy to predict. Kara and Ruby have been my friends since we were little, and we are always three peas in a pod when I come back for the summer.

The scorching summer heat has increased as it's nearing lunchtime now. I dig into my tote bag and pull out my sunscreen, squirting a bit onto my fingertips. I hold out the blue tube for the girls, and Kara takes it while I rub the thick cream onto my face and neck. We pass it around, and I squeeze a bit more, applying it to my shoulders. My skin tans during the summer months, even with sunscreen applied. We step through the bushes along the wooden path and take in the view. Small waves break the surface, so at least the ocean isn't calling me to run home and grab my board. We find a spot that has a bit of distance between other beach goers, and I shake out my towel to lie down on. The girls lay theirs down on either side of me and we enjoy the heat of the sun as it warms our skin.

My eyes flutter closed behind my sunglasses as I relax into my towel. The knot in my sarong slips loose. The soft fabric falls from my legs and settles at my sides.

"Oh, em gee, don't look, but there he is," Kara whispers beside me.

"Who?" I ask, leaning up onto my forearms to do the opposite of what she says.

"I said, don't look. Lie back down," she demands, pulling on my arm.

"Who is it, though?" I whisper back, scanning the crowd, not sure which direction I should be looking.

"Hottie at ten o'clock," Ruby tells me.

"Where is ten o'clock again?" I ask, confused.

"Heck, Lexi, wait till he passes, and I'll point him out," Kara tells me.

I scan the crowd while remaining unseen. There are too many people, so I can't tell who they're discussing. A few seconds pass before both Kara and Ruby lean up on their elbows.

"There. Dark hair," Kara says, directing me with her finger as it points to the back of a guy's head. Obstructing my view of his face is his dark brown hair, wavy and curling around his neck. His bare, toned back reveals lean muscles. White board shorts sit low on his hips, contrasting with his sun kissed skin from the season.

"Who is he?" The words leave my mouth, and I settle back on my towel, relaxing again.

"He's just the hottest guy ever," Kara chimes.

"He's some random guy who showed up in his van a couple of weeks ago. He pretty much sleeps in it. No one knows much about him," Ruby adds.

"I didn't see his face. You'll have to point him out again so I can see him next time," I tell them. Rolling over onto my stomach, I rest my forehead against the back of my hands, making a makeshift pillow. The girls follow suit and roll onto their stomachs as well.

"Don't worry, if you see his face, you'll know it's him. He's gorgeous," Kara gushes. I catch sight of Ruby's eye roll and hide the giggle, but Kara still catches it. "Laugh now, but you won't be laughing when you see that perfect angel face of his," Kara spouts, which only makes Ruby and me laugh harder.

Once we calm ourselves down, we lie in silence for a few minutes, the hum of the beach atmosphere soaking into me. The beach has always been my favourite place to be. The sound of crashing waves, kids laughing, and the salty ocean air relaxes me and makes me long for it. As if my soul needs it to survive. Right on cue, the ocean draws me towards it, and I jump up.

"I'm gonna go for a dip, you coming?" I ask, dropping my sunglasses onto my towel.

"Yeah, I need to cool off," Kara says, as she pushes herself up. She throws her shirt down and wriggles out of her shorts with her bikini underneath. Ruby does the same as her sundress gets pulled over her head, as her swimsuit is under it. Here, swimsuits are a must for every outfit. You never know when you might jump into the sea.

"Race ya," I yell, and their laughter follows me as I weave through the groups of people.

When the dry sand turns wet, Kara catches up to me, and Ruby isn't too far behind. We rush into the whitewater, then we lift our knees high to dive into the cold, salty current. The first wave hits me hard. The chill shocks my skin. Soon, the water warms up, feeling nice against my overheated body. We swim a little deeper until we wade, our arms slicing back and forth as our legs kick underneath us to keep us afloat. The crowded shoreline is in perfect view. There are a few surfers further down the shore, riding the waves that are bigger there. It's still not wavy enough for my liking, so I'm content to swim instead of surf for the time being.

I'm sure soon enough, there will be waves calling my name, I won't be able to resist.

CHAPTER THREE

<u>Dec 5th</u>

Alexis

Days here are carefree. They're spent rising before the sun to get a jump on the waves before too many people come out to the beach. The rest of the day doesn't follow much routine, and it's as easy as it's always been. After my morning surf, I join Dad for breakfast before we head our separate ways for the day.

"You know, Lexi, I'm short staffed for lifeguards at the moment, if you'd like to help your old man out a few days a week?" Dad's hopeful voice has my eyes peeking at him, as I hold my spoonful of cereal on its way to my mouth.

"How many days are we talking?" I ask, as I pop the crunchiness in and chew while I watch him.

"A couple of days would help me out, love bug. Plus, you'd get paid."

"Sure. It's not like I have anything major going on. Let me know which two days you need me, and I'll be there."

"Thanks, I appreciate it. If you know of anyone looking for work, send them my way. Buzz and Legs both moved away recently, and I haven't been able to replace them."

"I'm sure someone will come along to fill the spots, Dad. I'll ask Kara too." My hands wrap around the white porcelain bowl and lift it to drink. The best part of my cereal is the chocolate milk, and it's often wasted time trying to spoon feed myself. Much easier to drink straight out of the bowl. "Ahh," I add, which makes Dad shake his head with a smile as he turns towards the sink to rinse his coffee cup.

"Could you start tomorrow if you haven't got plans?"

"Sure, sounds great." He plants a kiss on top of my head.

"Thanks, love bug. I'm headed there now. You up to much?"

"Kara, Rubes, and I are going to the beach to soak up the sun. I'll see you down there."

"See you there. If not, I'll be here for dinner," he says with a wave, as he steps out the door.

My chair screeches as I push it back and walk to the sink. Thoughts of the beach distract me as my hands scrub our morning dishes before I gather my things and head out too. Kara and Ruby are both busy this morning, so they are meeting me later. A book in my bag will keep me occupied while I wait if I get bored while people watching.

Salt scented air hits me before I see sand, and I draw it into my lungs to savour it. I can never get enough of it, and I hope one day I can live this close to the beach.

It's only 9.00 am, and the beach is filling up with families and people looking to secure a good spot for the day. Wattle Downs attracts a lot of tourists during summer as the beach is one of the best on this side of the coast. I understand why they plan their summer holidays here.

Luckily, my small patch of sand I like to call my own, is free. I fling out my towel and lie down to soak up some of the sun before the heat becomes scorching. I slide my pale pink floppy hat over my face for shade, which heightens the surrounding sounds. Parents call kids back from the water. They suggest using sunscreen first. Laughter erupts from a group nearby. Waves crash on the shore, and seagulls soar above. A deep voice scolds Hugh for stealing food from strangers. A soft giggle escapes past my lips at the thought of this Hugh kid stealing food.

"Well, if it isn't one of my favourite people. I heard you were back in town. How you been, Cooper?"

My lips twitch at the sound of the familiar voice before someone pulls my hat off my face. I squint against the brightness of the sun. James' smiling face stares down from above as he stands, hovering over me. By his side, my pink hat dangles from his fingers while his amazing six pack blocks my view of the ocean. As my smile widens at the sight of his, I push up and fling my arms around his neck.

"I've been good. You?" His arms squeeze me tighter against him before he lets go and tucks a stray hair behind my ear.

"Better now you're here," he admits, which has my cheeks heating. His blue eyes sparkle as they stare back at me.

"It's good to see you, too." Dropping my butt back on my towel, he follows suit and sits on the sand beside me before popping my hat on my head.

"Are you keen on our usual summer arrangement?" he asks. His neck turns my way with hope in his eyes.

"Straight to the point, I see." A chuckle releases as he shrugs his shoulders.

"Just wanting to see where your head is this summer. You know me, I'm always down for our arrangement."

"Still haven't found a girl you see a future with yet?" I ask, and he holds my gaze for a few beats.

His eyes finally squinted as if his brain talked him out of saying anything. His eyes relinquish mine as he drops his gaze to the sand, shaking his head.

"Nah, no one around here," he says in a gentle tone.

James and I have had a thing since we turned eighteen. James is a local from Wattle Downs, like Kara and Ruby. He grew up with us and has been our friend from the start. But as years went on, I knew he started to crush on me. I like James, but he's always liked me more. At eighteen, we lost our virginities to each other. I thought it was silly to head to university, still a virgin. James was more than happy to be the one to help me.

Since then, we've spent the last few summers hooking up. It was an arrangement we kind of fell into without meaning to. Now, as I look at James and I know deep down he feels and wants more with me, I can't bear to lead him on. Even though it's going to hurt him, I'm only going to keep hurting him if I keep this arrangement up.

"Is it okay if we don't this summer?" I ask, my face scrunching up as I wait for his reply. His bare shoulder pushes against mine.

"It's fine, Coops. But if you change your mind, you know where to find me." He winks, and his perfect dimples peek through, which lightens the mood.

"Thanks, James. Oh, I was gonna ask, are you free for some lifeguard shifts? Dad needs some people to help since Buzz and Legs left," I ask, knowing James has worked as a lifeguard in the past.

"That would work. I'm not doing anything else since I'm on break, so I might as well make some cash out of it."

"Awesome. I'll let Dad know. Unless you want to go see him yourself. He said he'd be up at the tower today."

"I'll head up there now. You wanna join or you gonna keep baking?" he jokes, as he stands up. He wipes sand off his butt as I lie back down.

"Nah, you go. I'll be here if you wanna come, keep me company after. Kara and Ruby shouldn't be too far away either."

"Sweet. I'll be back soon, then."

My eyes track him through the crowd to the lifesaving tower on the beach.

Rising on my elbows, I scan the area, which has gotten jampacked within the last hour that I've been here. The sun's heat has risen, warming my skin. I dig through my tote and grab my blue sunscreen bottle. A few generous squirts of the ivory cream should be enough to cover me. I rub the lotion in until it leaves my skin shiny, and then finish rubbing it into my face.

People have always interested me. From a young age, I would watch and wonder what their back stories were. In my head, I'd make up my own stories about their lives. Some were princesses, hidden away in our small town. Others were regular folks, living ordinary lives as they passed through.

My gaze flickers around the people closest to me in search of someone to interest me. My hand searches my bag for my phone to listen to my latest playlist while my mind drifts elsewhere. I pop my earphones in and with a click of a few buttons, the relaxing instrumental fills my ears. When my back hits my towel, I relax into it and place my hat back over my face, settling in for a second time since someone interrupted me before.

CHAPTER FOUR

<u>Dec 5th</u>

Alexis

My skin burns from prolonged exposure to the sun. With no sign of the girls, I'll have to go for a swim alone to cool down. I wrap my earphones around my phone, then toss it into my tote. With confidence, I strut my way to the clear blue green waves calling my name. Cold water hits my feet first, soothing my heated skin. I walk further into the surf until the water level hits my ribs, then I fling my arms forward and dive under. A sigh releases as the refreshing cold coats my skin, providing a welcome change from the burn caused by the sun.

As my head pops back through the wave, I glance around. A few other swimmers are nearby, wading in the water too. Further down the beach, the waves are bigger, so that's where the surfers gather, competing for space and waves without taking each other out.

I'll have to come out tomorrow morning and catch some waves before it gets this busy. The smooth sand under me squishes between my toes as I push off and lay my body out flat to float. The sun's rays are blinding, so my eyes close, and a red glow fills behind my lids. It creates a feeling of warmth with the sun that runs through my body, heating my skin, even though it's in cold water.

With my arms wide, they stroke back and forth, keeping me afloat while I listen to the laughter of the people nearby. Time slips away as I drift into peaceful bliss. The sounds fade as people move away.

It's been long enough that the girls should have arrived by now, so I drop my body weight down to swim into shore. I've floated further out than I thought, with my feet not able to touch the sand. With a glance around, a wave bobbles me as they are bigger the further out I am. Time to head back to shore; I push my hands forward and glide my arms through the water in a freestyle stroke.

A sting on my waist has my head breaking the surface.

"Ahh, shoot," I wail, as the searing pain worsens. I rub my hands over my skin, trying to find the source of the pain. Then I notice a few smooth bodies floating nearby. Jellyfish. "Dammit," I grit out, before I continue swimming, trying to get away before the pain becomes too much. I need to anchor my feet, so I lower my body, searching for sand, but there's still nothing. I must be out deep still. Bobbing up and down, I keep an eye out for any more of the stinging culprits and try to keep my distance. When I think I'm clear, another sting hits my leg, and the pain pulls me under the water. Just my luck, I get stung twice.

A burning, prickling pain spreads across my skin. It's hard to stay afloat as the waves grow larger, the longer I'm out here. I choke on salt water as another wave hits me while I endure the pain. The people on the shore are unaware of the fight I'm having. I glance towards my dad's lifeguard tower, but it seems so far away, down the other side of the beach. I tap the top of my head. The lifeguards are watching the beach with binoculars, so I hope someone sees me and comes to help.

My skin burns from the stings, and I can't focus on much else. I glide my arms through the water, but the pain gets worse, draining my energy. My head dips below the surface again. Panic fires through me as I endure the pain.

When things can't get any worse, a commotion above the waves gives me a glimmer of hope. A stranger grabs me and hoists me into their arms.

"You okay?" a deep voice asks, as I wince at the pain.

"Jellyfish stings," I force out between gritted teeth.

"Hold on to me," he insists, as he grabs my arms and wraps them around his neck. He wraps my legs around his waist, but skims the place where I've been stung.

"Ouch. Sorry, they stung my stomach and leg," I inform him, and he nods. Even through the pain, I can't help but notice how close our bodies are. Lex, this is the most inappropriate time to be having dirty thoughts.

He takes my weight and swims us to shore, where the pain has left me drained.

"Do you need me to pee on it?" he asks, causing my eyes to bug out and my eyebrows to raise. And with that, my dirty thoughts are gone.

"What on this green earth did you say?" I ask, as I wriggle out of his arms.

"Do you need me to pee on it? It helps jellyfish stings, doesn't it?" his soft voice questions, and I look up at his face. His dark, wet hair sticks to his forehead as his deep brown eyes stare at me.

I admit he has a gorgeous face for someone who offered to pee on me.

"I don't know you. Even if I did, I wouldn't want you peeing on me. That's an old wives' tale about jellyfish stings. Plus, we are in a public space. Keep it in your pants and help me to the lifeguard station, please," I tell him.

He stares at me a beat longer, not responding to my snark.

"Ahh," I squeal, as the burn increases, and a wave of lightheadedness hits me.

"Come on," his deep octave whispers, before his firm hands wrap under my legs and hoist me back into his arms. He is getting too comfortable with me being close, but the pain makes that thought disappear.

I jiggle in his embrace as he jogs towards the tower, and I close my eyes and grit my teeth. My head tucks into the curve of his smooth neck, focusing on my breaths to distract myself from the pain. His feet hit the wooden ramp to the tower, and he slows down. I focus on his deep breaths instead of my pain.

"Thanks," I whisper, before the door flings open, and my dad's wide eyes stare at me and the stranger holding me.

"Love bug, what happened?" he asks, his voice fill with worry, as he reaches forward and takes me into his arms.

"Pretty sure I was stung by jellyfish on my stomach and leg," I tell him.

He walks through the door and lays me down on the bed they have in the tower for people throughout the day.

"Damn, you're the third one already today. We were about to put a warning out," he says, as he inspects my body. I glance down to check my stomach, and the red, angry welts stain my skin.

"Can you grab the vinegar bottle over there?" Dad asks the stranger who carried me in.

He grabs it and hands it over. Dad doesn't hesitate. He pours it over my inflamed skin and then soaks a small towel, which he lays over my stomach.

"Mozzie, can you grab some hot water for Lexi to soak in, please?" Dad yells out to the other lifeguard, who has been around since I was little.

"On it, boss."

"What's your name, kid?" Dad directs his attention to my saviour, which causes my eyes to follow. They rake up his tan, smooth toned body with wide shoulders until they land on his cute face.

"Casey, sir," he replies with that deep husk.

"I've seen you swimming out here the past week. You're exceptionally good," Dad admits.

"Thanks. I used to compete when I was younger."

"I haven't seen you around before; are you here on holiday?" Dad asks as Mozzie places a bucket of water at the end of the bed.

"Thanks, Moz," I say, making the man, who is like a second dad, wink at me.

"Hope it helps, Lex," he says, then walks away and pulls out his binoculars to scan the beach again.

Dad dunks another towel into the water before replacing the one on my stomach. He grabs my hand and pulls me forward, then lowers my leg into another bucket I hadn't seen filled with hot water.

"Just travelled for a bit and stopped here as it looked like a friendly town," Casey tells Dad.

"Well, if you're looking for work, I need some lifeguards if you're interested?"

"I don't know anything about life saving," Casey admits.

"We can teach you. Plus, you did what you needed today to rescue Lexi, so you're already off to a good start."

"Yeah. It sounds good. I could use the money, and I'm not doing anything else," he says.

"Great. If you hang around for a bit, we can talk more about it. Pipes over there can get you started on paperwork if you like." Dad points to where one of his other lifeguards sits, and Casey nods before heading that way.

"When I said send people my way, I didn't mean get injured, so they'd have to carry you in here, love bug," Dad jokes.

"Ha, ha, very funny. I'm enduring this awful pain just to complete your lifeguard team," I say, making Dad laugh.

"James popped in too and said you sent him, so thanks. Between you, the two guys, and hopefully Kara, I'll be fine for lifeguards this summer now."

"Glad I could be of help," I reply, as the pain lessens. "Can I start another day instead of tomorrow?"

"Yeah, sure. I'll work out the roster with you, James, and Casey on it and let you know where I'll fit you in. And can you let me know if Kara can help too?" Dad says, before replacing the towel on my side with another one. "Do you need me to take you home?"

"No, the girls were supposed to meet me here, but they must have gotten caught up with something else. I'll head back soon to my spot and see if they're there and ask Kara. If not, I'll head home."

"Make sure you head home and rest and call if you need anything."

"I will," I tell him, which makes him smile. I'm about to ask him if he'll still be home for dinner when Casey walks up beside Dad.

"Paperwork sorted, except Pipes needs my ID, but I lost it while travelling and haven't been able to replace it. Is that a problem?" His gaze flicks to Dad before he checks out my leg, still in the bucket of water. My cheeks heat from the intensity with which he stares at my leg.

"Would you be able to set up a P.O. Box at the post office and get it sent there?" Dad asks.

Casey's eyes widen as he stares at my leg in the bucket, and it's a beat before he replies, "Yeah, that should work. I'll get right on it."

"Sounds great. I was telling Lexi that I'll sort a roster and let you know. But if you come back tomorrow morning, I can put you on the shift then if you like?"

"Yeah, that suits me. I'll be here," he says, as his straight face looks at Dad. Dad pats him on the back twice in thanks, before Mozzie calls him away with an emergency out on the beach he's sighted.

The other lifeguards spring into action as someone dips under the waves and struggles to stay afloat.

"Get home and rest, love bug. I'll see you for dinner," Dad calls as he rushes out the door with Pipes hot on his tail.

Casey lingers in front of me, so I look up at him.

"Thanks again for the help. Sorry if I snapped earlier," I apologise.

"Nah, no need to apologise. You were in pain, so I don't blame you. If I had a stranger trying to pee on me when I'm in pain, I'd lose it too," he confesses, making me smile. "Do you need help to get home?"

"I should be fine now. I'm gonna head back and grab my stuff. Besides, home isn't too far."

"I'm heading out, anyway, so I'll walk you to your stuff at least." I nod, and he hands me a towel from the end of the bed to dry my leg off after I pull it out of the bucket.

"I'm gonna head out, Moz. See ya," I yell over to Mozzie, who is staring out the window, binoculars in his grasp.

"See ya, Lex. Stay out of trouble."

Casey and I walk side by side, out of the tower and down the ramp. My skin is still tender, and the bright red welts are still visible, but the sting isn't as bad as it first was.

When we hit the sand, Casey's voice breaks the silence, "I'm Casey, by the way. I should have introduced myself before."

"Alexis, but most people call me Lexi or Lex."

"So, you're from around here?"

"No, I spend my summers here with my dad, but the rest of the year with my mum."

"Oh, okay." He slows his steps to keep in line with me, as I'm slower than usual with my sore leg.

"So, where are you from?"

"Lexi," I hear yelled, which has me glancing around until I spot Kara and Ruby on their towels beside my stuff. Their eyes flicker back and forth between Casey and me, asking what I'm doing with him while not voicing it out loud.

"Casey, this is Kara and Ruby," I inform him, pointing to my friends. "Kara and Ruby, this is Casey. I got stung by jellyfish, and he helped me get to Dad."

"Oh my God, are you okay?" Kara squeals, pushing up from her towel, and Ruby follows. Both of their brows furrow as they inspect the redness on my side.

"Hey, I'm gonna head off. I guess I'll see you around." Casey draws my attention as my friends stare at him.

"Thanks again."

"No problem. Glad I could help," he says, before nodding to the girls and continuing down the beach.

The girls and I watch him, and to our surprise, a duck walks beside him as if they are together. Casey clicks his fingers, which makes the duck quack as if in response.

"Tell us everything," Ruby whispers, as if Casey could still hear.

"That's the mystery guy I was telling you about," Kara informs me, before she turns back to watch Casey walk away.

"That's the guy with the face of an angel?" I ask with a raised brow.

"Yes. He's gorgeous. Don't you think so?" Kara gushes as her eyes track him as he walks further away.

"He's cute, yeah, but I bet angels are cuter," I joke, which causes both to roll their eyes. My body flushes with the lie because if angels are good looking, then Casey would be right up there with them.

"Always so hard to please," Kara jokes to herself, making my own eyes roll.

"Someone is gonna break through that hard exterior of yours one day, Lex," Ruby adds.

"We'll see," I throw back.

"You never know. This Casey might be the one to do it," Kara adds. I raise both my brows at her.

"I thought you wanted him all for yourself," I question, making Ruby laugh.

"Well, he's gorgeous, so if something happened with us, I wouldn't turn him down. But if something happens with you two, it won't bother me. I don't even know the guy."

"Don't worry, I doubt anything will happen with us. I don't know him either."

"So, what happened?" Ruby asks again.

"Not much to tell. Like I said, he helped me when he saw I was in trouble, then he took me to Dad. Oh, and Dad asked him to be a lifeguard for the summer, which he's going to do. Before I forget, Dad asked if you're keen for some shifts yourself?" I ask, as I turn to face Kara.

"Yeah, I don't mind helping. Tell your dad to send me a roster. Did you talk to Casey much?" Kara asks.

"Not a lot. I was in pain, and then he walked me down here, and you guys were here. Dad said I need to go home and rest, plus I've had enough beach for the day. You guys wanna come, or you gonna hang out here a bit?" I ask, as I shake the sand off my towel before rolling it up and stuffing it in my tote. My pink floppy hat sits on my head as I sling my bag over my shoulder. Kara and Ruby look at each other before deciding.

"I'm keen to leave if you want company?" Ruby says, while Kara is already grabbing their things and packing up.

"Yeah, that would be nice. We can go veg out on the couch and watch a movie or something?"

"Let's go," Kara says, once she packs up all her stuff. Our feet push through the dry sand, making our way to the wooden path that will lead us towards the road home. I can't help my gaze wandering down the way Casey took in search of one more glimpse of the cute boy who helped me.

CHAPTER FIVE

Dec 6th

Casey

It's still dark out as my alarm on my phone wakes me. My hand scrambles to cancel the ringing melody that fills the van. Once silenced and with my eyes still closed, I draw five deep breaths into my lungs. The new routine I developed to begin my day is a healthier way than anything I've done in the past.

As the last breath pushes past my lips, I allow my eyes to open, ready to take on the day. I kick off the messy blanket with my sock covered feet. Then I scoot to the end of the mattress. I had the backseats taken out so I could fit a bed in here for my travels.

The dim lighting from the streetlamp that I'm parked close to lights up the tiny space of my Crombie van. Locating my clothes, I set out last night, I changed my outfit before removing my socks and sliding my thongs onto my feet.

Grabbing one of my full water bottles, I quench my thirst before I unlock the back door and push it upwards. Humid air fills my small space, making me sip another taste of water before I grab my toothbrush and paste. A few steps outside, I find the grassy hill in the small cove. I discovered it on my first night here a few weeks ago, and I've stayed here every night since.

As well as an amazing view first thing in the morning, it's peaceful. No one disturbs me out here. Very few people seem to venture out here at night, which is perfect for me. It lets me sleep.

"Quack quack," breaks the silence. My eyes drop to where my grey spotted friend stands next to me.

"Yeah, it is a nice day," I return.

Juggling my bottle, brush, and paste, I line up my brush with the thick white paste and scrub my teeth clean. With a large mouthful of water, I swish it around my mouth before spitting it onto the grass in front of me.

From this spot, the beach in view, there are already a few surfers making their way out into the sea. The sun, only now rising into the sky, is my hint to get a move on. I put my things away, including my friend, close the boot of the van and hop into the driver's seat. The short drive down a few side streets has me parked up on the main road to the beach in a couple of minutes.

My backpack sits on the passenger seat with a towel, hat, and sunscreen. Sliding the zip back, I throw in my phone, a bottle of water, and my sunglasses before getting out and locking up the van. I chuck the keys in with everything else and zip it up, slinging it over my shoulder.

My thongs pad down the wooden path before they hit the sand. My friend trails beside me, waddling.

"I'm gonna be busy today, so I'll meet you at the van later," I tell him. I like to believe he understands, as he's always there waiting for me at my van at the same time each day. Whether he does is another story.

"Quack," is his reply. He could be telling me to piss off for all I know, but I choose to believe he likes me. I nod in response and drop my bag on the sand. He wiggles himself into the sand next to my bag, getting situated while I head out to the water.

Further down the beach are a couple of surfers I saw from the cove. As I quicken my steps and dive into the water, breaking the surface, I watch them. I'm mesmerised by the way they control their boards, as if they are an extension of their bodies. Dedication to waking up this early, they must have a love for it.

I understand that feeling. When I was younger, I loved swimming competitively for years until I tired of it. I didn't want the pressure to compete or to be the best, as it was taking a toll. Early morning sessions and late nights spent in the pool every day are a hard effort when your heart isn't in it anymore. Swimming is still second nature to me, even though I stopped competing. My body still remembers.

Taking my eyes off the surfers, I let my body fall into muscle memory and glide through the water. Back and forth until I've done enough. With little effort, I swim until I've exhausted all I can while leaving some energy in the tank to get breakfast.

When I emerge from the water and walk up to the main road, the sun is still low. I've learnt where the mobile coffee cart likes to park, so it's my next stop. It's smart business that catches all the early morning surfers and swimmers before they begin their day. A delicious looking egg and bacon muffin catches my attention, and I order one along with my double shot latte to go.

With my hands full, I head back to the spot where I dropped my bag and take a seat next to my friend, who's fast asleep. Cold sand seeps over my toes as I push my feet into the sand and bend my knees. I turn the brown paper coffee cup back and forth, so it sits in the sand while I peel the white wrapper away from my muffin. Flakes of soft egg fall as I take a big bite, savouring the flavour. Two more mouthfuls, and I'm scrunching the empty wrapper into a ball in my fist.

My eyes roam across the surfers as my fingers graze my coffee before lifting it to my lips. The boiling heat burns my tongue as it still hasn't cooled, so I cradle the cup in two hands to let the heat warm my palms.

The surfers catch waves here and there, but there's one who stands out above the rest. Their body moves as if they are one with the ocean and have been surfing since birth. They must compete with the way they can ride every wave that they go after. It must be an innate ability to know which wave to choose, something I've never considered before.

As my drink cools, I take tentative sips while still enjoying the show. The sun has risen, lighting up the sand and surf as more people arrive. I keep glancing at the lifeguard tower in wait for someone. Before long, a few of them come in. I see Alexis's dad with his long braid down his back, so I push up from my seat.

"I'm off, bud. I'll see you later," I tell my feathered friend, who ends up shaking himself out of his sleep. He gives me a quack in recognition before I head towards the tower, ready to start my first day as a new lifeguard. I'm not sure whether this is the best thing, but I have no other plans, so it can't hurt. Right?

As my feet trudge through the sand, my eyes remain on the surfer that I had been watching. When they exit the water, I notice her long hair that runs down her back. With her board under her arm, she walks closer to me, and I see that it's Alexis. Realising it's her has me stopping in my tracks.

"Hey," I call out. The sound of my voice causes her eyes to look at me, and a small smile lights up her face.

"Hey, yourself," she replies.

"You looked great out there. Have you been surfing long?"

"Only since I was about four," she tells me, with a chuckle.

"Wow, that is a long time."

"Yeah, well, my dad has always surfed. He owns the local surfboard shop, along with being a lifeguard, so I guess it's in my blood. Are you off to the tower now?" she asks, as her head nods in that direction.

"Yeah, I am. How are you feeling after yesterday?"

"A lot better. The vinegar did the trick. I'm glad it wasn't pee, though," she jokes, before she winks at me. Her casualness about the situation has me laughing, which catches me off guard, and I cut my laugh short.

"Well, I'd better go. Don't want to be late on my first day," I tell her, and she nods as she hikes her board up in her arms to reposition it.

"See ya," she calls as I step away from her, and I can't help the wince that crosses my face when I turn away. I didn't make that awkward at all. I can't even talk to a pretty girl without making an idiot of myself.

Reaching the wooden ramp, I continue my way and push through the door into the tower.

"You made it," Alexis' Dad greets me.

I nod in reply, not sure what to say. I'm still feeling awkward from the conversation with Alexis.

"Come on, and we will get you sorted. We're about to go over everyone's positions for the day." I grab a seat like everyone else and listen as Corbin talks.

Corbin informs me I'll be following him for the day. At least I won't get thrown into the deep end. After everyone breaks up, he shows me around the tower and explains everyone's job. When we've run through all the basics, he has me sit next to him while he scans the beach with his binoculars. He hands me a pair of my own. Then, he points out things to observe. He suggests they might develop into something.

By the end of my shift, there haven't been many rescues, which Corbin informs me is a good day. He hands me a roster for the week before I leave and says he'll see me tomorrow.

It's only the early afternoon when I finish up, so I head down the beach toward the main street with all the shops. I grab a fish and some chips from the takeaway bar and carry the warm, wrapped parcel back to where my van is.

Flicking the boot open, I sit in the back with my legs up and my food resting on my lap, picking at it. It's a welcome meal since I hadn't eaten since the muffin this morning. Enjoying the view of swimmers and beachgoers around me, I lose track of time. It isn't until the familiar quack alerts me to my feathered friends' return that I realise the sun is setting.

I help him into the van, and then we set out on our way back to the cove for another night of summer sleep.

CHAPTER SIX

<u>Dec 7th</u>

Alexis

When Dad arrived home last night, he gave me the new roster and told me I was on shift today. So here I am, walking up the wooden ramp to the familiar tower to help Dad out. He's only got me on for two days a week, which suits me. I get to earn a little money, help Dad, plus still enjoy my summer holiday.

"Lex, great to have you on board today," Mozzie greets me, the moment I step inside the tower.

"Always good to be here, Moz," I tell him, smiling at one of Dad's oldest friends.

While I'm pushing my tote bag into one of the cubby holes in the back, I hear Dad's voice.

"I'm confident in your swimming ability to put you out on the sand today. You'll tail Pipes, and he'll help show you the ropes out there. The surf isn't looking rough at the moment either, so it's the perfect time to get you used to it."

Their heads pop around the corner as I finish putting my things away, and I see it's Casey he's talking to. His eyes glance at me, and he raises his head in a slight nod of recognition before his attention turns back to Dad.

"Hey, love bug, I'll have you paired up with Cheese today down one side of the beach, and Casey and Pipes will patrol the other."

"Sounds great, Dad." I smile his way before adding, "Morning, Casey. Don't worry, it's more fun being down on the beach than up in the tower." His lip twitches but lacks any hint of a smile. I realise then that I want to make him smile, so I add, "Don't pee on anyone and you'll be fine." His eyes shine back at me as his lips tug up. I also catch sight of Dad's raised eyebrows in my peripheral vision, but I pay him no attention.

"Don't worry, sir, I won't be peeing on anyone. It's an inside joke between me and Alexis," he stutters as he tries to reassure Dad.

"Call me Corbin, Casey. As long as you don't pee on anyone, especially my daughter, we won't have any problems," Dad teases.

The other lifeguards are gathering their supplies. They are packing bags for patrols in case we find someone injured. Having medical supplies and walkie talkies makes everything easier and faster, as we can contact base when needed.

"Okay, everyone, it's time to get out there. Call in any issues when they arise. Let's go." Dad's voice echoes in the space, and we all jump to attention and head out to our positions. Cheese and I head one way while Casey and Pipes head the other.

"Let's take the cruiser for a bit," Cheese suggests, so I jump in the passenger seat and throw my bag on the floor of the truck bed. The cruiser starts up, and I hold on to the side handle while I settle in for the bumpy ride down the beach.

"So, how have you been?" I make small talk as we travel around, keeping my eyes peeled for anything that may warrant our attention. It's still early out, so there aren't as many people here as there will be later. It's already in the high twenties and bound to hit the mid thirties by the afternoon. That's always a sign the beach will get packed with people wanting to come down and cool off. It's usually a given that most days of the summer, the beach is full. I can't say I blame anyone, as it's my favourite place to be as well.

"I've been good. Not much new is going on since I saw you last summer. How's Uni going?"

I release a sigh before saying, "Uni's good, I guess. Just not sure what I'm going to do after this final year."

"Are you still doing your engineering degree?"

"Yeah, still that. I'm not sure that's even the right fit for me anymore, though."

"You don't need to have it all figured out, kid. You're young, it'll all fall into place, eventually. Just remember to have fun along the way," he says, offering his advice, and I let it swirl around my head for a bit.

I've been worrying so much about the future that I'm missing out on all the fun. I should be looking forward to this last year of university, not dreading it.

"Thanks, Cheese." A peaceful smile lights my face as I settle on the decision to have more fun and not worry about the future for now.

We circle the beach in the cruiser, not noticing anything that needs our attention. Clear blue skies above are proving me right in that the beach fills up fast. With so many people around, the cruiser becomes more of a hazard, so we head back to the watchtower and park up.

After grabbing a quick bite to eat and a drink, we head back out on foot. It's only a few minutes into our second patrol of the day that Cheese's radio crackles with my dad's voice.

"A couple of people out in the water on the west end need help. Looks like one's dropping below the surface. I'm sending Waltz out with the jet ski if you and Lexi can swim out to reach them, too."

"Got it, boss," Cheese says. We've picked up speed and are sprinting down the west side. We scan the surf for what Dad spotted from the tower. "There," Cheese yells, as his finger points out over the surf. Two heads bob up and down while one pats its head, and the other keeps disappearing.

"Cheese," Pipes' voice sounds from behind, which causes us to turn. He and Casey come running up to us with their buoys slung over their shoulders.

"Casey and Lexi are with me. Cheese, you wait here and help Waltz get in the water," Pipes takes over directions, as he's second in charge after Dad.

Casey and I waste no time splashing through the whitewash until we are deep enough to dive under. We swim our hardest out to the victims. I can still see their heads bobbing in the distance when I lift my head to check I'm headed in the right direction. Adrenaline kicks in, and I use all the energy I have to keep my muscles moving, even when they burn from exertion.

"I'll get the one further out," Casey shouts, which makes me pause. He's already further out in the surf, having passed me. He is a strong swimmer.

I see the young woman within arm's reach, so grab her and help her hold on to my buoy until Waltz arrives with the jet ski.

"You good? I'll help Casey," Pipes says, and I nod, then he resumes swimming.

"It's alright. I've got you," I tell the woman, as she draws in deep breaths.

"My brother?" she asks, and my head whips in Casey's direction, where I see he's helping him onto his buoy, and Pipes is closing in on them. Casey catches me watching him and lifts a hand in the air to give me a thumbs up.

"The other lifeguard has him. Was it just the two of you out here?"

"Yeah. It got deep quick, and then neither of us could feel the sand, and we couldn't get back in," she puffs out between breaths.

"That's okay. Focus on slowing your breathing now. Help is coming, see?" I point towards the shore to show her where Waltz is out on his jet ski with Cheese coming out on his board.

Once Waltz reaches us, I give him a thumbs up so he knows I'm okay to wait for Cheese, and he can head to Casey, who is further out. Cheese doesn't take much longer to reach us, and then I help him get the woman on his board.

He steers the woman and the board towards shore with care, and I begin the swim back in. Waltz zips past with his passenger on the back, holding on tight to him. It's only a minute later, and I notice the powerful presence of Casey and Pipes gliding through the water beside me. Together we swim side by side into shore, but I'm sure if Casey wanted to, he could pass us with ease.

My feet hit sand, and Casey walks beside me while Pipes jogs to the two we rescued.

"You did well out there. You're a natural," I tell him. My knees lift and push through the waves while Casey walks with no struggle next to me.

"Thanks. It's a big adrenaline rush, that's for sure," he says, his laboured breathing the only sign he exerted himself out there.

"Yeah, it is. I don't know if you ever get used to it, either."

We find the others. They give the victims water and tell them not to swim too far if they aren't confident. We often scold people after we save them. But out in the surf, it can be life or death. Dad always says it's better for someone to feel hurt than to drown.

"You two, head back to the watchtower and take your breaks. We've got it from here," Cheese suggests, as he hands me a radio in case an emergency happens while making our way back.

Casey and I fall into step along the hot sand. No more words spoken as we each catch our breath.

"Great work out there, guys," Dad congratulates us as we enter the tower and pats Casey on the back. "Have a rest and something to eat before the last bit of your shift."

I walk over to my tote and grab out my sandwiches that I'd made this morning for my lunch. Casey grabs a muffin and a sandwich of his own out of his backpack, and we sit together at the small table.

"How long did you swim for?" I ask, breaking the silence.

He swallows his mouthful of water and says, "I've loved swimming since my parents put me in lessons as a baby. Then I got into competitive swimming, but I gave it up a few years ago."

"What made you give it up, if you don't mind me asking?"

"One day, I realised it was too much pressure, and I didn't want to live like that anymore. I was never going to make it to the Olympics or anything, so why continue to compete?"

I shrug my shoulders at him, not knowing what to say to his honesty. He averts his gaze after that and focuses on his water bottle. After thirty seconds of staring at it, he tips it and drains the rest. His hand flicks as he throws the plastic bottle away in the bin like a basketball player. He moves over to sit by Dad and watches out the tower window, talking to him about what Dad looks for. I'm not sure if he was expecting more of a comment from me about his swimming or not, but the way he left the table felt off. Either that, or the adrenaline from the save is wearing off.

Closing my eyes, I draw some deep breaths into my lungs. Calming my whole system down after a save has always helped me, especially if I need to go out and rescue someone again soon.

Cheese, Pipes and Waltz walk into the tower a little while longer for their breaks. The beach is quiet, so we relax until Dad spots someone else out in the surf needing help, and then it's all systems go again.

After the next rescue, Dad tells me and Casey to call it a day. I grab my things while Casey grabs his backpack, and we leave the tower together. My hand digs into my bag and locates my phone, which I turn back on. Ruby and Kara texted me about a bonfire party at the beach tonight, and they will meet me later.

Before Casey and I walk in different directions, I call out to him before I can rethink my decision.

"You free tonight?"

He stops his steps and raises an eyebrow at me.

"There's a bonfire party thing going on tonight if you want to meet some people. I'll be here with my friends." His silence lingers while he thinks it over.

"What time?" his deep voice finally asks.

"Around eight is when most people show up. I'll be here around then if you want to meet?"

"Sure. I'll see you then," he says, before turning his back and walking away down the path he took the other day. A small smile pulls at my lips as I watch him leave and begin the short walk home. Butterflies swirl in my stomach at the thought of seeing him soon, and I can't help my smile.

CHAPTER SEVEN

Dec 7th

Casey

The rest of the afternoon, I spent snoozing in the back of my van on the main street. I've learnt that this small town is very welcoming and the safest place on the planet. With the back of the van wide open, I can sleep away day or night if I choose, and no one would bother me or even contemplate robbing me. It's one of those towns where people leave their front door unlocked without a second thought about the boogie man coming to covet what's theirs.

After my much needed rest from an exhausting day, I walk along the main strip to find something for dinner. I had planned to relax tonight, but since Alexis invited me, I guess I'll show my face, if only for a little while. It doesn't hurt that I'll get to spend time with her outside of work.

I'm not sure what my plans are. At first, this town seemed unimportant. I was passing through. But after getting the lifeguard job and finishing my first shift, it's the perfect spot for summer.

It's the definition of stress free living here, and that's exactly what I need. Maybe it will help set me on the right path.

The crumpled burger wrapper soars into a nearby bin. I then finish my fizzy drink and toss that in, too. I'm not usually one to smash a burger, but with the calories I burnt today, it was very much needed.

I jump into the van and close my white frilly curtains for privacy. I put on my dark denim jeans and a plain black tee. There's no point in wearing sneakers around here, I've discovered, as you end up dragging sand around in them. So, I forego mine and slide my thongs on again, which are fast becoming a favourite item of clothing.

Before I left the city to travel, I was very much into labels and appearance. Everything had to be perfect, not a hair out of place, but here no one cares. I didn't bring many clothes with me when I left in a hurry either.

I run my hands through my now shaggy hair in the mornings, and that's the best it's going to get. It seems it's more common here, too. The old me would be more out of place here than ever.

A couple spritzes of my cologne that hardly gets used these days, and then I'm done. A light, warm breeze flows past me, so I take a seat on the stone wall that separates the road from the sand. My feet sway back and forth as they dangle above the sand, and I watch the last beach stragglers of the day.

Soft music plays from the beach. As the sun fades, more people come with foldout chairs, coolers, and drinks. A few people help each other roll big barrels across the sand before they set them up for the bonfires. There are five of them spread out across the sand, which they light up. This must be a regular occurrence over the summer, as they've perfected the setup to take the shortest time possible.

It's not long, and more people are joining. I remain perched on my spot on the wall, not wanting to mingle. I may have agreed to come, but it wasn't for me.

I hear infectious laughter and follow it. It leads me to the three girls. They joke around while going down the wooden path, dragging their cooler.

"Alexis," I call, and her head turns my way.

The slow, warm smile stretches across her beautiful face when she notices me on the wall. She changes direction and walks towards me. Her friends see her and follow.

"You came."

"Didn't have anything better to do, so thought I'd check it out. Hey," I say, once her friends reach us, then I offer them a head nod and jump down.

"Kara and Ruby, you guys remember Casey?" She gestures to me with her hand, and they nod with their big smiles on their faces.

"Casey, tell us about yourself. What brought you out here to little Wattle Downs?" Kara asks as she links her arm with mine and pulls me towards the barrels, closer to other people.

Ruby and Alexis walk beside us, getting stuck with lugging the cooler.

"Do you need help?" I offer, but Alexis shakes her head my way, so I turn my attention back to Kara. "Nothing really. I was passing through and it looked like a cool place, so I stopped and haven't left. Was thinking of spending the rest of the summer here before I move on," I tell her.

"Ooh, there's James and the gang," Ruby says beside me.

"Let's go introduce you." Kara pulls my arm, and I glance over the top of Ruby's head to Alexis with raised brows.

She shakes her head and lowers her eyes, but I see the smile she tries to hide at my misfortune.

"Lexi," the guy says, before I turn to see a picture perfect blond surfer guy as he takes a few steps towards her.

Her welcoming smile shines at him before he bends and wraps his arms around her calves, hoisting her straight up into the air. The way his loving gaze watches her as she looks at him from above makes it obvious that he's her boyfriend.

"James, put me down," she laughs, and he does, but not before spinning her around, which makes her laugh louder. She looks carefree from up there, and for a second, I wish I knew that kind of freedom.

He lowers her and then slings his arm around her shoulders, drawing her close to his side. His eyes focus on me, but he doesn't utter a word.

"James, this is Casey. Casey, this is James. James is another lifeguard on shift, so you two will probably work together," Alexis introduces us, and I nod my head in response.

"Sup," he says, before his attention turns back to Alexis. His arm around her shoulders moves across her collarbone, so he's holding her back to his front. "You want a drink?" his voice carries over the open space.

She turns her head and whispers something in his ear, then his arm loosens from around her. Ruby ends up pulling her away, and they both grab a fizzy drink from the cooler.

"Casey, do you want a drink?" Alexis asks me, with raised brows.

"I'll take a cola if you've got another," I reply, noticing that's what she holds in her hand.

She fishes through the cooler and hands me a cold one. Water droplets drip off it from the ice that's keeping it cold.

"Thanks."

"Guys, come sit with us," Kara calls from her spot, with the rest of the group.

Alexis stays near me as we settle around the others, who have scattered chairs surrounding a barrel, giving off heat.

"Take a seat if you like," Alexis suggests, so I take one only after she sits down in another. She and Ruby park the cooler between our chairs, and Ruby lays a beach blanket down to sit on.

"That's Marcus, Elle, Steph, Clayton, and Grotto." Alexis points each one out as they talk in their different conversations.

"Grotto?"

"Don't ask," she laughs, as she lifts her can to her lips and takes a sip.

"What's up with all the nicknames people have around here?" I ask.

"It's a thing everyone does. Don't worry, I'm sure the other lifeguards will have an embarrassing one for you soon enough," which she laughs at. Her jovial mood is infectious, and I can't help but bask in the warmth she brings. If I hang around her enough, will it rub off on me?

Everyone falls into conversations about old memories, and I enjoy listening to the stories they share. The way they joke around with each other, you can tell that they've been friends for a long time.

More people arrive as the night sets in, with a humid air circling us. At least it's not cold being so close to the sea. Some of the group are drinking beers, and you can tell which ones when they get louder as the night progresses.

Lost in my thoughts, I observe the group. They all seem welcoming enough, except James is a tad standoffish. I do notice that he doesn't come over to Alexis again, and it makes me wonder what she said to him earlier.

"Quack, quack," sounds behind me, and I stand up so fast my chair falls over.

"Shit. Sorry, dude, I forgot." I apologise as I pick my chair back up.

"Quack."

"Are you talking to the duck?" Alexis asks, and as I turn her way to reply, I notice the group has gone silent, all watching me.

"Yeah, he's kind of my pet. Well, pet slash friend, you could say," I explain, as I shrug my shoulders.

"You have a pet duck?" Alexis asks, with wide eyes.

"Yeah, I came across him a few months back while I was travelling, and he had a broken leg. We were stuck in the outback, and there weren't any vet clinics around. So, I did the best I could, and I healed him up. His gait is quirky now. We usually go our way during the day but meet up at night. I forgot about him while thinking about meeting you." My cheeks heat at the slip of tongue about how I was thinking about her, but she doesn't seem to catch on.

"Aww, does he have a name?" she gushes.

"Hugh Quackman," I tell her, which has her and the rest of the group bursting out with laughter.

"And you were talking to us about nicknames," she laughs.

Hugh settles himself into the sand next to my chair and burrows down, content to sleep, while he waits for me.

"That is so cool, man," the guy named Marcus says, which the others agree with.

"Yeah, he is pretty cool, and he's low maintenance too," I tell them.

Alexis keeps her gaze on him, a wide smile on her face. Her eyes finally lift to mine, a radiant glow shining in their depths, and my lips pull up in response. I can't help but become mesmerised by her.

Everyone settles back into their conversations, and it isn't long before the exhausting day catches up with me, even with my nap.

I haven't swum full on for so long that the extra bout of exercise has drained me. It won't take long before I'm used to it, but today is not that day.

"Hey, I'm gonna head off," I say in a low voice, to avoid drawing attention to myself. I rest my hand on her bare shoulder, wanting physical contact with her.

"You sure?" Her hand reaches up and slides on top of mine.

"Yeah. It was a long day," I say, as my mind focuses on her hand touching mine.

"Okay, well, I'll either see you on shift or see you around, I'm sure," she says, as her fingers trace lazy patterns on the back of my hand.

"Night, and thanks for inviting me. I had fun," I tell her. I haven't been around other people lately, so it was nice to get out of my comfort zone and meet new people.

"Anytime," she replies, as she holds eye contact with me. With a last squeeze on her shoulder, I release my hand, but my fingers linger against her fingertips. It doesn't go unnoticed the way her breaths deepen at my touch.

I stand up and say, "Hugh, let's go," which startles him awake. He shakes off his feathers before he waddles up next to my feet.

"I'll see you guys around," I tell the group, and a range of farewells ensue. They even add in some goodbyes to Hugh, which pulls a smile out of me.

"Quack," is his response, which has the guys laughing and the girls gushing. I shake my head at my pal before walking away with him hot on my heels with his wonky waddle. I can't help but turn around to catch one last glance of Alexis, and I find her watching me as I walk away. She lifts her hand in a wave, which I return, which makes my heart thump in my chest.

We reach the van, and I put Hugh in before driving to our cove to sleep. I change out of my jeans and into some baggy shorts before I lie down. With Hugh curled up next to me and a hand under my head, I can't help the smile that forms. Tonight was a good night.

CHAPTER EIGHT

Dec 8th

Casey

The next day, I'm back at work, but instead of waking early, I changed my alarm to an hour later to sleep in. I skipped the morning swim to save energy for my lifeguard shift. If I have enough energy later, I'll swim tonight.

I'm not rostered on tomorrow, so that would work out better. The coffee cart calls my name as I pass it, so I grab a double shot latte and a delicious muffin. This time I ordered the banana choc chip, and it's my new favourite.

When I arrive at the watch tower, I'm greeted by a light hearted vibe from the other lifeguards.

"Morning, Casey, how did you pull up this morning?" Corbin asks, as he looks back from his place at the window. He's already scouting the beach for incidents requiring help.

"Pretty good," I tell him.

He nods before saying, "You'll get used to it. The action packed days are thrilling but also draining. Let me know if they take a toll and you need an extra day to recoup, or anything, okay? We need everyone on their A game while they are out there."

"Will do, boss," I tell him, which makes him smile. I put my backpack in a cubby hole before I head back over to him to gaze out the window a bit too.

"Have you sorted the P.O. box and your ID yet?" My throat dries, making me gulp harshly.

"Not yet, but I'll get on to it tomorrow when I have the day off."

"Awesome. Make sure you do, kid," he says, as his eyes flick back to his binoculars for a minute before he places them down on the counter in front of him. "Gather round, everyone. I've got your assignments."

When we all circle him, I notice James on the other side of the room. I catch his gaze and offer a head nod, which he returns with a straight face. No smile. Nothing. I don't know what I've done to step on his toes, but it feels like he's not happy with me.

"James, you'll be with Casey for the morning, then we'll switch," Corbin informs us. Just my luck, I get stuck with the guy who doesn't seem to like me. He lists off everyone else's partners and jobs, and then it's all go.

"Guess I'm with you today," I say to James, as I step over to him, offering him a friendly smile.

"Looks like it," he replies, but says nothing further. We grab our buoys, which we fling over our shoulders, and a radio each. James tosses me the backpack with medical supplies, and I follow him down the ramp towards the same side of the beach as yesterday. I grab his shoulder and spin him to face me.

"Did I do something wrong or step on your toes, cos I'm getting a weird vibe from you, man? Can we clear the air?" He lets out a deep exhale before he scrunches his eyes and stares at me.

"It's nothing. I take a while to warm up to people. Nothing against you, man." I feel he's not being completely honest.

"Cool, man. Well, if you've got any life saving tips that may help me, I'm all ears. I don't know much about any of this, but how to swim."

"Really?"

"Yeah, I only got the job cos Corbin was desperate, and I helped Alexis when she was stung by jellyfish the other day," I explain. His hand grasps my shoulder as his feet stop.

"Nah, Corbin must have seen potential in you, as he doesn't hire just anyone," he says, as he offers me his first genuine smile.

"Well, again, if you've got tips to help me learn, I'm ready to hear them," I tell him again, earning a chuckle before we walk again.

As we walk side by side, he offers me some of his tips he's learnt along the way. He tells me I'll gain a lot of knowledge on the job. It's one of those roles where you must experience things to grasp what's needed. He also says it's not all about saving people in the water. A lot of incidents happen on the sand, if not more than in the water.

We are about to pass near the skate park, which borders the far east side of the beach, when a crackle comes over the radio.

"James, race down to the west side. Three figures in the water," Corbin's voice comes through. We turn to race back towards the tower when a loud shriek sounds behind us. The kid lay at the bottom of the skate ramp, holding his elbow, crying.

James calls Corbin back, "Boss got a suspected broken arm at the skate park. What do you want us to do?"

"James, you stay with the break as you know the protocol and send Casey down to the water past the watchtower. Tell him he'll see the boat on the sand where they are."

I nod at James before I hand over the backpack of medical supplies, and then I'm racing back to the tower. My feet push as fast as they can through the dry sand. I manoeuvre my way towards the wet sand where the tide has been, as it's easier to run in and gain speed. The boat comes into view, surrounded by beachgoers watching the action. Waltz is beside the boat, along with Cheese on the other side, as they push it out. My radio sounds from my hip, so I unclip it to listen.

"Casey, swim out to the first person. The boat is heading to the two further out," Corbin tells me.

"Got it," I reply, before dumping my radio on the sand and heading into the water when I reach the spot where the boat was. As I run in, I look up and see the boat further out, passing the first person designated to me. With a burst, my arms dive out ahead of me and stroke through the water as fast as I can.

The person is about to drop under when I reach him, and he coughs out water. Situating him with the buoy, I turn on my back and hold his back to my front and swim us backwards towards shore. He continues to cough, and as my feet hit the sand, I stand up and pat his back as we walk onto dry sand, where he drops.

My eyes turn back to the boat, which is heading in as well, and has the other victims on board. Both had only swallowed some water and nothing life threatening. I spot my radio on the ground, so I pick it up, clipping it back to my hip. The small crowd disperses when they see that the action is over and people are safe.

Corbin's voice comes over the radio again. He's spotted another person going under the surf, back down the east side of the beach.

"I've got it, Cheese," I yell, as I take off again, exerting more energy. Corbin directs me where to go, and I see the young girl struggling. No time to waste as I lunge into the water and push myself harder than I did before. I lift my head to make sure I'm on the right trajectory and notice she goes down twice before not popping up again. The adrenaline pumping through me pushes my limbs even harder as I dive under the water, eyes peeled. I find her and pull her up, but she's unresponsive.

"Shit," I cuss, as I turn her head to the side. I drag her body the best I can while hoping she expels the water she must have swallowed. My heart beats faster as panic sets in. The firm sand meets my feet, and I'm running. I'm close to the skate park, and I can see James still there.

"James," I scream, which he hears over the beach noise. His body turns, and when he sees the girl in my arms, he races over.

By the time he gets to me, she's already on the ground, and I'm doing compressions on her chest. I hear James on his radio calling for backup. Two quick breaths in her mouth and back to compressions.

"Keep going. You're doing great," James encourages. Out of the corner of my eye, he takes her wrist in his hand, feeling for her pulse. It's another two breaths and a round of compressions, and then her chest heaves and water is expelled. We thrust her onto her side, so it all comes out.

"That's it," I tell her, as I rub her back, not sure what else to do.

"Good save," James' soft voice says, as he pats me on the back.

The sound of an ambulance arriving has James jumping up to lead them to us. Once they take over, I step back, and that's when it hits me. I expel the contents of my stomach onto the sand, not able to hold it in.

"It's okay, man," James says as he comes up beside me while I puke my guts out. "Happened to me on my first save, too."

61

When I can't vomit anything else up, I stand and wipe my mouth with the back of my hand. James pats my back as we watch the paramedics load the young girl into the ambulance. As she's pushed inside, a distraught, grey haired man runs down the beach, screaming for his granddaughter. At the sight of her, he breaks down in tears. He clasps both my and James' hands, thanking us before he jumps in the ambulance with her.

"Let's head back," James suggests, so I follow him back towards the tower, as water drips off me with every step.

"Did the break get sorted?" I ask.

"Yeah, the paramedics were with him when I heard you call out. He broke his forearm by the sounds of it."

Walking into the tower, they greet us with a loud round of applause, slaps on the back, and congratulate me on a good save.

"Awesome work, Cheetah. I knew I saw something special in you," Corbin tells me, which has me raising an eyebrow.

"Cheetah?"

"Well, you're fast. I thought you were a fast swimmer, but you're fast on the sand, too. And it's either that or Pipes suggested Hippo," he tells me, raising his eyebrow.

"Cheetah it is," I accept, making him let out a loud laugh.

"Cheetah it is," he says, and this time a huge, genuine smile lights up my face. I may have embarrassed myself with the vomit, but I sense this is where I need to be. And that's all right with me.

CHAPTER NINE

Dec 8th

Alexis

After a long day of perusing the markets with Kara and Ruby, I need to reset. Back home, I'm not used to being on the go all the time, surrounded by people. It's usually only Mum and me. I have a few friends, but we aren't in each other's faces every day like everyone is here.

My favourite way to reset is through water. Swim or surf. I don't mind, but surfing is my preference. There's still enough time before the sun sets to see if there are any waves worth going out for. If not, I'm more than happy to leave the board on the beach and swim instead.

Walking barefoot on the familiar path, I step around the last few people on the beach. The heat of the sun is fading, so families are packing up for the day to head home. The surf is calm, not a good wave in sight, so I head to my little spot on the sand and set my board down.

I drop my butt onto the warm sand, satisfied to sit for a minute and enjoy the salty air. It's still a little humid, so it isn't long before a slight perspiration adorns my skin. I wore a wetsuit down here, as I prefer to surf in one, but there's no need for it now. I could still swim in it, but I'd like the water to cool me off. Standing up, hand over my shoulder, I reach behind me as I grasp the strap for the zip. Pulling it down, I claw the tight material away from my body until I'm left in my pea green one piece.

The wetsuit hits my board with a thud as I drop it and sit back down. The sand is scratchy on my bare skin now. With my focus on the waves, I'm mesmerised as they glide in and out. Hypnotised and lost in thought, I pick up handfuls of sand, letting it drip through my fingers repeatedly.

"Love bug," Dad's voice breaks me out of my trance, and I glance in the direction it came from. "You going for a surf?"

"Nah, waves aren't looking good, but I'll head in for a swim."

"You want me to take your board? I've closed, so heading home now to make dinner," he offers.

"Yeah, that would be great, thanks. I don't think I'll be too long," I tell him, as I stand and hand him my wetsuit and board.

"Could you do me a favour before you head home?" he asks, and I raise my brows, waiting for him to continue. "Casey finished a hard shift. He had a close save, and I don't want it getting to him. I saw him down the beach there. I thought you could talk to him. Bring him home for dinner if you can talk him into it," he suggests.

"Sure, Dad, I'll check on him. Make extra in case I rock up with him," I tell him, then lean forward, kissing him on the cheek.

"Thanks, love bug. He seems like a good kid."

"Yeah, he does," I agree. I gather my bag I had with me and walk off in the direction Dad said Casey was. The air has cooled a little from when I first arrived, and there's hardly anyone left out on the beach now.

It isn't far from the watchtower that I catch sight of him seated on the sand. Knees bent with his arms crossed over them and his chin resting on his forearms, eyes on the water. A melancholy surrounds him while he looks so serene.

I've never been one to mince words, so I jump straight in, "Where are you? You seem like you're a million miles away." His eyes flick up towards me at the sound of my voice. A sadness laces his face before it's pulled back to leave his expression neutral.

"Hey Alexis, you out for a surf?" I drop down next to him before answering.

"Yeah, but the waves are non-existent, so I'm thinking about going for a swim instead. What are you doing out here?"

"Just thinking," he replies, as he lowers his chin back onto his arms in the same position, I caught him in when I arrived.

"Whatcha thinking about?"

"Are you always this nosy?" he asks, as I copy his position.

"You get used to it," I tell him, which gets a hmm sound in reply. The silence stretches, neither of us talking before I break it. "You wanna talk about it?"

"Not really."

"You sure? I'm a good listener."

"You sure about that, cos you seem to talk a lot," he deadpans.

"Hey, I can talk and listen. It's quite the skill. Come on, lighten the load," I coax, as I lean over and push my shoulder to his.

"You ever been unsure if you're doing the right thing?" he finally asks.

"Like what?"

"Today was intense with a close save. I felt good about it until an hour or two ago. Now, I'm not sure if I should stay or go home," he says, keeping his eyes on the water.

"Hard saves come with the lifesaving territory. It can be one of the most fulfilling jobs in the world, saving someone's life, but then there's the flip side. If you're not careful, it can drain you. I learnt to compartmentalise it all. Try to keep things separate from your emotions or else it'll become too much," I explain.

His head turns my way, so I follow suit and face him, our heads close as we stare at each other. I can't help but think that Kara is right about how gorgeous he is.

"And how did you do that?" his deep, husky voice asks.

"By distracting myself with something else when I'm not on shift," I tell him, but scrunch up an eye as my cheeks heat. Both his brows raised as he noticed my reaction.

"What is this distraction you speak of that has you blushing?" he asks, causing a light laugh to escape.

"Promise you won't judge?"

"I promise," he says, even softer.

"Sex," I whisper, as my whole face scrunches up this time.

"What?"

"Sex, okay? It's a good stress reliever," I tell him, as my entire face heats with this conversation.

"How does that help keep your emotions separate? Aren't your emotions tied in with sex?"

"Well, not when it's a friend with benefits arrangement and you have clear boundaries. Then it can be a beneficial agreement for both of you."

"Hmmm," he replies.

"What's hmm mean? You promised you wouldn't judge?"

"Not judging, just wondering who it was you had this friend with benefits arrangement with?"

"I'm not sure I want to tell you," I say, looking back out at sea.

"Why not?" he asks, his voice back to its normal pitch.

"Because you sound a little judgey," I tell him, as I stand. I pull my hair tie out of my hair before my fingers make quick work of plaiting my hair while he watches me. When I'm done, my hands rest on my hips.

"I wasn't judging," he says, before he stands facing off with me.

"Your tone implied there was judgment," I say, while I squint at him.

"Maybe you don't know my tones yet. There was no judgment," he defends, as he takes a step closer.

"I beg to differ," I argue, as I tilt my head to the side.

"Well, I think you need to cool off and have a think about it," he says, before he reaches out, grabbing my hips. I'm flung over his shoulder, bouncing against his back as his feet pound through the sand towards the water.

"Casey," I squeal, as his feet hit the water and it splashes. Droplets hit my face as I laugh at his playfulness. "Casey, put me down."

"As you wish," he replies, before he lunges forward with me still over his shoulder.

The cool water hits my body, and I stop myself from laughing in time, so I don't swallow a mouthful of seawater. His hands hold my hips, pulling me forward in front of him under the water. I pop up for air at the same time he does. A big smile lights up his face, while I can feel mine reflect his back. I take the moment to lunge forward with both hands, landing on his head. I push down so he goes back under, dunking him.

His hand on my ankle pulls me down with him as we tangle and wrestle in the water, trying to outdo each other. I'm not sure how long we play fight, but we are both panting by the end. Calling a truce while we catch our breaths.

The heavy sadness has gone from his face, replaced by a lightness. A wave of happiness washes over me, knowing I could do that for him. So, I gave him what he wanted on the beach.

"James."

"James?" he questions, with a tilt to his smile, knowing exactly what I'm telling him.

"It was James, the friend with benefits," I say, shrugging my shoulders.

"So, he isn't your boyfriend then?" he asks, creeping closer.

"No, what gave you that idea?"

"The way he greeted you at the bonfire," he says, his voice quiet as I notice the sun has set and darkness surrounds us.

"No, we're just friends now with no benefits," I tell him, rolling my eyes.

It's not until his hand grasps my wrist in the water that I realise how close he's gotten. With a light tug, he pulls me into his arms and on instinct, my arms and legs wrap around him.

"So, does that mean you need another friend you can benefit from?" His voice mixes with the light lull of the water surrounding us.

"Is that you offering?" I ask, my heart beating fast as my fingers travel to the base of his hairline, where his wavy hair hangs.

"Do you think it will be a problem with James? I don't want to make things weird. Plus, your dad is my boss. Perhaps this isn't a good idea," he rambles.

"James won't be a problem. We've been friends forever, and he knows our relationship was never more than physical."

"I doubt that was the case for him."

"What does that mean?"

68

"It means I've seen the way he looks at you, Alexis. I'm pretty sure he has feelings for you." Releasing a sigh, I rub my forehead.

"That's why I put an end to our arrangement, cos I know how he feels, and I don't feel the same. Don't worry about him. We can keep it a secret, so he won't be a problem."

"Are you sure?"

"Yeah. I'll deal with him if anything arises, but I'm sure it won't."

"And what about your dad?"

"What about him?"

"I don't want to lose my job."

"Weren't you just wondering if you were in the right place? Now you don't want to lose your job?" I tease.

"Hmm. I guess I do want to be here." A smile spreads across my face at his revelation.

"Don't stress about my dad. This arrangement is supposed to be about releasing stress, not causing it."

I wait as he stands there thinking before he says, "Okay, if you'll have me, I'm in," and his gaze dips to my lips.

"Just for the summer," I tell him.

"Just for the summer," he parrots.

"No deep conversations."

"Perfect."

"No falling in love. It's just sex," I remind him.

"No falling in love. Got it."

"Then okay, I'll have you," I tell him, and as soon as the words are out, his thick arms wrap around my waist, drawing me closer as he presses his lips to mine. My hands dive into his hair, angling his head to deepen the kiss as I swallow his moan. My body warms in the cool water from the way his mouth relishes the sensation. Minutes pass before I pull back, both of us panting. "We'll have to continue this another time, cos my dad invited you

69

for dinner." My wide smile shines at him as he lunges forward, pecking me before I dunk him under the water again.

I swim a little to shore before he gains on me. My feet could walk in, but I use my hands to propel myself forward by digging my fingers into the soft sand. Being in a playful mood myself, I don't want the moment to end once we get out of the water, like I know it will.

Glancing behind me, Casey stands a short distance away. I turn to face him, laughing as he grabs my ankle, pulling me back. He slides on top of me and wraps me in his arms, rolling us around as the whitewash hits us. Our laughter fills the air around us as he takes in a mouthful of water from not shutting his mouth fast enough. His coughing makes me laugh harder, which only makes him laugh and cough at the same time.

"Now I'm covered in sand," I laugh, as I step back into the water and dunk myself to get the sand from the whitewash off.

He copies me, removing the sand covering him.

"Come to dinner?"

"Yeah, dinner sounds great. I haven't had a home cooked meal in ages," he tells me, as he flings his head back, shaking his hair out of his eyes.

We walk back to the spot he sat in and grab our things. We both pull a towel out of our bags, drying off before wrapping them around us.

"I've got my van. I'll drive us," he suggests, so I follow him to where he's parked.

"Hey Hugh," I greet his cute friend, who waits with patience on the grassy patch in front of his van.

"Quack," he replies, and I can't help but laugh. He gathers Hugh in his arms and walks around to the driver's seat. I pull the passenger door open and hop in.

He drops Hugh into the back of the van, which I notice has a mattress and clothes strewn all over the place. Some packaged food and water bottles sit to the side as well.

"It's not much but handy for travelling around," he tells me, as he turns the van on and pulls out onto the road.

"Sounds like fun. The road taking you wherever you want to go. I can see the appeal. Follow the road. I'll tell you when to turn."

He follows my directions, and a few minutes later, we are pulling down the bumpy driveway, parking beside Dad's car. I jump out, and Casey follows and removes Hugh from the van, placing him on the porch.

"Dad, I'm home and we have company," I call out, as we walk through the door. Dad's smiling face pops around the wall.

"Cheetah. I'm glad you came." His happiness washes over him.

"Cheetah?"

"Did you not tell her your nickname?" Dad teases.

I let out a loud laugh as Casey's cheeks darken.

"Told you it wouldn't be long before you got a nickname," I laugh, which has Casey rolling his eyes. "So why Cheetah? Wouldn't Hippo suit you better, cos you're fast in the water?" I question.

"That's what Pipes said, too. But he's just as fast on the sand," Dad says.

"I say we put it to a vote," I tease.

"No. No way. Cheetah is bad enough, so we'll keep it to that, thanks," Casey states, which has Dad and me laughing.

"Set the table and I'll dish up," Dad tells me, as he turns his back on us. Casey uses his cheetah speed and steps into my back and tickles my sides while I try to hold my laughter in.

"Not funny," he whispers.

"Whatever you say, Hippo," I tease, and he tickles me harder, making me let out a louder laugh. The smile on his face is worth the tickling torture, though.

"Come on, you two. I'm starving," Dad calls, and Casey releases me.

I walk over to the cabinet and grab plates and cutlery, handing half to Casey to carry to the table. We set it up, and I tell Casey to take a seat while I fill some glasses with some of Dad's latest batch of lemonade. I hand one to Casey, which he sits next to his plate.

Dad places the serving plates of chicken pieces, steamed veggies and rice down and tells us to dig in. We waste no time passing plates around, and then we are quiet while we all enjoy the food.

"So, Casey, are you enjoying Wattle Downs?" Dad asks, as he leans back in his chair once he finishes. His arms rested on his belly.

"Yeah, I am. Everyone is super nice," Casey says. He pushes his finished plate forward, and he and Dad fall into a simple conversation while I finish my meal. They continue to talk and, once I'm done, I stand and gather their plates with my own.

"I can help," Casey offers, but I shake my head.

"No, it's okay. Sit and relax," I tell him, and he offers me a small smile. The water heats as it fills the sink and bubbles while I push the scraps into the bin. Hot water stings my fingers as I scrub the dishes and make quick work of them before I stack them to dry. I clear the little leftovers we have and wrap them up before placing them in the fridge.

"Do you guys want another drink?" I ask. My eyes flicker between the two as they both accept my offer. I refill their drinks and set the glasses in front of them before I sit back in my seat.

"So, where have you been staying?" Dad asks.

"I've been sleeping in the van. I've got a mattress in the back and it's all I need," Casey explains. Dad bites his bottom lip while he thinks.

"How about you sleep on the couch tonight? Any time you wanna crash there, you are more than welcome to. If not, you can keep the van parked in the driveway here and sleep there. For this old man's peace of mind," Dad explains.

"Thanks, Sir. I appreciate it."

"Hey now, none of that sir stuff, remember? How about I set up the couch for you tonight? You can grab a shower, and if you need to wash any clothes, we've got a washing machine and dryer," Dad offers.

"Thanks, that sounds great," Casey says.

"How about I show you the bathroom and the laundry while Dad sorts the couch?" I offer, which has Dad nodding as he pushes out of his chair. I lead the way down the short hall and point to the toilet door, the bathroom, and then the laundry.

"Towels are in here," I say, reaching up to the cabinet above the laundry sink and grabbing one down for him.

"Do you think your dad will care if Hugh sleeps in the house, cos he's slept with me ever since I found him? I don't want to leave him alone," he says, as his eyes concentrate on the ground.

"It'll be fine. Dad will get a kick out of Hugh," I tell him, smiling.

"Cool, I'll go get him and introduce them," he says, before turning and heading back that way.

I walk into my room and grab my pyjamas and a towel of my own for a much needed shower. When I step out of my room and take a few steps to the bathroom, I hear Dad's loud voice.

"No way. You have a pet duck?" and I can't help the giggle that escapes me as I peek down the hall and catch sight of Dad reaching out a hand to pet Hugh. It's with a smile on my face that

73

I relax and wash all the beach and the busy day away. Then I throw on my pyjamas and step back into the lounge. Dad sits cross legged on the floor, cuddling a tame Hugh. I can't help but feel giddy seeing the childlike look on Dad's face.

"He'll never want you and Hugh to leave now." My arrival has them both looking up at me with similar joyful expressions on their faces.

"I'll have a shower if that's okay. You good with Hugh?" Casey asks as he stands from where he sits on the couch.

"Yeah, yeah, go ahead. I've got him," Dad encourages, as he continues to stroke Hugh. Casey and I nod at each other as we pass by, and he heads to his van. He comes back with a laundry sack filled with his clothes and a spare set of clean ones to put on after his shower.

"I'll show you how to work the machine." I follow Casey back down to the laundry room. The machine is empty, so he tips all his clothes into it and sets his bag down. I close it, about to show him how to use it, when he stops me.

"Hold on. I wanna wash these," his husky voice says. He reaches forward and grabs the towel I'd given him and wraps it around his waist. He holds my gaze with a hint of a smile as he reaches underneath and removes his shorts and drops them in the machine. Then he grips his now dry but dirty shirt and pries it away from his body, and my pupils dilate at the sight. Trim, toned muscles fill my vision.

Casey must see something in my eyes cos he reaches forward, grabs me by the wrist, and places my fingers against his abs. My fingers explore, running over the ripples of muscle before his body pushes me back into the machine.

"I'm going to enjoy this friend with benefits," he whispers, right before his full lips lay a kiss on my neck.

I arch my neck, giving him a better angle. He delivers kisses right down the centre of my throat, stopping where the top of my pyjama top lies against my skin.

"Another time," he chuckles, before he delivers a quick kiss to my cheek and then pulls his warm body away.

"Definitely another time," I heave, which only makes his smile grow. "Okay, back to laundry." I show him what to press, add the washing liquid and set it to start. He walks out of the room first and steps into the bathroom. I head back to Dad, who is in the position I left him in, gushing over Hugh still.

"This is the raddest thing ever, Love bug," he exclaims, making me giggle even more. I finish tucking the sheet around the couch, cos it looks like Dad got too distracted by Hugh to do it. I throw some pillows and a blanket down too before I take a seat on the floor next to Dad.

"You want to hold him?" Dad asks, and I nod, curious what it feels like to hold a duck. I hold my hands out, and Dad passes him over with the greatest care.

"Quack," Hugh grunts to the two of us, disturbing him, but he settles in my arms once I have him. Cuddling down into my lap, he tucks his head in, content to sleep, while I pet his feathers with the back of my fingers. Casey finds us a few minutes later when he comes out of the shower.

"Well, I see Hugh is getting spoiled," he jokes, which only makes me and Dad laugh behind our hands so as not to wake Hugh.

"The couch is all set for you, and your washing shouldn't be too much longer. Do you wanna watch some TV while we wait?" I ask, and he nods.

"Okay, kiddos, that's my cue to hit the hay. Neither of you is rostered on tomorrow, are you?" Dad asks as he stands up.

"Nah," we both sing out.

"Well, get a good night's sleep then. Night," he says, before walking away.

"Night," we say in unison. Casey takes a seat on the couch next to where I sit on the floor.

"The remote is on the table there if you wanna put the TV on. I'm guessing you haven't watched anything lately if you've been living in the van for a while."

He grabs the remote and points it at the screen. It lights up and is on the movie channel. Casey seems content enough to leave it on whatever movie it landed on.

"It's been so long since I've been in a house. It's nice. Thank you," his husky voice says, as he reaches over and scratches Hugh's head. I angle my head back to catch his eyes.

"Like Dad said, whenever you want, the couch is free. Even if you want a shower or something, just pop over." He nods in reply. The beeping of the washing machine cycle finishing grabs our attention.

"I'll get that," he says, before hopping up and walking down the hall like he's been in the house more than a couple of hours. A few minutes later, he's back, and I hand over Hugh.

"I'm heading to bed. It's been a long day, and I wanna try to get up early and catch the waves since I didn't go surfing tonight," I explain.

"Do you mind if I join you in the morning? I usually have a morning swim if I'm up."

"Yeah, sounds good. I'll wake you in the morning," I say, as Casey lies down and pulls the blanket half over him. Hugh snuggles into his neck, and I can't help but smile.

"Perfect," he replies, holding my gaze. His hand reaches up to grasp my fingertips. He glides his rough pads over mine before he drops his hand down. "Night, Alexis."

"Night, Casey," I reply, before I turn and walk away. I flick off the lights and glance back at the guy on my couch. His duck snuggled against his neck. I can't shake the feeling that my heart might be in trouble. It's not just Casey's body that draws me in.

CHAPTER TEN

Dec 9th

Alexis

My room is still dark when the ringing of my alarm wakes me. I silence the alarm before tossing the covers aside. That's my cue to break free from my bed's warm embrace. Every summer, I've fought the battle of early risings. If I don't leap up at the first beep, sweet slumber will lure me back.

The creak from my bedroom door hinges is the only sound that fills the hallway. On light feet, I step towards where Casey is lying on the couch. The closer I get, Hugh can be seen still curled against his neck and Casey's slight movements.

"You awake?" I whisper.

"Yeah. Not used to sleeping somewhere other than the van," he says, as he removes Hugh from his neck and sits up.

"I'm gonna head out. You still keen to join me?" I ask, walking backwards towards the kitchen.

"Yeah, a swim would be good." I open the fridge and grab an up and go, and with the light of the fridge shining, I hold one up to show him.

He nods, so I throw the chocolate milky drink his way, which he catches. The fridge closes with a light thud. I rip my straw off before poking it in the hole and drain the drink.

"I'm gonna brush my teeth, then change," I tell him, as I throw my empty carton in the bin.

Casey heads outside with Hugh while I head to the bathroom and then back to my room to change.

As I'm coming out of my room, Casey enters the bathroom, and I head back to the lounge and fold the blanket he used while I wait. I have my tote over my shoulder that is always packed, ready for an impromptu surf session. He exits a couple of minutes later, and I nod to the door so he follows me.

My board lies against the side of the house, so I grab it, ready to walk the short distance to the beach that I usually take.

"Leave your van here, and we can come back after," I tell him.

"Sounds good," he says, then he steps back into the house, leaving his van keys on the buffet table beside the door. Hugh waddles around on the gravel outside, so Casey bends and says, "I'm going for a swim, but I'll be back soon. Wait here."

I can't help the smile that lights up my whole face as he stands up and stares at me.

"What?"

"You and your duck are cute, is all," I say, as my smile grows.

"Cute, huh? You sure you don't mean manly?" he asks, his voice dropping deeper, and I let out a laugh as I walk down the driveway.

"No, I was right the first time. It's cute," I tease.

He comes up beside me and plucks the board from my arm, offering to carry it for me without asking.

"You know, with this friend with benefits, you don't need to do coupley stuff," I tell him, as we head down the quiet street. It's nice to have someone to talk to on my normal walk. It's usually just me unless Dad has a day off work and can join me this early. Otherwise, he sleeps in until he has to get up for his shift.

"Just my gentlemanly tendencies. Wasn't even thinking of benefits actually," he confesses, as he shucks his shoulder to mine.

"Good. Don't want the lines getting blurred," I tell him.

"No lines blurred here," he says, with a straight face. "Our relationship is based on pure animal sex." His answer makes me pause for a minute. Then his devilish smile appears, and I crack up laughing.

"Okay, FYI, I'm not into any hippo sex," I tease, making him laugh.

"Come on, it's Cheetah, and even that is bad enough. Do you think I can get them to change it to something more manly, like Kong or something?" he ponders.

I laugh even harder as we push through the bushes that lead to the beach path.

"What? Like King Kong with the big dong?" His light laugh sounds, and I love the ease of the banter we have fallen into.

"You'll see soon enough," he replies before he winks at me, which only makes me laugh harder.

As we trudge through the sand, I stop at my normal spot and put my hands out for my board. He passes it over, and I push the tip into the sand as I examine the ocean. The waves are decent enough, and only a few surfers are out at the moment.

"I'm gonna head in. Meet back here when we're both done?" I ask, as I plait my hair behind me before yanking my board back out. I bend and attach the strap around my ankle as Casey pulls his shirt over his head one handed. The sight makes my skin heat.

"I'll be here," he tells me, before he ruffles my hair and runs off before I can stop him. With a serene smile on my face, I walk over, closer to where the other surfers are, and make my way into the water.

Casey is sitting in my spot when I emerge from the water, holding two brown takeaway coffee cups. I push my board into the sand, then I pull my towel from my tote. I dry my face and wrap it around my waist. Finally, I sit down next to him.

"Got you a latte. Not sure if you drink coffee or not. And it's a friendly gesture, nothing more," he comments, as he holds the cup out in front of me.

"Thank you." I take the cup from his fingers and hold it to my lips as I take a tentative sip to test the temperature. It's not burning hot, so I take a bigger mouthful. "That's good. Yes, I drink coffee. Especially when getting up early to surf. I usually need a good caffeine hit by the early afternoon."

We sit side by side, content with the silence as we consume our beverages and gaze out at the water. The sun is up now, and other early morning swimmers are emerging.

"You ready to head back?" I ask, after I finish my coffee.

"Yeah, let's go." We both stand, and Casey holds out his hand for my empty paper cup, so I hand it over so I can grab my tote and board. We pass a trash can on the way out, which he dumps the cups into, and then we walk the way back that we came. As we reach the driveway, Dad is walking down, heading to the tower.

"How was the surf?" he asks, as he passes.

"Great. Hopefully not too rough for you today," I tell him, as he leans forward and delivers a kiss to my cheek.

"You sleep well, Casey?"

"Yeah, I did, thanks."

"You're more than welcome to crash there again tonight. I'm cooking lamb chops for dinner if you're interested," Dad says, as he keeps moving down the driveway.

"Sounds delicious. I'll be here," Casey tells him, making Dad nod before he disappears.

A quack sounds from the side of his van, and out waddles Hugh.

"Good boy," Casey tells him, then he walks over and pets him.

"I'm gonna jump in the shower, then you're free to have one." I put my board back in its place against the side of the house.

"My clothes are still in the dryer, so I'll grab those."

He trails behind me as I walk into the house.

"We've got cereal if you are hungry as well." I point to the kitchen while I head down the hall to wash up.

It doesn't take me long to finish, and then I find Casey sitting at the table with two bowls of cereal, one waiting for me. I take the seat that's placed in front of me and give him a smile in thanks. His lips pull up in a seductive smirk across the table before his spoon meets his open mouth and closes around it. How he makes eating cereal look hot, I'll never know.

We finish up, and I take the dishes and wash them while he walks down the hallway to the shower. I walk into my room, and the cleaning bug hits, so I put things away. The dirty clothes go in the hamper, while I also place my clean clothes in their rightful drawers. I also make my bed, which is usually forgotten if I leave early for a surf.

Light knocking on my open door turns my head from where I'm bent, tucking the end of the blanket under the mattress. Casey's playful smile hits me in the chest as he kicks the door shut, and I know what's coming. He lunges forward and tackles me to the bed, drawing a giggle out of me.

"So with this arrangement, do we wait for it to happen, or are we like booty calls to each other?" His eyes stare down at me from his position above me.

"Both, I guess."

"Maybe we should have a code word or something?"

"Hmmm, maybe King Kong with the big dong?" I try to say it with a straight face, but my laughter ends up erupting out of me.

"You think you're so funny?" he accuses.

"Maybe a little."

His hand raises as the back of his finger slides across my temple to push a stray hair out of the way. My laughter dies as his gaze falls to my lips, and his weight presses into me. His face lowers, and I close my eyes in anticipation of his lips touching, but his nose runs along the length of mine in a slow motion upwards.

Warm lips press the softest kiss to the side of mine, out of reach. He draws his lips away and does the same on the other side. I want his lips on mine, but he teases me by leaving a trail of these soft kisses along my jaw. My lower body wriggles, wanting to feel him move against me, but he holds still, building the tension inside of me.

His lips trail down the other side of my jaw, and when he reaches my chin, I tilt my head to capture his lips and suck on his top lip hard. He gives in, and our tongues tangle together as we both take what we need. His hand grabs my thigh to lift my leg. He grinds against me as I run my fingers through his hair. I dig into his scalp to keep his mouth on mine.

One handed, he removes his shirt, discarding it somewhere. My hands explore his taut body as our movements get more needy. Putting space between us, he grabs the bottom of my shirt, so I take over pulling it off along with my sports bra.

His eyes fall to my breasts before he lowers his mouth and delivers sweet swipes of his rough tongue against my nipples. My back arches to give him more access.

The sharp tone of my phone ringing has Casey pulling away and holding his weight up as he looks at me.

"Damn it. That's my dad's ringtone. Hold up," I tell him, as I reach for my phone on my bedside table. With a swipe of my finger, I answer, "Hey Dad."

"Love bug, would you be able to fill in today, please? Pipe's daughter is sick, so he has to stay with her, so I'm short a lifeguard," he says. Casey's eyes smoulder at me as his lips pull up in a smile before he tries to attack my nipple again. My palm pushes against his face as a laugh bubbles up.

"Sure, Dad. I'll be there as soon as I can," I ramble out.

"Thanks, love bug. See you soon," he says, before hanging up.

"You are trouble," I tell a smirking Casey, as he captures my lips again.

"The best kind of trouble," he whispers, between kisses.

"Well, trouble, this is going to have to be short and sweet, cos I have to go help Dad on shift now," I tell him, as I drop my phone on the mattress.

"Short and sweet, I can do," he says, which makes me laugh. He leans back and hooks his fingers in the sides of my shorts and underwear, removing them before he pulls his clothes off.

My hand waves to the side to locate my drawer handle. I pull it open and grab the box of condoms out to get one. Holding it up for him, he takes it from my fingers, tears it open with his teeth and sheaths himself.

"Tell me what you need," he says, as his mouth moves back to continue his ministrations on my nipple. He uses his other hand to glide a finger down my wet slit before using my wetness to rub at my core. I moan at the sensation and he releases my nipple to suck on my neck.

"That's good," I draw out, which has his finger continuing. My hands wander over his firm body, getting their fill. He pulls back and hikes my leg back up as he shuffles forward and lines himself up with my centre. His eyes remain on me as he pushes his length in, and the urge to throw my head back and close my eyes is strong, but I keep them open. The delicious stretching feels good, and it's even better as I watch, mesmerised as he closes his own eyes at the sensation.

We let out soft moans when he is completely inside me. As he pulls out and thrusts back in, I close my eyes, lost in the sensation.

After a few pumps, he rolls us over so I'm hovering over him.

"Ride me," he instructs, so I do as he moves his thumb to continue rubbing the little bundle of nerves. His other hand digs into the flesh of my ass, helping me keep rhythm. "So beautiful," he adds, and my eyes fall to his. My heart flutters at his comment, and I realise if I'm not careful, I could end up falling for him, so it's best to nip it in the bud.

"You don't need to talk sweet, you know. It's not part of the deal," I tell him, as I speed up my motions with this help.

"Still true," he admits, which makes my skin heat. Pushing any emotions aside his words cause, I focus on the physical instead.

"Keep going," I tell him, so he keeps the same pressure as he rubs circles. My movements get messy as my release gets closer. The feeling builds before it explodes inside me, working its way up inside of me. Once I'm finished, he rolls us back over as his thrusts speed up, seeking his release. My hands splay over his ass helping him and moments later his eyes scrunch closed as it hits him. His eyes finally open as a lazy smile crosses his face.

"See, short and sweet," he comments, which makes me laugh.

"Okay, Casanova, off now, cos I gotta get a move on," I tell him.

He pulls out and lies down on the mattress to catch his breath as a light sheen of sweat covers his skin. Our clothes are scattered around the room from being flung in our frenzy. I gather them all up and dump them on the bed before pulling mine back on.

"You can stay here today if you like, or else dinner is around 6.30 pm," I inform him, as I pull my hair out and plait it with my nimble fingers.

"I'll head out and find something to waste the day away on," he says, as he pulls the condom off and then yanks his clothes back on.

"The markets up on the pier are quite good if you haven't checked them out already."

"Cool, I'll do that."

"Can I get your number?" I ask, as I gather my tote and check through it to make sure it has all my things.

"After round two already, are you?" his cocky voice says, and I can't help but smile.

"Something like that," I say, which makes him smile back. I hand over my phone for him to take, and he grasps it between two hands while he inputs his details. A low buzz sounds from his pocket as he explains he sent himself a text to get my number.

"You better hurry before your dad gets suspicious," he says, and I nod. "You want a ride?"

"Nah, a little jog won't kill me," I tell him, as I sling my bag over my shoulder. I throw the condom in the bin in the corner of my room and lead the way out of the house. Hugh waits on the grass off to the side of our driveway. "I'll see you later." He lifts his hand in a wave, which I return. I turn and pick up pace as my sandals thud against the ground in a jog. A smile shines from my face the whole way to the tower, and even though I'm puffing by the time I enter, it still doesn't disappear. I can't help but feel this summer got a lot more interesting.

CHAPTER ELEVEN

Dec 9th

Alexis

"What's got you glowing?"

I jump from Kara's voice behind me as I'm stuffing my bag into a cubbyhole. "What? Nothing," I deflect, as I turn away and head to where my dad is.

He has binoculars glued to his eyes as he peers out the window. It's a little overcast today, so the beach isn't as packed as it usually is. Still a lot out there, but the weather forecast predicts a storm coming in later. The big red and yellow flags are set up on the beach, too, as there's a rip out there that people need to be aware of.

"Thanks for coming in, love bug. I've paired you with Kara today since you're helping me out. For now, can you inform people to swim between the flags?"

"Sure, Dad. We're on it," I tell him, as I turn back to Kara. She hands me a buoy, and she shrugs her arms into the backpack with medical supplies in case it's needed.

"Soooo, you gonna spill the beans or what?" she asks again, as soon as our feet hit the sand. I wince before turning to face her.

"Promise you won't get mad?"

"Pfft, I doubt there's anything you could say that would make me mad, now spill," she demands, as we stand under the tower, her hands resting on her hips.

"I kind of might have somehow made a teeny weeny tiny little friends with benefits arrangement with Casey," I tell her, as I scrunch one side of my face, bracing for her reaction.

Her eyes widen as my words sink into her brain before she lunges, and her hand grabs my wrist. She pulls me under the shelter of the tower for privacy.

"You didn't?" She whispers, her mouth hanging open.

"I'm sorry. Are you mad?" I ask, grinding my teeth together.

"Are you kidding? No way. Bit gutted it wasn't me, but it's not like we had a love connection or anything," she admits, as she shrugs her shoulders. I push out a big exhale in relief.

"I was dreading telling you, given the way you talked about his angel face," I tell her, laughing. My feet push into the sand, and we walk away from the tower.

"Well, he still has an angel's face, and I'm glad one of us can enjoy his body. There are plenty of other hotties I've seen around here lately, anyway. So, have you guys done it yet?"

"Maybe," I say, as my cheeks heat and I turn away from her.

"Oh my gosh, you have, you little minx," she teases, giving my arm a playful whack. "Tell me everything."

"Not much to tell. I set the rules. Last night, he stayed on our couch at Dad's request. This morning, he came with me to surf. Afterwards, we went back to my place. Then, one thing led to another."

"Are you sure you understand your own rules, cos him sleeping on your couch is a bit close, don't you think?" she says, as she grabs my arm and halts my steps.

"It was Dad's idea. Think he's worried about him sleeping in the van all the time. It's fine. We'll be okay as long as we both see it's just sex." Yet, I can't help but wonder if she's right about him being too close. It was fine with James cos he didn't stay at my house, and it was only if one of us hit the other up; otherwise, we didn't do coupley stuff. I don't know why I'm worried. It's not like anyone has penetrated my heart so far in all my twenty one years. I'm sure I'll be fine.

"If you say so. I don't have a problem. It would be good for you to let your guard down and let someone in," Kara says, which I roll my eyes at. "What? We both know your walls are so high around you, not even a fire breathing dragon could get through them."

"Come on, let's go tell people to swim between the flags and worry about my guarded heart later."

She lets it go, and we split up. This way, we can cover ground fast and inform more people about the flags. Most are following the rules, but a few small kids in the whitewash are jumping over waves. I need to go out and get them to move. Can never be too careful with the ocean.

We walk back and forth along the beach, making sure everyone knows about the flags. The clouds overhead darken a lot, and it's around lunchtime when the first crackles of thunder sound in the sky. That alone is a deterrent for most people, but there are still a few stragglers who stay out hoping the weather will clear.

My radio at my hip sounds, and I hold it to my ear to listen.

"Team, clear the beach, we are gonna close it. The storm looks to be setting in. Get the ones out of the water first, then focus on the ones on the sand," Dad commands, and we spring into action.

Kara and I race to the flags, where there's a group of five people in the water, wading quite close to shore.

"Hey, we're closing the beach, so you need to come in now. It's not safe," Kara calls out to the swimmers.

They ignore her and continue swimming.

"Dad, they aren't listening," I say into the radio. Mozzie joins us before Dad can reply, and lightning shines across the sky.

"Get out of the water now, or else you'll each get a ten thousand dollar fine. If you can't afford that, I suggest you hustle," Mozzie's deep voice thunders across the beach, and the swimmers finally walk out of the water.

We stand watch as they walk back to their things, pick them up and then head off the sand. Leaving the beach deserted except for all the lifeguards.

"We can't hand out fines, can we?" Kara asks.

"They don't know that," Mozzie replies, as he winks at her. We all laugh as thunder sounds overhead again, and it gets us moving back towards the tower.

"Good work, team. We need to put up the closed beach signs as we go, but otherwise that's it for the day," Dad tells us, as everyone gathers their things to finish their shifts early.

"You hanging around?" I ask Dad.

"Yeah, I'll hang back a little to make sure no one is silly enough to venture down, but the storm is big, so people won't want to be out in it. Then I might pop into the shop and see Mike."

"Okay, I'll see you at home for dinner. I'm gonna head there now," I tell him, as I hike my bag high on my shoulder.

"Make sure you stay there too, or let me know if you leave."

"Will do, Dad. Love you," I say, before I reach up and kiss his cheek. "You ready to make a mad dash home, Kara?" I call across the room to where she's bent, grabbing her bag.

"You know it," she says, as we both smile at each other. It's happened a couple of times now that we've been on shift together in the past, and a storm has struck. We are lucky we both live close enough that it's not that far of a run for us.

I take off my thongs and push them into my bag, and Kara does the same, as they will only slow us down.

"Let's go," I yell, as we fling the door open and tread with ease down the ramp so as not to slip. Then our laughs fill the stormy air as we race across the sand while pelted by raindrops. Water drips down my face as our feet splash through the puddles down the street.

"I'll see you later," Kara calls, as she continues while I turn up my driveway. I wave back at her, which she does in return. Down the dark driveway, I find refuge on my verandah, where I glide my hand over my face and hair to get it out of my eyes. Wiping my feet back and forth on the welcome mat, I dry them the best I can before I enter.

My tote is completely soaked, so I empty it and put it in the wash along with my uniform. Then I wrap myself in a towel and go take a hot shower. When I'm finished and changed, I snuggle down on the couch to put a movie on, since there's not much to do on rainy days like this.

As I flick the button on the remote, my mind wanders to Casey and where he is. Holding my phone in my hands, I debate texting him to check on him. He is coming over for dinner, so I guess it isn't too much if I tell him to come back over now, so I know he's safe. That isn't against the rules, right? I'm worried about his safety.

My fingers race across the keyboard, typing the text and then sending it. It sits in my hand while my knee bounces in hope of a reply, but nothing comes. It's about fifteen minutes later when I hear the hum of a vehicle coming down the driveway.

I walk to the door to check who it is, and I'm greeted with a very wet looking Casey holding a contented Hugh.

"Quack."

"I take it he likes the rain?" I laugh as I step aside for them to enter.

"We went to check out the markets like you said, and he was following me around until the rain hit. The stalls started closing up to protect their stock, but not Hugh; he started splashing around in the puddles, taking a bath. Took me forever to catch him after I saw your text," he rambles.

"I'll get you guys a towel," I say, as I jog down the hall and bring two back with me.

"And yes, I'd love to come hide out from the storm here if that isn't already obvious," he states, as he lets out a sigh while he rubs Hugh dry.

"You don't say," I tease. "You're free to shower and warm up, too. I'm sure we have popcorn and stuff to munch on while we watch movies."

"Sounds great. I'd love a shower. Can you watch him while I grab some dry clothes? He's likely to get back out into the rain if I don't watch him like a hawk," he says, so I hold out my hands to take Hugh. Funny little thing sounds like such a handful over a bit of rain.

Casey jogs to his van and gathers his clothes, and is back inside within a couple of minutes. I close the door behind him before placing Hugh on the ground so that he can't escape.

"I'll shower."

"I'll start the popcorn," I tell him, as we part ways.

Seated on the couch with a big bowl of popcorn and both dry, we settle in for an action movie that is starting. Neither of us preferred what to watch, so we clicked on the first one that was available.

Casey sneezes next to me.

"Bless you," I say, before he sneezes again and then a third one. "You got the sneezles?" I laugh.

"Just a thing I do," he comments, and I can't help but laugh harder.

"You've got the cute thing down pat, you know that, right?"

"What do you mean?" he asks, with furrowed brows.

"Apparently, you have this angelic face, and you get the sneezles, and you have a pet duck. It's a pretty cute package," I tell him, as my eyes leave him and focus back on the screen. He snatches the remote off the table to pause the TV

"Back up, what is this about an angelic face?" he asks, with a huge smile on his face as my face heats.

"I said, apparently. It was not me commenting about your face either way. I'm saying some people, not me, think you have the face of an angel," I explain, with my arms crossed over my chest and pursed lips.

A beat passes before he releases the loudest laugh, and Hugh joins in with a quack.

"Great, now your duck is laughing too," I tease.

"Now I'm thinking that you're thinking about me naked with a little bow and arrow on my back like Cupid," he states, while holding his belly laughing.

"Ugh, forget I said anything. It wasn't me who thought it, anyway. FYI," I huff at him.

"Don't worry, I'm sure my angel looks will grow on you," he mocks, as he flutters his lashes at me, and I can't help but laugh at him.

"Just watch the movie," I say, as I whack him with one of the couch cushions.

"Oof," he exaggerates, as he grabs the cushion and holds it to his chest. His body wriggles as he settles back down into the couch, and we continue to watch. The room heats with the storm raging outside, so I open up two of the windows to let some air in, which is cooler with the rain still pouring.

"I gotta say the rain is quite nice," Casey says, as I take a seat beside him.

"Yeah, I don't think I've noticed much rain lately. It sucks that all the rain seems to come in the summer."

Back to watching the movie that isn't holding my attention at all, I soon find my head drifting.

"Love bug," I hear called, and I jump up, forgetting where I am for a second. Dad stood at the open door while I had fallen asleep, and my head was resting on Casey's shoulder. Casey lets out a yawn beside me that makes me think he must have drifted off to sleep as well. "Umm, you two might want to come see this?" Dad suggests, so we both get up and walk to the door.

There outside is Hugh paddling back and forth in a big puddle, having the time of his life.

"He must have escaped out the window," I guess, as Casey scratches his head.

"I can't take him anywhere. I swear," which has Dad chuckling.

"Leave the door open for him. When he tires, I'm sure he'll come in. I'm gonna get dinner on after I shower," Dad says, as he walks dripping down to the bathroom. I head down to the laundry and grab an old towel to dry the floor behind him.

"You wanna try watching another movie?" Casey asks, as I shuffle back and forth, cleaning up the water drops.

"Yeah, sounds good, although not action. That one put me right to sleep."

"Same," he agrees. He flicks through until he finds a romantic comedy that we settle in to watch and stay awake for. Dad even joins us to watch after he's got dinner cooking in the oven.

We spend the rest of the stormy night watching movies and only take a break when Dad announces he has finished dinner. Hugh finally comes waddling in with a quack when he's done, and as soon as Casey dries him down with a towel, he cuddles up on his lap and falls straight to sleep.

After the third movie, we call it a night, and Casey takes the couch again. Dad leaves, and when I hear the click of his door closing, I say good night to Casey as I walk backwards down the hall. From his spot lying down on the couch, he wriggles his index finger for me to go to him. With a bubbly feeling in my gut, I step back to him. He hooks a finger into my top and pulls me down. His lips press softly against mine.

"Good night, Alexis. Thanks for today," he whispers in a gentle tone, as I push back up.

"Good night, Casey," I whisper back, as I turn around. It's then that it hits me that Kara has a point about us being in each other's space a lot more. How can I keep my walls up if he is always around, waiting to pounce?

CHAPTER TWELVE

Dec 10th

Alexis

Sunlight streaming through the gap in my curtains pulls me from my blissful sleep. Rain and stormy weather always cause me to have restful sleep. I'm unsure if it's because it's like white noise to a baby and sends me to a deep slumber. As I stretch my arms and legs out, my muscles release the tension they hold.

My phone lies face down on my bedside table, so I grab it and glance at it. I didn't set my alarm last night because of the storm. There was no point in waking up early if it was still going this morning.

The blankets gather at my feet as I push them off before I get out of bed. I first head to the bathroom to relieve myself, then head to the kitchen.

"Morning," Casey greets me as he sits at the kitchen table with my dad. Both are holding a hot mug of coffee in front of them.

"Kettle's boiled if you are after a cup, love," Dad informs me.

I grab a mug of my own before making a cup of coffee and taking a seat beside them.

"What are your plans for today?" Dad asks, before he takes a sip from his steaming mug.

"I was thinking I could teach Casey to surf if you're keen, that is?" I ask, as I turn to Casey and wait for his reaction.

"Really? That would be awesome," he exclaims, which brings a smile to my face.

"Yeah, I was thinking if you leave this town with nothing else but the ability to surf, then at least you'd be taking a piece of Wattle Downs with you."

"Well, how can I say no when you put it like that?" he says, as his smile widens.

"You can use any of the boards I have stored in the garage, too, if you like," Dad suggests.

"Thanks," Casey replies.

"Since you guys have plans, I'm gonna head out. I'll be at the shop today. Pipes is in charge of the beach, so I'll be home in time for dinner," he says. I nod as he leans in and kisses my head. He places his finished coffee mug in the sink and walks out the door with a wave.

"I'll make some toast for our breakfast, and then we can head out too before the beach becomes too packed with people. It's looking like a nice day after the storm."

"Sounds good. I'm gonna change," he says. I grab four slices of bread from the bag and place them in the toaster. When they are brown, my knife glides butter across them, and I watch as it melts. Casey's footsteps sound behind me, so I put two on a plate for him and keep two for myself. We eat in silence before we place our plates in the sink and gather our things.

"It doesn't matter which board you use today. We are only going to start with the basics, so I'll grab one," I explain, as he pulls the door to the house closed. I jog to the garage and grab the closest board to the door before returning to him with it.

He grabs it out of my grip and moves it under one arm as we begin our walk to the beach.

The beach is still quite empty as the sand is still wet from the storm last night. It will be dry in no time, and then the beach will buzz with people again. So we'd better make the most of it.

"You can drop the board here," I instruct Casey, as we reach my spot of sand. He does as I say and places the all blue board down on the sand. My fingers work to braid my hair, just as they have a million times before, and then I remove the hair tie from my wrist and secure the end. "So today we are starting at the very beginning, and all you are going to practise is pop ups. You lie flat on the board as if you are paddling out to sea, and then you use your body to push yourself into a crouch position. I'll get you doing it over and over until it becomes second nature." He nods before he drops his body and lies face down.

"Like this?" he asks.

"Yeah, great. Put your legs together. It makes it easier to paddle if your feet are together, so you aren't creating extra drag in the surf with your legs hanging off the board," I explain.

His legs clap together as he listens, which makes me smile.

"Keep your chest up as you look ahead and pretend to paddle." I continue, and he follows my instructions one by one.

He pays no mind to the people who walk by and look at us, either.

"When the wave hits and you feel the push, paddle a bit more. Then, put your hands flat on the board under your chest. Push your chest up and tuck your toes onto the board," I say, watching him follow my instructions with precision. "That's great. It might be easier if I show you the pop up first, so let's swap positions for a second."

He stands and steps to the side, and I lie face down.

As I go through the motions, I explain what I'm doing.

"Place your hands under your chest. Push your chest up and tuck your toes under. Then, push up and float your legs so your front leg is under where your chin was." My body moves as muscle memory sets in, and I end up with my legs bent and body turned like I'm surfing a wave out at sea.

"You make it look effortless."

"I've been doing it a long time, so remember that. It might take some time to learn, but if you practice on a flat surface during your free time, you'll get the hang of it. I remember Dad put a board on my bed for me when I was little and had me practise on that every night before bed." A smile spreads across my face as the warm memory washes over me. I have a million happy memories from my summers here, but the ones that include mum and dad are by far my favourites.

"Practice makes perfect, huh?" Casey's voice cuts through my reminiscing, pulling me back to the present.

"Yeah, something like that. You wanna see it again, or you good?"

"Watching you in a bikini is worth it, so one more time won't hurt," he jokes, which makes my eyes roll and a smile form.

"One more time, so watch closely."

"That won't be a problem," his voice whispers, which only makes my smile grow before I run through the steps with him again. Once I'm done, we switch positions, and he gives it a go.

He moves in slow motion as his leg gets caught the first time he tries. The second time, he falls over into the sand, and the third, his hand slips out from under him, and his head hits the board.

"Ouch, you okay?" I ask, as I crouch beside him.

"Yeah, I'm fine. My ego took a hit, though," he says, as he sits on the board and rubs the red spot on his forehead.

"I told you I've been doing it for years. That's why it looks so easy. Trust me, once you practise, you'll be doing it in your sleep," I say as I pat him on the back. "Come on, let's go again."

He moves into position and lies face down, and begins all over again. I spend the next hour with him, repeating the motions. He becomes better each time. Still a beginner, but at least he isn't slipping and hurting himself anymore.

"Come on, let's head in for a swim before we head back to mine." I walk backwards towards the water.

His lazy eyes rake up my body before they land on my eyes, and he follows. I turn as he stands, then I take off running towards the beach as the sound of his feet hitting the sand sounds behind me. Two steps away from the cool water, and his arms wrap around me and haul me into the air as I squeal. He carries me a few feet before his body drops into the sea and takes me with him.

The water silences our laughter before we break the surface, spitting out water. My hands push water towards him, splashing him in the face. Unable to look away, I watch him fling his wet hair from his face. I must admit, he is cute. He catches me gawking, and a smile lights up his face before he sets his sights on me and comes my way. I turn and run, but he's faster and catches me before dunking me.

We spend the next few hours in the surf, playing and enjoying the freedom that comes along with the summer.

CHAPTER THIRTEEN

Dec 13th

Alexis

Stabbing pains in my stomach have me curled up on my side while I take a moment to breathe. Eyes scrunched tight, I draw a breath in, hold and release it. Dreaded Shark Week. You would think it would get easier, but it doesn't. Plus, I'd been so occupied with my current friends with benefits arrangement that I've completely lost track of the days.

Eating half a block of chocolate last night should have hinted at what was coming. But I'm too focused on a penis to think about what's happening with my vagina. Ugh, cramp.

Hand on hip, I stumble to the bathroom, wincing as I rummage through the cabinets. My heart sinks as the products I need elude me.

"Damn it," I hiss, as I can't find any sanitary products. I don't know why I thought Dad might have some stored here when I'm only here for a quarter of the year. Back in my room, I rifled through all my bags, finally finding a crumpled up pad in the back pocket of my handbag. Well, that will have to do until I can buy supplies.

My phone buzzes in my pocket, and I pull it out to see it's Casey ringing, so I swipe to answer it.

"Hey," I grunt, as another cramp takes me by surprise.

"You okay? You sound funny," he comments, and I want to say, of course I sound funny as I'm haemorrhaging out of my vagina, but I hone my rage in and keep that to myself.

"Just period cramps. What's up?" I throw out.

"Well, I guess that puts a damper on my plans," he says.

"Oh, this was a booty call?"

"Well, yeah, sorry."

"No, don't be sorry. Just the goodies have closed up shop for the week," I tease, laughing.

"That's the least of my worries at the moment. You okay? Do you need me to get you anything?" he asks.

"Actually, if you wouldn't mind getting me some pads or tampons or something. I'm out of everything, and with these cramps, it will be a literal pain to go up to the shop to get some," I explain.

This is a simple friend request, right?

"That I can do. Do you have a preference or anything that you want?"

"Ones with wings will do," I tell him. "Thanks for this. I appreciate it," I grumble, as another cramp pulls at my uterus.

"I'll be as fast as I can," he rambles, before he hangs up. As soon as he's gone, an awkwardness washes over me at having to depend on him for such a personal matter. Another stab to my stomach clears that thought as soon as it arrives. Desperate times call for desperate measures.

I walk to the bathroom and put the crumpled up pad to use. Then back to bed I go, where lying in the foetal position helps lessen it a little. Time slips away from me until I hear a knock on the front door and Casey calling my name.

"In here," I call back.

Another knock sounds on my door before it opens. In walks Casey, carrying two big brown paper bags filled to the brim.

"What on earth?" I ask, with my eyes bugging out and brows raised.

"Okay, let me say, do not go to the local pharmacy, as little old Dorothy there will talk your ear off if you let her. She talked so much, I ended up buying whatever it was she threw my way," he rushes out, as he deposits the bags on the bed.

Grabbing the first bag, I tip it upside down and out pour four packets of pads and four packets of tampons. They aren't ordinary packs. No, they are all multipacks. I have enough sanitary products to last me months. When I glance at Casey, who stands there with his hands on his hips, huffing as if he ran the entire way here, I can't help the burst of laughter that escapes me. I hold on to my stomach, half from the cramps and half from the fit of giggles he's sent me into.

"Oh my gosh, what is it? Are the ones you wanted not even there?" he asks, which only makes me laugh harder.

"Casey, you got me ultra, super, regular and light tampons. Plus, you got me maternity, nighttime, super and regular pads. This will last me forever," I tell him, as I try to hold my laughter in.

His cheeks redden before he reaches forward and dumps out the contents of the next bag. Another four packets of pads bounce on the bed, and I pull my lips into my mouth, this time to hold the laughter in.

"The others don't have wings, but these do," he explains, as every inch of his face turns red.

I stare at him as my face heats from holding back until we both crack up with laughter.

"I am never buying sanitary products again," he exclaims, once we quieten down.

"It's the thought that counts, and this must have cost you a fortune. I'll pay you back," I tell him.

"No, you will not. It's the least I can do. Plus, I got the multi packs cos Dorothy told me about the sale they were having. That woman, I tell you. She's one heck of a saleswoman cos she must have known I was buying excess when she was ringing it up. No wonder she got employee of the month three months in a row," he states, and I can't help it as I'm hit with another giggle fit.

"Well, it is much appreciated," I say, as I hop off the bed and kiss him on the cheek before wrapping my arms around his waist.

He pulls me in tight to his chest as his arms wrap around my back. He glides one hand down my hair, brushing it off my face.

"How are you feeling?" he asks, in a gentle tone.

"Pretty crappy, actually," I admit.

"Well, I got some other stuff that might help, too. I told you Dorothy was one hell of a saleswoman," he states, before his lips lower to my forehead. He releases me and takes a step out of my door before coming back in with another bag and handing it over. This one contains a wheat bag to heat for my stomach, two blocks of chocolate, some painkillers and a pack of tissues.

"Aww, this is thoughtful. Thank you," I say, gushing at him and pulling him in for another hug.

"Yeah, well, thank Dorothy." His statement makes me laugh again.

"Poor Casey, it sounds like she traumatised you," I tease.

"Yeah, when she talked about her day and how they didn't have these sanitary products, my brain went on alert. Then she talked about what they used instead, and I froze. I ended up loading the basket with whatever she recommended," he says.

"She must say that to all the boys," I joke.

"Ha ha," he deadpans.

"Jokes aside. I appreciate it. I don't know where I'm going to store it all, but I appreciate it."

"You're welcome. Do you want to hang out or something?"

"If you don't mind hanging around here, then sure. I don't feel like venturing out today."

"Yeah, not a problem for me. Whatever you wanna do, I'm here for it," he says, which has me banging my teeth together.

"We aren't blurring the lines, are we?" I ask.

"Hmm, well, we are friends and I did a friendly thing for you, so no, I don't think so," he says, as his bottom lip pouts out and he shrugs his shoulders.

"Cool, just clarifying. You can chill in here. I'm gonna take a shower."

"No rush," he says.

I scoop up all the packets of products and haul them down to the bathroom with me to store under the sink. Dad will wonder why I've invested money in a sanitary care company, but oh well, the joys of having a daughter.

Like Casey said, I take my time in the shower as the hot water helps soothe the cramps. I pop some painkillers before leaving the bathroom, too. When I walk into my room, feeling renewed and freshened up, my heart can't help but beat a little faster at the sight. Casey and Hugh are lying down on my bed with Hugh cuddled up into Casey's neck. He's scrolling through his phone while Hugh sleeps.

"You look comfortable."

"I am. This mattress feels amazing. Last time I was on it, there was a lot of bouncing, so I didn't get the full effect," he states, which makes me chuckle. Hugh's tucked up on one side, so Casey hangs his other arm out.

I take the invitation and cuddle up on his side. He brings his arm back around me to rub my back.

"Feeling better?"

"Yeah, the shower helped."

"I wasn't sure if you'd want the wheat bag, but I read the instructions and heated it in the microwave for you," he says, as he pulls the bag off the bedside table.

Holding my chest, I say, "Gosh, a guy reading instructions is a man after my heart," which has him cracking up with laughter.

"Well, I didn't want to blow up the microwave, did I, smart ass?" he explains. He passes the pink warm wheat pack, and I place it across my stomach where the heat sinks through my clothes and into my muscles.

"That feels nice," I tell him, as I close my eyes to relax more.

"You wanna play solitaire on my phone with me?" he asks.

"You know the purpose of solitaire is to play by yourself, hence why it's called solitaire?"

"Yeah, but we can battle to see who can get the most done or something. That way, we don't have to move from here."

"Okay then, but prepare to eat my dust," I challenge.

"Competitive are we?"

"Extremely," I admit.

We dive right in and take turns seeing who can get the fastest times. We begin at the easy levels and progress to the master level. There, we help each other by calling out any moves we think are wrong. It isn't until Hugh quacks that we realise a good chunk of the day has disappeared.

"That's my sign to get going before your dad comes home. I know he lets me stay, but I doubt he'd appreciate finding me in your bed," he says, as he pulls away and stands up.

"You're welcome to stay tonight if you like. On the couch," I quickly add.

"Nah, I don't want to overstay, so I'll spend a few nights in the van," he says, holding my gaze.

I ignore the drop my stomach makes and pass it off as period pain instead.

"Well, the offer is there anytime. You know that, and thanks again for today."

"Don't mention it. And don't get up. Relax and rest. Hugh and I can make our way out. I'll see you later, kay?"

"Okay. See you later," I say, as he delivers a kiss to my forehead before walking out the door with Hugh hot on his tail. The rumble of his crombie pulling down the driveway fades away, and I can't help but wonder why the room feels a little emptier without him in it.

CHAPTER FOURTEEN

Dec 16th

Alexis

It's been a few days since I've seen Casey. The last time was when he was sweet and bought the complete section of sanitary products for me. Over the worst of the period pain, I'm more myself today, so I've walked over to Ruby's to see what the girls are up to today.

With two knocks on the white painted door, I wait. The click of the lock has my eyes looking up to see who is behind it.

"Hey Lexi, you're just in time. Kara arrived like five minutes ago," Ruby greets me. I kick off my thongs, leaving them on the porch before I step into her house.

"What are we gonna do today?" I follow Ruby down the hallway to the kitchen, where Kara sits at the table.

She gives me a nod as she takes a huge bite of her green apple. Her cheek putts out as she chews, and I sit down at the table opposite her.

"Hey, Kara."

She chews faster, then swallows before she replies, "Morning, chicky. No, Casey today?"

"Nah, I got my period a few days ago and haven't seen him since. Have you guys seen him around?" I grab an apple of my own from the fruit bowl sitting in the middle of the table.

"He was on shift with me yesterday. Seemed a bit, I don't know, off, you could say. Like he wasn't his usual happy self that I've seen."

"Oh, really? He seemed fine the other day. I wonder if something happened," I say, as my thoughts escape my mouth.

"Should we head to the beach? That kite show is on today, isn't it? Maybe you'll see him down there. He's got the day off too," Kara suggests, and I nod, lost in my thoughts and hoping Casey is all right.

"Oh yes, I forgot all about that. Let's do that," Ruby adds. She rushes out of the room and is back a minute later with her tote slung over her shoulder.

Kara and I throw our apple cores in the bin before we all walk out the front door, and Ruby closes it behind us.

We talk as we walk the familiar path to the beach. We catch up on what's happened in the last few days. Marcus and Courtney had a big fight the other night, so they may break up again.

As the beach comes into view, you can see all the vibrant colored kites in the air. At first glance, there's an octopus, a crab, a dragon and a Rubik's cube.

"So pretty," Kara whispers beside me, in awe.

I nod along as my eyes stay fixed on the kites above. They span along the length of the beach, filled with patrons watching the show.

"Let's find somewhere to sit," Ruby suggests.

We follow her as she leads us through groups of people to a spot we can take. I'm thankful I'm not on shift today, as the days there are big events like this are more chaotic than ever.

We bypass my patch of sand that a family with small children has occupied. I can't help but smile at the excitement that shines on their little faces as we pass. We trail after Ruby before she stops closer to the lifeguard tower, where there's a spot big enough for us each to lay a towel down. It's free as the tower blocks the view of some kites further down the beach, but it doesn't bother us. We shake out our towels before taking a seat and settling in for the show.

My eyes gaze over the beautiful kites as Ruby passes her bottle of sunscreen to me. I squirt a big dollop onto the palm of my hand before I pass it along to Kara. With my finger, I dab the cream over my face, arms and legs before rubbing it in, so I'm covered.

"Ooh, look, there's a Spiderman one," Kara gushes, and I follow her finger. Iron Man and Captain America float close by as well.

"Is that Casey over there?" Ruby asks.

"Where?" I ask, as I follow in the direction she now points.

"Is that the back of his head?"

"I'm not sure."

"You want me to go have a look and invite him to sit with us? He's all alone," Kara suggests.

"Nah, I'll go. I'll be back." My feet pick up pace as I head in his direction.

His head has dropped forward, looking at the sand instead of the amazing spectacle of colours in the sky. As I get closer, I come around the side of him and realise it is, in fact, Casey.

"Hey," I say, as I drop beside him on the sand. His eyes shift to mine before he moves them back down in front of him.

111

"Hey," he replies, his voice lacking its usual warmth.

"You good?"

"Yeah, why wouldn't I be?"

"I don't know, because you're sitting here staring at the sand when the excitement is in the sky?" I tease, trying to coax a reaction out of him.

He releases a sigh before he moves his forearms across his bent knees and rests his chin there.

"Just missing home a bit," his soft voice confesses.

"Ah, the dreaded homesickness. I feel like that whenever I leave Wattle Downs at the end of the summer. I miss Dad, the beach and my friends. It lasts a few weeks too, but I always try to distract myself with Uni, and before I know it, the feeling has gone. If you keep yourself busy doing stuff, you'll feel it less. Or you could always head home. You're travelling, right?"

"Yeah, I could, but I don't want to," he says, releasing another sigh.

I gather there's more going on than he's saying, but I don't want to pry, so I change the subject instead.

"The girls and I are sitting back there. Why don't you join us? At least having others around would distract you for a bit," I say, as I push my shoulder against him.

"I'd rather wallow by myself over here. I'm not good company at the moment."

"That doesn't bother me. Come on. I won't take no for an answer," I say as I flutter my eyelashes at him until I catch the smallest hint of a smile.

"Okay, I'm coming. Don't flap your lashes like that again. It's scary," he jokes.

"What? I'm not pretty when I do this?" I ask, as I continue to flutter them.

"No, it's creepy," he states, as he stands. He holds out a hand for me, so my fingers curl around his as he pulls me up.

"Fine, I'll stop since you're coming to sit with us." I wipe the sand off my butt as we turn and head towards where the girls are still seated. As we walk through the groups of people, I say, "You can leave anytime you want. If you want to be alone, say you gotta do something. I won't take offence."

"Thanks, Alexis," he says, as he gives me a small smile.

"You know you can call me Lexi. You've seen me naked, so I think we've moved into nickname territory."

"I like Alexis, though," he states, and my cheeks burn.

My lips squish to the side as I nod, which only makes his smile grow.

"Welcome, Casey. You can sit here if you like," Kara says as she moves over to the edge of her towel, which makes room for Casey to sit next to me between the girls.

"Thanks."

"It's such glorious weather for the kite show this year. Remember last year's rain cancelled the show?" Ruby says, and we all fall into an easy conversation.

Casey doesn't talk much, but he listens and answers if one of us directs a question right at him. He sits with his legs crossed in front of him and leans back on his hands.

An hour passes as the sun shines above us, and we watch and point out different kites that catch our eyes.

"Do you want to reapply sunscreen?" Ruby asks as she holds out the bottle for me. I squirt more into my palm before handing it to Casey, who takes it. He sits forward and squeezes his own into his hand before handing it off to Kara. We're all quiet as we rub the lotion into our skin.

Casey stays close to my side, and his fingertips trail along the skin at my back between my shirt and my jean shorts. My breath hitches at his touch. I catch the small chuckle he releases as his fingertips glide along my sliver of skin. We stay like that with the girls unaware as he caresses my skin. Their light chatter remains, but my focus is now on where his finger touches me, and nothing else matters.

"You good, Alexis?" he whispers beside me, and my face turns to look at him. A teasing smile lights his face, and the gloomy cloud that surrounded him earlier has drifted away. I nod, not able to speak, which only makes his smile grow. His eyes turn back to the sky, where he gazes over the kites while continuing to torture me with just a fingertip.

Another hour passes before Ruby mentions she has to go to meet her mum for some last minute Christmas shopping. So we pack up and all walk back towards my house. Casey included.

"We'll see you guys later," I say to Ruby and Kara, as we reach the end of my driveway.

"Yeah, see you guys. Have fun," Kara says with a wink, which makes my cheeks heat as she and Ruby smile at us before turning around and heading towards their own houses.

"You are such a tease," I tell Casey, as soon as the girls are out of hearing range.

His carefree smile widens before he grabs my hand and pulls me further down the driveway. Hedge covers one side from view, while a wooden fence surrounds the other side. Casey wastes no time in pushing me up against it. His mouth lingers over mine, still teasing, so I close the gap and bring my lips to his. One hand slides into my hair while his other hand wraps around me and pulls me flush against him. We release the built up tension caused by his finger into our kiss.

"You know what would be a good distraction," he says between kisses. I know what he's hinting at.

"I've still got my period," I say back, as our mouths continue kissing each other.

"I guess we'll have to kiss until our mouths hurt, then," he states, as he squeezes me tighter still.

And that's what we do. We lose ourselves in our kisses against the fence, hidden from view. When we finally pull apart, his pink, swollen lips stare at me. He swipes his thumb across my lower lip as his gaze follows the movement.

"Thank you for today," he says, as his eyes stare into mine, some of the sadness surrounding him returning.

"You're welcome. Do you want to come for dinner tonight?"

"No, I think I need that time alone. But raincheck?"

"Yeah, you bet." I don't want him to spend time alone with the sullen mood that's following him, but I also don't want to push it too much. "Message me if you change your mind, though."

"I will. Thanks again," he says, before he pecks my cheek, and then he steps out of my orbit and heads down the driveway. I draw in a deep breath as I lean against the fence, and can't help how my heart beats faster as I watch him leave.

"Casey?" I yell.

"Yeah?"

"If you want, we can have another surfing lesson in the morning?" I watch as his smile grows.

"Sounds good. I'll be here bright and early," he says, before he lifts his hand in a wave and turns back around. A few more steps and he's gone from view along the footpath.

I release a breath and pull myself away from the fence, tracing my thumb over my swollen lips, relishing the feeling.

CHAPTER FIFTHTEEN

Dec 17th

Casey

"Hands under chest, chest out, tuck feet and pop," I say to myself, in the confines of the Crombie van. It's not ideal working on my pop ups on the mattress in the back of the van, but it's the best I can manage without people staring at me.

Plus, I couldn't sleep at all last night. You can only toss and turn for so long before you've had enough, and then the only option is to get out of bed early. There is no point in lying there when your head is a mess and the thoughts won't stop pounding their way through. So pop ups it is.

I also wanted to show Alexis that I wasn't as uncoordinated as she thinks I am. I know she says that she's been surfing for a lot longer, but it still makes me want to prove I can do it. I repeat the motions over and over, hoping I look a lot smoother than in our last lesson.

"Quack."

"Okay, I'll let you out now," I say, as I look at Hugh, who stares at me from his perch on the passenger seat, waiting to go outside to do his business. With a sigh, I press up and push the boot of the van open. Hugh follows me, and I place him on the grass. We are back at our cove, having spent the night here again last night. Alexis offered dinner, but I meant it when I told her I needed space. My head still isn't great.

Part of me wants to run back home, while the other part wants to head in the opposite direction and put more distance between us. I'm battling with which half of my heart will win, and I don't know which piece that will be.

The crinkle of my muesli bar unwrapping peaks Hugh's interest as he stares at me. I finish it in two bites before walking to the rubbish bin and throwing the wrapper away. The day is grey with a chilly wind. A huge contrast to yesterday's blue sky and blistering sun. The waves already look quite rough as I look out at the sea. It isn't a problem for me, though, as I doubt Alexis will say I'm ready for the water yet, anyway.

Picking Hugh back up, I put him in the back of the van, close the door, and begin the drive to Alexis's house. It's still early, but I'm hoping she's already up.

The bright lights of the van shine down the driveway, so as soon as I reach the house, I flick them off. I grab my phone out of the centre console and send her a text telling her I'm here. She replies with a smiley emoji and then appears at her door a couple of minutes later. She holds up a finger to tell me to wait while she grabs the same board from the other day.

I step out of the van with Hugh and place him down, then take the board from her.

"Do you want to walk? It's not far? Hugh can hang out here," she suggests.

"Sounds good."

We fall into step beside each other as we head down the driveway and along the footpath.

"Did you have a good sleep?" Alexis asks, as a yawn escapes me.

"Yeah, but a coffee wouldn't hurt," I lie, not wanting her to worry about my lack of sleep.

"Surfing lesson first, then coffee."

We walk down the path she always takes and find the beach empty. It's only after 5.00 am, so I don't blame people for not being out, especially with little sun. The cool wind blows harder as we step onto the sand, losing the shelter from the bush we had near the path.

"I should have worn a sweatshirt," I murmur more to myself, than to Alexis.

"We can make it a quick lesson. I heard a storm is in the forecast," she says, as she stops in the same area I realise she likes.

"Does it always storm around here? Seems like it rains more than anything," I say.

"Yeah, the summers are always like this. Never know what you are going to get. It could clear by the afternoon or turn into a big hailstorm. Who knows," she says, as she shrugs.

I drop the board on the sand and rub my arms to warm them against the harsh wind.

"We'll practise pop ups again," she instructs.

I lie face down, and she runs through the movements that I've memorised. We do it over and over until she's happy.

"See, you're getting better."

Pride sounds in her voice, and warmth floods through me at the compliment.

"I would suggest we try you in the whitewash, but the surf is pretty rough today. So, how about we grab some coffees from the cart and observe the surfers that are already out there? I can point out some things while we watch."

"Yeah, that sounds good," I admit, more in need of the coffee than anything.

We walk over to the cart and order a latte each, a double shot for mine. With our coffees in hand, we head back to the spot and take a seat next to each other. There are about five surfers out in the ocean at the moment, with the waves quite high already. It isn't long before a few more cars pull up with surfers. The harsh wind may not be great for swimmers, but it's like candy to a baby for surfers who want the bigger waves.

"Hey, guys," we hear called, and we both turn to find Marcus wearing a wetsuit and a white board tucked under his arm. "You're not coming in?"

"Hey, Marcus. Nah, I'm teaching Casey to surf, but it's too rough for him to practise, so we're gonna watch instead," Alexis explains.

Marcus nods in understanding, before saying, "Yeah, good plan. Don't want to dissuade you with the rough waves. It is fun once you get the hang of it."

He leaves us with a wave as he jogs towards the water, places his board down, and slides on. I watch as he paddles himself out to where all the other surfers wait and try to lock it in my memory, how he grasps the board when a wave comes. This observation is a good idea instead of throwing myself into the deep end.

We drink our coffees as Alexis points out different things to watch for, like the things about certain waves she likes or the way one surfer moves his body. She explains surfer etiquette and how to stay out of each other's way, and, most of all, to have fun.

The coffees finish, and the grey skies still hang overhead, not looking like they are going to disperse at all, so we pack up and head back to hers. The first sprinkle of raindrops hit us as we reach her driveway, so we quicken our steps until we were under the safety of her porch.

"Come on in, Hugh," I call, as he sits out on the grass, waiting for a puddle to appear for his enjoyment. He ignores my request, so I leave him be.

"Hey, did you guys go for a swim?" Corbin greets us, as we enter the house.

"Nah, we were having another surfing lesson, but it looks like a storm is brewing. Are you heading down there now?" Alexis asks.

"Yeah, I am. If a storm sets in and you leave home, let me know where you are, love bug. You're welcome to stay here Casey, especially if a storm starts."

"Thanks," I tell him, as he kisses Alexis on the head and then leaves us.

"You all take storms seriously here," I tell Alexis. She grabs bowls from the cupboard and fills them with cereal.

"Yeah, it's because the streets around here can flood if we get too much rain, which has happened in the past. You don't want to be out in the flood waters as the conditions can change in a flash. That's why Dad worries. I'll spend the day here. You wanna hang too?"

I nod as she pushes a bowl of cereal and milk towards me.

We eat in silence, and our breakfast finishes when the first sound of thunder crackles outside.

"I'm gonna grab Hugh." I walk to the door and call for him, and wait until he waddles inside. A bright flash of lightning streams across the sky as I close the door.

"Dad's probably gonna be closing down the beach, so I'm guessing he won't be out long, but if you want…" Her words trail off as she lifts her shirt over her head, leaving her standing in the kitchen in her navy blue bikini top. Her warm smile shines my way.

A few steps are all it takes before I'm in front of her. My arms wrap around and pull on her bikini string, and she yanks it over her head. Her breasts are on full display. My mouth finds hers, and her hands slide my shirt up and over my torso before I pull it off, dropping it to the floor with her top. Our lips reconnect, and we stumble our way down the hall as we tug at our shorts and underwear, in a hurry to feel each other's flesh.

She pushes her bedroom door open, and I pick her up, throwing her on the bed with a yelp. Her hand thrusts open her bedside drawer in search of a condom, which she retrieves. I grab her ankles and pull her down the bed before I spread her thighs open, mesmerised by her bare pussy.

Her chest heaves as her wanton eyes stare at me, and my lips tug up before I lower my mouth for a taste. My tongue strokes up, causing her back to arch. My hands tighten their grip on her thighs, holding her open for me to devour. I lap at her juices, taking my time until I find the spot I'm after and suck hard. Her soft moans urge me on, and I pick up the pace as her hands glide into my hair, pushing my mouth harder against her. She holds me in place as I continue, listening to her moans for confirmation that I'm doing what she likes.

Her moans grow louder, and my movements pick up speed until she arches higher and finds her release. I continue working her until her moans cease and she sounds out of breath. My eyes peek up at her. A lazy, sated smile looks my way, making my heart rate increase. Her hand pulls me towards her before she kisses me. Not caring that the taste of her is on my lips, she takes what she wants.

We break apart, she rips open the condom, sheathes me, and then I ease myself inside her. My moan sounds in the room as I drop my head into her neck and enjoy the sensation of her before I move. Our mouths suck and bite at each other as my movements increase. I hook her leg over my shoulder, pushing deeper. Harder. Then my release comes, and my eyes close as I relish the high. My sated smile pulls at my face as I look down. Her hair surrounds her, having come out somehow in the chaos of it all. The sight of her beneath me makes my heart pound. Not wanting to dissect those feelings right now, I pull out and immediately sense the loss.

My tired body drops beside her, and I wrap her back to my front as our laboured breaths fill the air. My lips deliver a kiss to the back of her neck as I squeeze her against me, feeling sleepy.

"You can grab a shower. I'll have one and get changed in case Dad comes home." The sound of thunder outside awakens me more, and I realise her dad could be home any minute if the storm rages on.

"Sounds good," I say, as I squeeze her once more before releasing.

She moves out of bed, grabbing new clothes from her drawers before leaving me on the bed. I head into the kitchen, where I collect my clothes and pull them back on and take hers to her room.

She's out in a few minutes, and then we switch, and I rush through my shower. Once I'm out, I find her in the living room, in search of something to watch on the TV.

"I've got some cards if you want to play Last Card or something?" she says, which has a smile growing on my face.

"I haven't played cards in ages. Sounds fun," I confess, which makes her cheeks blush. She grabs the pack from the cupboard, and we set ourselves up sitting cross legged on the floor on opposite ends of the coffee table. We go over the rules, and before we begin, her dad barges through the front door, drenched from the rain.

"It's looking like a big one today. You guys all right?" he asks, looking between us.

"Yeah, we were about to play Last Card. You want to join?" she asks him, and his eyes light up.

"Yeah. Let me shower, and then I'll be out," he says.

"Quack." Hugh makes his presence known from his spot where he's cuddled up on the couch.

"Don't worry, Hugh. You can curl up on my lap in a minute," Corbin tells Hugh, which seems to please my feathered friend as he curls back into himself.

"Who is looking after the beach?" Alexis asks.

"Cheese and Mozzie are on patrol, but it's getting bad, and the forecast has it going all night. I told them to monitor it, but if the beach stays clear and the storm gets worse, to head home to safety. Hopefully, people aren't stupid enough to go out in this weather."

He walks down to the bathroom, and when he closes the door, I crawl my way to where Alexis sits. Her raised brows greet me as I sit back and pull her onto my lap.

"If your dad is going to be here all day, then I'd better kiss you while I can," I whisper in her ear, which makes her grin before her lips find their way to mine.

My hands glide through her hair, angling her face as our tongues move together. We lose ourselves in the moment. It's not until I hear the bathroom lock click that we pull apart. Then I head back to my side of the coffee table. Luckily, Corbin walked in the opposite direction with his wet laundry to the washing machine. A close call, that was.

Once he returns, we settle in for card games, and we spend the rest of the day playing. Somehow, with these two taunting and laughing at each other, I'm lighter than I've felt in days. So I revel in the feeling. When I fall asleep on the couch that night, I can't help but smile.

CHAPTER SIXTEEN

Dec 18th

Casey

Alexis was gone this morning when I woke up, and since I'm on shift with Corbin, I walked to work with him. The storm scattered debris and broken tree branches all along the footpath. He explained we would clear any rubbish from the beach today.

Strong winds blow around us as we walk, and I find it comfortable around Corbin. He doesn't push me for information, just asks in casual conversation. And I'll be forever grateful that he offered his couch to me. His actions spoke volumes.

"I know you didn't get to the post office because of the storm, but don't forget about it. You could even put our address down if you wanted," he suggests, as we step onto the sand.

"Thanks, I'll do that if you're sure it's okay?"

"Yeah, it's perfectly fine," he says. "Going to have our work cut out for us today with all this mess," he grunts, as his eyes scan the beach.

"Wouldn't be so bad if it wasn't as windy," I say, watching two wrapper packets blow past us from the wind.

"The beach will remain closed today, so at least there won't be many people around getting in the way."

"Why do you keep it closed after a big storm?" I ask, curious.

"The pipes along here flood with heavy rain, and then the sewage can leak into the sea, so it's safer to keep patrons off the beach while it clears."

"Avoid the water today. Got it," I say, which earns me a pat on the back as we walk up the ramp to the tower. "Do you know where Alexis went this morning, if she couldn't surf?"

"Oh, she took my car up the coast about an hour away. She has a habit of doing that if she can't surf here," he explains, and I nod. He unlocks the tower, and we step inside.

I place my bag down, and he turns on the lights and checks that everything is in working order. The other lifeguards trail in one by one, and I give James a head nod when I see him.

"Hey," he says as he puts his bag down.

"Gather 'round, everyone. It's a clean up day today. Grab bags, gloves, and rubbish pickers, and split up. If you see patrons coming down, they can stay on the sand, but they have to stay out of the water, so warn them it's not safe. Mozzie, can you watch the skate park too, as there are bound to be kids there today? Radio, anything you need help with," Corbin directs, and we all break apart.

The radio clips onto my belt as I pull on a pair of thick black gloves to protect my hands. I grab a roll of rubbish bags and a picker, and then I follow James out of the tower.

We head in the same direction, towards the pier, but taking different sections of the beach. He's further down towards the surf while I stay near the road. The tool is a breeze for picking up most clutter effortlessly. Only a few things do I have to bend to pick up with my hands. The black rubbish bag fills fast, and we aren't even finished with this side.

"I'm gonna take mine to the skip. You want me to take yours?" James calls out.

"Yeah, thanks, that would be great," I call back, which sends him in my direction. I tie my nearly full bag off and hold it out to him when he reaches me.

"Keep heading down towards the pier, and I'll catch up. There's a lot down there from the markets."

"On it," I tell him, as I extend another bag out and open it. Eyes on the ground, I continue on my way, lost in my thoughts. I never thought my summer would include picking up trash, but I can't say I'm disappointed when I surprisingly don't mind it. This cosy little town is growing on me.

I make fast work of the top side of the beach that I am sticking to and reach the pier in no time. I still haven't seen James. If he doesn't show up before I'm done here, I'll walk back along the beach and collect what we've missed.

"Casey," I hear a call behind me, which has me turning around.

"Alexis? What are you doing here?" I ask with my brows pulled in, as she's not rostered on today, but she's in uniform.

"I told Dad I'd help because I know what the beach can look like after the storms," she says. With the pier above us and the huge wooden pillars holding it up, we are cast in shadow when she reaches me. A quick scan shows me there's no one in our close vicinity, so I clasp her wrist and tug her behind a pillar as I lean against it.

"You didn't wake me this morning?" I whisper as I tuck a wayward hair behind her ear, as she gazes at me. I rest my arms around her waist, holding her close.

"I knew you had work today and thought you might need the rest. You looked peaceful," she says, as her own hands slide up my body before resting around my neck.

"Still could have woken me for a kiss goodbye," I say even quieter.

"Is that so?" she whispers.

I nod, as I whisper, "I'll never say no to a kiss from you."

She pushes up on her toes and closes the distance. My grip around her tightens as I pull her to me. The kiss starts soft, a feather light touch, but quickly becomes deeper, more intense, as our lips remain locked together. I suck her lip hard before turning us and pressing her against the pillar. Her soft moans float away with the wind that blows harsher down here, adding to the cold in the shadows.

My lips trail a line down her throat, and she arches her head back. I grasp her behind the knee to hike her leg up and wrap it around me. Our bodies grind against each other, deepening her moans as I lavish her neck and suck under the collar of her shirt. A primal instinct takes over, and I want to mark her, so I don't stop until the skin turns a slight purplish red colour. Her pants become more hurried, making me harder.

Leaning back, I stare at her, but keep the words beautiful in my throat, but that's what she is. So beautiful. But this isn't about sweet words or sweet moments. That wasn't the agreement. The words die in my throat as I take her lips again, tasting her.

"Casey?" I hear hollered, and pull back to stare at Alexis' wild eyes.

"Shit, that's James," she whispers.

I close my eyes as I step further back, breaking the connection and trying to calm myself down.

"Fix your hair," I tell her, so she pulls the hair tie out, which only makes me want to pull her back into my arms, so I turn away and close my eyes, taking deep breaths.

"Casey? You 'round here, man?" James calls again. I bend to pick up my forgotten rubbish picker and step out from behind the pillar.

"Yeah, over here," I call. Alexis remains hidden behind the large pillar, so I step towards James, hoping he will head back with me so Alexis can escape unseen. "Sorry, man, didn't hear you over the wind. I'm done here. We can head back and finish your side," I tell him, and luckily, he follows me.

"I saw the guys on the other side of the beach. They're almost finished, so we should meet back at the tower when we're done."

"Sounds good," I tell him, as I focus on picking up trash again. A large blue wrapper flies by us with a gust of wind, and James turns to chase it. He stomps on it with his foot before he bends to pick it up. We are a little way from the pier, but at that moment, Alexis emerges from the pillar we were at and dashes towards the other side of the market.

James' blank face stares at me, having put two and two together.

"You and Lexi?" he asks, as his jaw clenches.

"It's not serious, man," I try to tell him, but it only makes his jaw clench more.

He lets out a fake laugh before speaking, "Yeah, it's never serious with her."

"What's that supposed to mean?" I growl as my hands clench into fists.

"Whose idea was it to be friends with benefits? Cos that's the deal, right?" he asks, as he crosses his arms over his chest.

"Hers," I tell him.

"Exactly. She'll use you and spit you out when she's tired of you," he grunts at me, as his chest heaves. "Don't get attached to her, cos trust me, you'll think she feels something for you, but then she'll pull the rug out from under you once summer is over."

I nod, not knowing what to say, and I want to diffuse the situation as I can feel both his anger and mine wafting around us. I'm not sure if he's mad at me or Alexis, but I don't want to deal with this right now. My unwelcome feelings have me on edge, too.

When he realises the conversation is over, he turns his back on me and continues picking up rubbish again. It isn't until Alexis comes down from the stone wall as if she only arrived that his hackles go up again.

"Hey guys," her cheery voice greets us, with a wide smile.

"Hey, yourself," James huffs out, before stomping away towards the tower, the rubbish forgotten.

"What's his problem?" Alexis asks, as she turns to me.

"He knows about us. He saw you run off from the pillar," I tell her, watching as her eyes widen.

"Damn it. I didn't want him finding out like that," she whispers, as her eyes track James down the beach.

"Yeah, he seemed pretty mad about it. You sure there wasn't more to your arrangement with him than I know about?"

"I told you I thought he had feelings for me and wanted more from me than I could give him. He knew the deal we had, though," she states, as she nibbles on her bottom lip.

"He'll get over it eventually," I mumble, as I pull a glove off. I step closer to her and pop her lip out from where she's biting it with my thumb. My head leans down, and I press a soft kiss to her lips before I pull back. "Come on, let's finish this side of the beach."

130

She nods, and I pull my glove back on. We work in silence until our side of the beach is clear, and then head back to the tower. I can't help that James' words swirl in my head, and I hope I'm not stepping on his toes too much.

Alexis finishes up after the beach is clean, as there's not much left for her to help with, since there aren't many patrons around today. The skies are still grey, but by afternoon, the sun shines bright again. More people come out to soak up the rays.

As the sand fills with people, Corbin sends us out with instructions to warn them away from the water. It's still off limits for today. I'm paired up with James, but he's not in the mood for talking.

"We cool, man?" I ask, after we leave a family who are building sand castles.

"Yeah, whatever," he says, as he shrugs his shoulders. I know part of me should say if Alexis and I are a problem, then I won't see her, but I don't know James and I don't want to stop seeing Alexis, so I keep my mouth closed.

For the remainder of the shift, he gives me the cold shoulder. He leaves in a hurry when we finish, not saying goodbye to anyone. I grab my things and head to sit on the stone wall as I watch the rough waves flow back and forth.

Wattle Downs was supposed to be an escape from my reality. Drama free and easygoing. Maybe this arrangement with Alexis isn't the best thing, but the allure of her is too much to make me stop.

A quack pulls me from my thoughts, and my hands push off to jump down to the sand to pick up my friend.

"Where have you been?" I ask him, as if he can tell me all about his adventures. I hold him to my chest and walk back to Alexis' house, where I left the van. The house is quiet when we arrive, so I place Hugh in the van and we head back to the cove.

131

After today, I need a bit of space from Alexis. It's as if this arrangement is more than friends with benefits, and I need to put the boundaries back in place. I don't know if that's possible as they become more blurred by the day.

CHAPTER SEVENTEEN

Dec 22nd

Alexis

Since James found out about my new friends with benefits arrangement with Casey, they've both been avoiding me. I was on shift with James the day after he found out, but he ignored me the whole time. Dad partnered us together, but James asked if he could switch with Cheese, so I didn't even get a minute to speak to him about it.

In all honesty, I don't know what I would say to him. There's nothing I can say that would make it better. I knew he had feelings for me, and instead of being selfish, I should have broken our agreement off years ago. That's what I get for thinking I can have my cake and eat it too. Now all I've done is wreck a friendship.

Things will be different with Casey, though. He's only here for the summer, so we both know there can't be anything going on further. I should never have agreed with James, as he's too close to home. Casey is a better choice, as there can't be a future for us. I hardly know anything about him, and it works better that way.

Casey hasn't been around either since James found out, though. He's avoiding me, too. I messaged him the other night to ask if he wanted to join us for dinner, but he declined, saying he'd already eaten, and that was the last I heard from him.

I worked today as well, and Kara was on shift with me. The beach gets crowded as Christmas approaches. Many people are on holiday, and locals come out to enjoy the time off. Dad closes the surf shop for the public holidays, but apart from that, it stays open like most of the shops on the strip do. Holiday makers passing through make for good business.

Today was a hard day. My body felt tired more than usual, and my head was pounding, but I pushed through to complete the shift. Dad gave me a worried look when I walked into the tower late in the day, as he knows when I'm pushing it too hard, but he also knows not to mention it in front of the others. Endometriosis is debilitating some days, but on the days that aren't as bad, I push through because that's the only thing I can do. And manage the pain the best I can.

With adrenaline still running through me, I'm antsy, and I doubt sleep will come soon. I had dinner with Dad earlier, and he lectured me about not pushing myself. I said I'd try not to. He's taken me off tomorrow's shift and said he'd find cover instead, so now I've got another free day. I know Casey isn't on shift tomorrow either, so I hope he's awake to keep me company.

With my lamp on, I grab my phone from the bedside table and open our text messages to type out a text.

A: Hey you awake?

My index finger taps the side of my phone while I wait for a reply. I gave up hope when a text came through.

C: Are you booting calling me?

134

His reply makes me laugh.

A: Actually, I wasn't. I can't sleep and wondered if you were up. Haven't seen you for a few days.

C: Ah, I see you're missing me.

A: Haha, whatever. I might go to sleep now, then.

C: Wait. Hold on.

I wait for him to elaborate.

C: I'm keen for company if you want me to drive and pick you up. I can't sleep either.

Warmth floods my body as my mouth turns up.

A: Park on the street and message when you're here.

C: See you soon.

I throw my blankets off and dig through my drawers until I find a hoodie and my black tights. I roll some deodorant under my arms, even though I'd only applied it a few hours ago after my shower. My pyjamas sail onto my bed as I strip out of them and change into the hoodie and tights. My thongs are outside on the porch, so I sneak to the bathroom, brush my teeth, and use the toilet before my phone vibrates in my hoodie pocket. I pull it out to see that Casey's outside.

A: Coming

The bathroom door creaks as I open and close it, and then I stand in the hall, straining to hear Dad's snores. A few moments later, the low whistle of his sleep sounds, and I know I should be able to escape without him noticing. It doesn't stop me from stepping down the hall on the balls of my feet, though, just in case. I peel open the door and close it behind me. Picking up my thongs with my fingers, I step down to the driveway, drop them, and slide my feet in. Then I'm off. I run on tiptoes down the darkened driveway, finding Casey in his van with it running, waiting for me.

Gripping the handle, I fling the passenger door open and close it before looking at him.

"Hey," I puff, as I catch my breath.

"Hey, you good?" he asks, as he pulls the van away from the street, flicking the lights back on now that I'm in.

"Yeah. Couldn't sleep from the adrenaline today," I tell him.

"You wanna head back to the cove with me?" he asks, as he turns down another street.

"Yeah, sounds good."

He drives us there in silence and parks the van in what I assume is his usual spot. Hugh is fast asleep in the back, on the mattress. Casey steps out of the van after taking out the key, and I follow him. The humidity outside feels stuffy, but the warmth is better than the cold right now. There's a park bench he leads us to that sits on the grass and faces out to sea. You can't see much now as it's dark, but the stars above are on full display.

That's one thing I love about Wattle Downs. The air is fresher and clearer without pollution. So, the night sky shines brightly. I can see the stars much better here than in the city where I live with Mum.

The sounds of the waves hitting the shore are like a lullaby, and I close my eyes to relish the sound. A sense of peace washes over me as I draw a deep breath in before releasing it.

"Did something happen today?" Casey's voice breaks through my peaceful moment, and I open my eyes. I pull my feet up onto the bench and wrap my arms around my legs as I rest my head on my knees and face him. His own body is all spread out, legs wide and arms thrown over the back of the bench, taking up as much room as possible.

"Have you heard of endometriosis?"

His face turns to me, and he shakes his head.

"The lining of my uterus can grow outside of it. That's why my periods hurt more than others. It also causes pain in my body during the month. Plus, I suffer from migraines."

"Sounds horrible," he says. I let out a light laugh.

"Yeah, that's putting it mildly, I guess," I say, as I turn to face back at the sea.

"So your body was hurting today?" he asks, having picked up on what I didn't say outright.

I release a sigh before I speak, "Yeah, I pushed myself through it, but it drains me when I do that. Now mixed with the adrenaline from a few close calls on shift, I guess, has messed me up, and I couldn't sleep."

"Are you hurting now?" he asks, as his back straightens and his eyes scan me over.

"A little, but I took some painkillers earlier that helped."

"Come, let's lie down in the back of the van," he suggests, as he stands and holds out a hand for me. I grasp it, and he links our fingers and leads me back. He pulls the back of the van open, and we climb onto the mattress. "Come here," he says, as he holds an arm out for me to lie on. I snuggle into his side, and he wraps his arm around me while we gaze at the stars from our vantage point. "Let me know if the pain gets bad, as I've got some pain relief you can take if you need." A warmth spreads through me at his thoughtfulness.

"Thanks," I whisper, as I squeeze him closer.

"Aren't you on shift tomorrow?"

"Dad knows I pushed myself too hard, so he's given me the day off and is going to find someone to cover for me."

"Good. It sounds like you need to rest."

"Well, yeah, that's not always possible, though. Sometimes I need to push through or else I won't get anything done," I tell him.

"That must be hard," he says, as he rolls onto his side and wraps both arms around me. We stare at each other for a bit, and my heart picks up pace.

"Yeah, it is hard, but I manage." My voice is quiet in the still night.

"Is there anything your doctor can do about it?"

"Not really. They haven't got a cure for it yet, and there are procedures they can do, but I haven't looked into them further. Maybe down the line I will, but for now, I'm dealing with it the best I can."

"It sucks that you're in pain and there's nothing they can do about it," he says, as his finger slides from my temple to my chin.

"I'm used to it."

"Still doesn't feel right."

"I know, but it is what it is."

His lips press a soft kiss against my own. Nothing more before he pulls back.

"You got plans for Christmas Day?" he asks, changing the subject.

"I'm rostered on. I usually spend the day in the tower with Dad anyway, as he likes to work and give the other guys with families the day off, if possible.

"Oh, I'm rostered on too, so at least we can make it fun on shift together."

"Are you still missing home?" I ask, and his body tenses under my arms before he releases it.

"Yeah, it's hard around the holidays as we usually have a big Christmas party every year, but I'm looking forward to a nice chill Christmas this year. Big parties can be draining."

He smiles at me, but tension still surrounds his eyes, and I'm curious about what made him leave his home. He doesn't talk much about it, and I don't want to ask right now as I'm physically and mentally drained, so I don't have the energy to help if he confesses something. So I make a mental note to ask another day when I'm feeling more up to it.

"Try to sleep, Alexis. We can call this booty call cuddles," he jokes, which has me laughing before I squeeze him tighter.

I close my eyes and listen to the sound of the waves, letting the soothing sound lull me to sleep.

CHAPTER EIGHTEEN

Dec 23rd

Alexis

Warmth surrounds me as a heavy weight presses on my legs. My head nuzzles into my pillow, the firmness of it setting off my internal alert system, as it doesn't feel right. As my eyes flutter open, the rest of my senses wake up. The inside of Casey's van, his weight against me, the smell of the morning surf, the wind blowing past, Casey's breath in my ear and the fuzziness of my mouth.

My body stiffens in his embrace as he wraps himself around me with my back to his front. His arm acts as my pillow under my head. No wonder it felt firm. The warmth that transfers from his body to mine is soothing to my sore muscles, and I wriggle back, trying to steal more of it.

His arms tighten around me as he pulls me closer to him, and his hardened length grinds against me.

"Morning," his husky voice murmurs in my ear.

"Morning," I reply, as I turn to hide my morning breath from him.

"What are you doing?"

"Nothing," I mumble out the side of my mouth, which has his deep laugh echoing in my ear before he nuzzles my hair.

"Here," he says, before he releases me with one arm, and rustling sounds from behind us. Then he hands me his toothpaste, making my face heat.

"Thanks," I grumble out as I take it. I squirt a small dollop on my index finger before scrubbing my teeth the best I can with it. That will have to do for now. I hold the tube behind me for him to take, and he does the same, scrubbing his teeth before I turn around in his arms.

"Good morning," I say, which makes him laugh again.

"Worried your morning breath will scare me off, huh?" he teases, which has me reaching under his shirt to pinch his taut skin on his waist.

"No, I'm worried about yours, actually," I tease right back. With a wide smile, he rolls us so I'm under him.

"Hmm, is that so?"

"Aha," I mumble as he distracts me by grinding himself against me. My eyes close to the sensation as he continues his movements.

"Quack," Hugh interrupts from the passenger seat, which makes us both look his way. The duck perched there watches us as if he's not happy we'd forgotten he was in the van with us.

"Come on, then. I'll put you out," Casey says as he moves off me. He grabs Hugh and puts him out on the grass, the back of the van having been open all night. It's still early, as the sun is only now rising. He comes back and pulls the door closed behind him. "Now, where were we?" His playful smile gazes along my body before landing on my eyes, where he stays.

"You know, I've never hung around for the morning breath phase," I say, as my brows furrow. The words pop out of my mouth before I can stop them. His own brows furrow, and his body stops in its tracks as he stares at me.

"Is that a problem?"

"No. I don't think so. James and I never did sleepovers, is all," I explain.

"Ah, I see," he says, as he leans away from me. I push up onto my elbows, not liking the space between us.

"You see what?" I ask, as my eyes flick back and forth between his eyes.

"Are we blurring the lines, then? With actually sleeping together?" he asks, as his own eyes search mine.

I drop onto the mattress as we stare at each other. My heart beats faster in my chest, but I push the voices in my head to the side, ignoring the fact that he might be right. So, I lie.

"No, I don't think so. Plus, you can't have morning sex if there is no sleepover," I say, as my lips scrunch to the side. His smile returns as his body leans over me again.

"That is true."

"It's too early for thinking," I murmur, as his body weight presses into me.

"That is true, too," he mumbles, as his smile grows before his lips press against my jaw.

"Yes, that's very true. Let's leave the thinking for later, shall we?"

"Good idea," he whispers, and the words stop as his full weight drops onto me. My legs wrap around his waist as his mouth lowers down my throat, along my collarbone. My mind continues to wander to thoughts about whether he's right, and the lines are getting blurred, but I push them away and focus on feeling the sensations his touch ignites in me instead.

In a hurry to feel each other's bodies, we pull and toss our clothes. Light sweat covers our skin, and as he puts on a condom, all thoughts vanish the moment he penetrates me. The rocking of the van is bound to attract the eye of anyone passing by, but it's still early enough. I hope no one is out there. His movements increase as we both chase our release. His groans fill my ear as he drops his head to my neck.

His sated face smiles at me when he finally moves away from my neck, and I raise a brow at him.

His smile drops, "You didn't come?"

"What do you think?" I ask, making his smile grow.

"Sorry, I couldn't hold back. Your turn now," he says, as he slides out of me. He drops onto the mattress before pulling my back to his chest, holding me close. One hand glides down my body and hooks my leg over his, giving him better access. My breathing picks up pace as his hands work me over where I need, and then I'm falling apart in his arms, finding my release.

His fingers stop while I catch my breath for a minute, then he whispers, "Come again," and his fingers move over the sensitive spot. They pick up pace, working me fast as I squeeze my core, chasing the feeling again. It grows fast before it washes over me, and my body jerks in his arms for the second time.

My eyes remain closed as my sated smile crosses my face, and his fingertip dips into my belly button before swirling around my stomach.

"Morning sex is good," he whispers. I nod in agreement.

"Hmmm," I mumble.

One hand releases me as he finds his blanket and pulls it over us.

"Sleep sounds good now," his faint voice says.

I nod as my body relaxes back into his. He pulls me closer still, and his breathing evens out before his light snores sound in my ear.

My body wants to sleep, but my mind has other ideas and is wide awake. I lie in his arms for a while, enjoying the sensation of his hold, before I decide to leave. I peel his arm off me and roll away from him as best as I can while he sleeps. A serene look across his face has my finger swiping the hair back from his forehead for a better look.

With as little noise as possible, I pull my clothes back on and then climb to the front seat and exit, closing the door with a soft click behind me.

"Quack," Hugh greets me from the grass, as if to say, "Where are you sneaking off to?"

"I'll see you later, Hugh," I whisper, as I walk away from the duck and his owner, who I'm becoming tangled with. As my feet get further away, the thoughts thrash in my head. By the time I get home after the long walk, I've convinced myself that things are fine and that the lines aren't blurred.

So, what if we slept together? Any feelings that are occurring can be easily extinguished. No more sleeping together, and we will be fine.

When I reach home, Dad has already left for the beach, so I change and grab my surfboard to head that way, too. One thing I know is that the surf will calm my thoughts. It always has. Whenever something is going on, I head out there, and it settles whatever is brewing inside of me.

I reach my patch of sand, drop my bag, and grab my board as I walk towards the surf, feeling my soul settle as I do.

CHAPTER NINETEEN

Dec 25th

Casey

"Merry Christmas, everyone. Thanks for coming in today." Corbin begins our meeting for the day before our shift by saying, "I know it's always hard to be rostered on Christmas day, but let's hope it's a good day out there and everyone gets home safe to their families tonight." Alexis walks around the circle, handing out Christmas hats for us all to wear while we patrol the beach. She hands me one, and a slight blush colours her cheeks.

"Thanks," I whisper, as I take it from her and place it on my head, pulling the elastic under my chin so it holds it in place for the day.

"We never know what to expect, so let's expect the unexpected. It may be quiet, it may be busy, but whatever happens, focus, and then you can all enjoy your night and your days off tomorrow. Let's go," Corbin finishes.

"You're with me today, cheetah," Cheese calls, and my head hangs as I release a groan, making Alexis laugh.

"Is there any way to get rid of the nickname?" I whisper as I pass her.

"No. You're stuck with it for life, so there's no point in trying," she teases, which only makes me groan more.

"Come on, cheetah, or we will change your name to slow poke instead," Cheese teases, as he winks at Alexis.

"How come she doesn't have a nickname?"

"Because I refused to have one," she says, as she slings a backpack with supplies over her shoulder.

"Well, I refuse too."

"You can't. It's too late," Cheese adds. Alexis's smug smile lights up her face as she pokes her tongue out at me.

"Come on, let's get out there. You can worry about names later."

"Fine." I sling my backpack on and follow him out the door. At the last second, I turn and find Alexis watching me, so I poke my tongue out at her, which makes her laugh. As I disappear out of the tower, a smile stretches across my face as her happiness infects me. It's Christmas after all, so best to enjoy the day.

It's quiet for the first half of the day until after lunch, when more families find spots to set up for the warm afternoon. I can't blame them, as it is a nice day outside. They're all full of their festive lunches, and what better end to the day than spending it out on the beach?

When it's time for the shift to end, we head back to the tower for our debrief. There have only been a few minor injuries, with a cut foot, a twisted ankle, and someone with heat stroke. Luckily, there were no incidents in the water today.

Corbin runs through our debrief, then wishes us a safe night before everyone disperses to their families.

"Hey, Casey?" he calls as I'm bent down, retrieving my bag from the bottom of the cubbyholes.

146

"Yeah, boss?" I ask, as I straighten to my full height.

"Come round for dinner tonight, yeah? It's only Alexis and me, so there's always heaps of food left over," he says. I can't say no when he puts it like that.

"Sounds great. Do you want me to grab anything?" I ask, as they are always feeding me. It's only fair if I return the favour.

Corbin must see something cross my face as he stops what he was going to say.

"Love bug?"

"Yeah, Dad?" she says as she walks over to us.

"You know that Ambrosia your mum makes?"

"Yeah?"

"Casey here wants to contribute to our Christmas dinner, and I'm thinking your mum's ambrosia would be perfect for dessert. Could you show him what to get?" I turn to her as she looks between us and nods.

"Sure, we can head there now. See you at home?" she asks, as she turns back to her dad.

"Yeah, I won't be long and then I'll get the ham cooking," he says, as he ruffles her hair.

"Come on then, cheetah. Let's go," she teases.

"Not you too," I groan, making her laugh.

There's a small grocery store on the main street, so we walk over to it from the beach. Following her down the aisles, she hands me ingredients to hold before taking me to the checkout. I pay and put them in a paper bag, then carry them back to my van.

Luckily, Hugh is grazing on the grass, waiting for my arrival, so I pick him up and place him in the van with our food. With Alexis in the passenger seat, I drive us back to her place.

"Okay, we need to whip the cream," she directs.

After washing our hands, I follow her instructions as she hands me the beater. She cuts up all the strawberries while I finish whipping the cream, and then she slides them all off the chopping board into the bowl.

"Drain the can of crushed pineapple for me." I grab the can and pull the tab back, before pushing the lid forward to drain the juice into a mug she hands me. She cuts the marshmallows next.

After draining the pineapple, I hold it up for her inspection; she nods, so I spoon it into the cream mixture. She then slides all her cut marshmallows on top and stirs.

"Looks delicious," I say, as she mixes it altogether.

"It's one of my favourite things mum makes. Dad loves it too, and I'm guessing he hasn't had it in a while," she says, as she finishes. She drops the spoon in the sink after licking it clean and then covers the bowl in cling wrap before placing it in the fridge.

As the door of the fridge closes, the front door opens and in walks Corbin.

"How about you kids relax for a bit while I get the ham on, then you can both help with the sides," he suggests.

"Sure," we say in unison. I spend time with Hugh outside for a bit, as I've been so busy lately, it feels like I don't spend as much time with him. I'm not sure whether it bothers him. He's a duck, so I doubt he thinks of things the way I do.

Alexis finds me twenty minutes later, petting him on her front steps, and we switch positions so she can keep Hugh company. I shower, change and then talk to Corbin in the kitchen.

"Is it okay if I wash a load of clothes?"

"Yeah. Go ahead. You don't need to ask. Whenever you need, the washer and dryer are there," he says.

Before heading to the van, I nod and retrieve my laundry bag, which was getting full. I didn't want to impose on them, and it had slipped my mind the last few days to look for a laundromat. I heave the bag down the hallway and set it to wash before joining them back in the kitchen, where I'm put to work.

We laugh and chat as we work in the kitchen, putting together a salad, bread rolls, and some veggies to roast. The time flies, and then we are digging into our yummy dinner. It makes me thankful I took him up on the offer to join them.

"What do you guys usually do for Christmas?" Corbin asks.

I gulp down the mouthful of food I had before I speak, "We usually have a family breakfast and then my parents would host a fancy Christmas dinner for all their friends." I shovel in another mouthful, hoping this line of questioning ceases.

"Well, sorry you are missing out on spending time with your family, Casey, but I'm glad you get to spend the summer here. It's been nice having you around the place, and you sure make a great lifeguard."

My cheeks warm at his compliment, and I nod, not knowing what to say. I avoid making eye contact with Alexis, but I can feel her gaze on me, too. The conversation dies down after that while we continue eating, and I'm grateful, as I don't like the spotlight on myself.

After we are full, I head down the hall and move my clothes from the washer to the dryer and join them in the living room. Alexis has pulled out some board games for us to play, and the sight of them setting one up makes my heart jump. It brings back memories of my brother and me playing board games with my parents when we were younger, before we got older and lost interest in them.

"Have you played this before?" Alexis asks, as she looks over her shoulder at me.

I glance down at the table, seeing that it is Risk that they have set up.

"I have, actually, so prepare to get beaten," I taunt, which makes her eyes widen and a gleeful smile show. Corbin laughs as he takes a sip from his beer bottle that he's cracked open.

"We'll see," she taunts back, and I take a seat, rubbing my hands together. Hugh curls up on the couch where he'll sleep for a while.

"Do you want a beer, Casey?" Corbin asks.

"No, I'm good. I'll grab a Coke, though," I tell him, and he nods.

"I'll grab them. I wouldn't mind one too," Alexis says, as she jumps up from her seat. She rushes to the fridge and comes back with two cans in her hands. She hands me one, and as she passes it to me, her finger lingers against mine for a beat longer than necessary, causing my lip to pull up a fraction.

We settle in for the game, and once Corbin's daughter defeats him, it's the two of us competing. It goes on for a while until we both relent and give up, neither of us making much headway at all. So, we call it a draw.

"Let's have ambrosia," Corbin says. As soon as the words are out of his mouth, he is out of his seat, rushing to the kitchen to retrieve three bowls and dishing it up. He hands out a bowl each, and we all moan at the yummy dessert.

"That's so good," I tell them.

"Hmmm," is his reply as he's shovelling the food in fast, and Alexis is no better. I contain my laugh at the two of them and focus back on my dessert. We finish, and then I offer to do the dishes.

"I'll help you," Alexis adds.

"Thanks, you two. Well, I'm off to bed. Casey, take the couch for the night, kay?" Corbin says.

"Sure."

He nods before kissing Alexis on the head and walks down the hall.

"I'll wash you dry?"

"Sounds good," Alexis says, as she grabs a tea towel. I fill the sink, and then we get to work.

"Thanks for today. I appreciate you guys having me around so much," I tell her, as I hand her a plate.

"We like having you around. It's no hardship on our part," she says.

I nod to myself, thankful that I came across this special little town. When I finish the last dish, I hand it to her and drain the sink before wiping my hands on another tea towel. She finishes drying the plate and putting it in the cupboard. While her back faces me, I hook my finger into the top of her jean shorts and tug her back to me. She falls against me, and I wrap my arms around her waist as I kiss along her neck.

She angles her neck away from me to give me better access to her skin. I continue trailing my lips to her shoulder.

"I gotta say, this is a pretty good Christmas," she murmurs, and I hum in agreement. I turn her around and press my lips to hers. She slides her hands around my neck, and then my tongue finds hers. We don't get carried away, as her dad is only down the hall. So, after a few minutes, we pull away, panting while still holding onto each other.

"Merry Christmas, Alexis," I say, as I stare into her eyes.

"Merry Christmas," she replies, before kissing my cheek goodnight and then releasing me to head to her bedroom.

CHAPTER TWENTY

Dec 26th

Casey

Alexis invited me to what she called a small backyard party at Kara's tonight. She said they usually have a few of them over the summer, and it'll be the people I met at the bonfire.

She said I could park my car at her place and walk over with her. So here I am, putting the car in park while she stands on her porch. At first glance, my heart stutters at the sight of her. She's wearing a red sundress with white flowers on it. Her braided hair hangs over one shoulder. No makeup or accessories, but she doesn't need them.

Her relaxed smile shines my way as I exit the van and put Hugh down.

"Hey," she says as she steps down the stairs to me.

"Hey."

"Dad's inside if you want him to watch Hugh," she says, and I nod. She jogs up the steps and opens the door to call out, "Dad, can you watch Hugh?" His giddy excitement reaches my ears from the driveway.

"Yeah, of course. Bring him in," he exclaims, which makes me chuckle. Hugh's gathering quite the fan base around here.

"In you go, boy," I tell Hugh, and he needs no more instruction as his wonky legs waddle him straight inside the house as if he owns it.

"Bet he cuddles up with Dad in his bed by the time we get back," Alexis says, while we watch Corbin pick him up with a huge smile.

"Have fun," he calls, and we wave before leaving.

Walking down the driveway, we don't say a word, but the light touch of her finger grazes against my hand as we walk. Before we reach the footpath where the road will lead us to Kara's, I grab her hand and pull her into me, not able to resist her any longer.

"You look so good in that dress," I mumble, as my lips press kisses along her neck. "Do we have to go to the party right now?" I ask, wanting to go somewhere private with her instead. The sun set an hour ago, so it's already dark out and anywhere with her is sounding better than this party.

"What do you have in mind?" her teasing voice whispers in my ear. My hand wraps around her butt, hoisting her into my arms. "Ahh," she squeals at the movement, laughter in her voice. She peers down at me with a cheerful expression on her face as her legs wrap around my waist and her hands push my hair away from my forehead. I squeeze the soft flesh of her ass, which makes her smile grow.

"I have a lot of things in mind," I whisper back, as we stand in the shadows in our bubble. Her smile fades as her head drops to mine, and I slide a hand around the back of her neck, holding her lips to mine. Our soft moans swirl around us in the dark, and I wish we didn't have somewhere to be right now.

She pulls away first, and my lips reach forward. I grab her bottom lip with my teeth, grazing it, making her laugh.

"Later, lover boy. Come on, let's go," she says, and I can't help but pout, which only makes her laugh more. One more squeeze of her ass, and then I lower her feet to the ground, and she smooths her dress down before we walk again.

Before we reach Kara's, we hear the soft melody of music and laughter coming from there. Alexis leads us around the side gate to her backyard, which is overflowing with people. When she said the same people from the bonfire, I thought it was that small group, but this is a lot more than that.

Fairy lights surround the outside guttering of the house. There are a few outside oil lanterns that keep the warmth in the yard, even though the air is still warm from the season.

"Lexi," comes from somewhere in the crowd, and then Ruby and Kara push their way to us.

"Hey, guys," Alexis greets, and I nod my head as they both look at me.

"You drinking tonight?" Kara asks us both, and I shake my head while Alexis says she'll have one or two. Kara steps to the cooler on the concrete patio and pulls out a Canadian Club and hands the dripping wet can to Alexis. She pops the tab and takes a swig of the alcohol before Ruby and Kara pull her into the crowd. She turns back to me and nods her head for me to follow, but I shake it and shoo her with my hand, wanting her to enjoy herself with her friends. I can't monopolise all her time this summer, and I'm fine on my own.

They disappear into the crowd, and I scan my surroundings, not recognising most of the people here. Everyone knows everyone, though, and I get a few looks my way as I must look out of place. People either stand or sit around, laughing and drinking.

154

I haven't touched alcohol in a while now, and don't plan to break that tonight.

"Hey, Casey," the voice says, as they walk up beside me. I turn and recognise the guy from the bonfire.

"Marcus, right?" I ask. His smile widens.

"Yeah. You good? Where's your duck?" he asks, as he looks around the ground as if Hugh will magically appear.

"He's with Alexis' Dad," I tell him, and he nods as if that makes perfect sense. "What?" I ask.

"I heard about you and Alexis," he states, as he sips from his can.

"What does that mean?" I ask, as my guard goes up.

"Nothing, man, James mentioned it. He was pretty cut up, is all. He and Alexis have had a thing for years, and he was hoping it would turn into something more, you know?" he explains, and I nod my head.

"Is this your way of saying I should back off for your friend's sake?"

"Nah, man. You do what you want. I ain't gonna stand in your way. I thought I'd give you a heads up if you notice James being a bit of a grump around you. It's nothing personal, and he will get over it eventually."

"Yeah, that's what I keep hearing," I tell him, which makes him chuckle.

"Don't worry, man. Enjoy your summer, then you'll both be going separate ways anyway, and it will all be a distant memory," he says, as he pats me on my back.

My eyes scan the crowd, locating Alexis. She's facing Kara and Ruby with what I notice is a tight smile on her face. A distant memory. Why does that feel so final?

"I'm gonna go mingle. Catch you later," Marcus says, before he wanders off into the crowd himself, drinking another mouthful as he goes.

Feeling a little off from Marcus' comment, I turn and check the cooler and find a can of cola, so I pull the tab and skull half of it in one go. Holding a drink makes me feel less awkward. I finish the rest before chucking it into the bin and decide it's been long enough by myself.

I angle my body through the crowd, which has grown before I make it to the centre of the yard, where there are more seats. The music is louder here, and some girls sway to the beat with drinks in their hands. Kara and Ruby are two of them, laughing as they move. Alexis isn't with them, and I scan the crowd in search of her. I can't see her, so I step towards her friends instead.

"Hey, have you seen Alexis?" I ask, as I touch Kara's shoulder. She turns to me with a lazy gaze.

"Oh yeah, she went to sit down somewhere. She said a migraine was coming on," she informs me, which pulls my brows together.

"And you aren't worried about her?" I ask.

"Migraines are normal for her. She's used to it," Ruby adds, and I nod as I step away in search of Alexis. A few steps through the crowd, and I find more chairs. Marcus and James sit together laughing while Alexis curls up on another fold out chair with her eyes shut.

The sight has me quickening my steps to her and bending down in front of her chair.

"Alexis?" I ask, as I stroke her arm so as not to alarm her. "Hey, you alright?"

"Don't stress, man. Alexis usually ends up like this at parties," James's drunk voice says, as he turns back to Marcus.

My skin itches with the annoyance that everyone flogs Alexis' pain off like it's nothing.

"Just cramps and a migraine. Honestly, it's normal for me," Alexis grunts, her eyes still closed.

"Come, let's go," I say, so she hears me.

She peeks her eyes open and squints against the light. I stand and hold my hand for her to take. Her other hand wraps around her stomach as she holds it tight. My hand clasps around hers as I lead her through the crowd and to the side gate, not saying goodbye to anyone.

As soon as we step away from the crowd, I turn and lift her into my arms. She cuddles against me as her eyes screw shut.

"Like they said, don't stress. This happens all the time," she tells me.

"Yeah, well, you're obviously in pain, and it doesn't sit right with me that they all blow it off like nothing," I grunt, not having realised how angry I was until I was away from them all.

"It's normal to them now," she defends, and I stop walking to look at her.

"Just because it may be your normal doesn't mean you aren't still in pain. I don't know much about endometriosis, but it bothers me that they don't try to help," I say, feeling my anger rise. It stabs at my heart that she's in pain and there's nothing I can do to help her. I hold her to me as I carry her the rest of the way home.

When we reach her door, I hold her still and open it to find Corbin on the couch with Hugh.

"Love bug, you, okay?" he asks, as he stands from the couch and rushes to us.

"Yeah, Dad. Just migraine and cramps," she tells him, and he nods.

157

"I'll get you some painkillers," he says as he disappears down the hall.

I continue to carry her down to her room. I flick the light on, but she asks me to turn it back off, so I do.

"The light makes it worse," she tells me, and I nod even though she can't see through her scrunched up eyes. I lie her on the bed with care, and she curls up into a ball, cradling her stomach.

"Here, love bug," Corbin says as he walks in with a glass of water and some pills. He hands them to her, and she downs them before handing him the glass back, and she lies back down. "Let me know if you need anything else."

"Thanks, Dad," she says, before Corbin leaves the room. I sit on the end of the bed, watching her, and the pained look on her face pulls at my gut.

"Is there anything I can do?" I whisper.

"Nah. Thanks for bringing me home, though."

"You're welcome. I'll leave you to sleep," I say, and she gives me a slight nod. I stand and lean over her to deliver a kiss to her head before pulling back. My heart tells me to stay, but my head tells me to leave, and my head wins out as I walk out and close her door behind me.

"You're welcome to sleep on the couch," Corbin says from his spot there with Hugh.

"I'll sleep in the van tonight, but thanks. Can I stay in the driveway, though, if that's cool?" I ask.

"Yeah, of course, that's fine. Thanks for bringing her home," Corbin says, looking into my eyes. I nod before turning to walk out the door. I hear Hugh quack before Corbin puts him down, and he waddles my way, coming to join me.

"Night."

"Night," I reply, as Hugh and I leave and hop into the van and settle down on the mattress. I toss and turn for a long time before I decide to text her.

C: Hey. Wanted to let you know I'm sleeping in the van, but I'm still in the driveway if you need me. Hope you get some sleep.

After I hit send, I reread the message and wonder if this is blurring the lines again, but my worry for Alexis wins out, and for tonight, I won't delve too much into the boundaries of our relationship. After moving around until I finally feel comfortable, I fall asleep, worried about the girl inside the house.

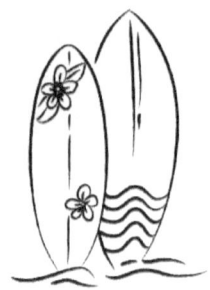

CHAPTER TWENTY-ONE

Dec 27th

Alexis

"How are you feeling today, Love bug?" Dad asks as I drag myself to the table for breakfast.

Turning my back on him, I grab the plastic cereal container, pour myself a bowl of the chocolate balls and follow it with milk before answering, "The migraine is better now. You heading to work?" I take a seat next to him, scooping the cereal into my mouth to finish it before it loses its crunch.

"No, I've got the day off, so I'm gonna head to the shop instead and give Mike a day off."

"You need a day off from working, too, Dad," I tell him, as he's always working.

"Yeah, I've got next weekend off, so I was thinking we could do something if you don't have other plans."

"I've got nothing, so some time with my old man sounds perfect," I say, as the thought brings a smile to my face.

"Who are you calling old?" he asks with a raised brow, making me laugh.

"Don't worry, young at heart is all that counts," I tease, and he shakes his head at me before clearing his bowl of cereal.

"I'd better go, so I make it in time to open. You gonna get up to much today?"

"Didn't plan on it, but I'll let you know if I won't be around for dinner. I'm sure I will be, though," I tell him, before he delivers a kiss to my cheek.

"Take some painkillers if you need, and I'll see you after work. Love you."

"Love you more."

Dad opens the door, and I hear him chatting while I finish my cereal and then begin on the dishes. The creak of the door opening grabs my attention, and I turn with soapy hands.

Casey walks in, followed by Hugh.

"Your dad said you were up, so I thought I'd come check and see how you were," he says, as he closes the door behind him.

"Thanks, I'm feeling better today. Head isn't so sore now." I turn back to the dishes to finish them.

He steps up beside me and grabs my forearm. My eyes gaze up at him.

"Here, sit down while I finish this, kay?"

I wait a beat.

"Please?" he adds, which has me nodding in acceptance.

I wipe my hands on the tea towel while he takes over, scrubbing and rinsing.

"Do you want something to eat?" I offer, as I sit back down.

"No, I'm fine. Are you feeling better?" he asks, as he finishes up and pulls the plug to drain the sink.

"Yeah, I was about to take some painkillers, but I'm better than yesterday."

"Where are they? I'll get them for you," he says, as he wipes his own hands dry.

"You don't have to do that."

"I want to."

"Why?"

"Because someone should," he states, his voice sounding harsh.

"They're used to it," I say, as I wring my hands on the table.

"Yeah, well, that's still not an excuse to not offer any help when you're in obvious pain. Now, where are these painkillers?"

"Bathroom drawer," I say. He retrieves them and returns. Then he fills a glass of water for me to take my pills. I swallow two down and clear my glass away once I'm done. "Thank you," I say, as it's been so long since someone has cared. I know my pain is a regular occurrence, so everyone has gotten used to it, and I handle it as it's my normal, but it is nice to get acknowledged and cared for.

"Now, what's your plan for the day? I have the day off too, so if you're up for it, I thought we could hang out?" he asks, as he takes a seat opposite me.

"If I'm being honest, my cramps are still bad, and I usually will feel drained and tired, but I could do something this morning if you like."

"Are you sure? I'm more than happy to sit on the couch and watch movies if you want the rest." His concern for me warms my body without him even touching me.

"No, let's go do something, and we can come back to the couch later," I tell him.

He winks at me, and it makes my face heat.

"Not what I meant," I chuckle, which earns me a wide smile from him.

"I saw a bike by the side of the house. Up for a ride? I can pedal you around?"

"Really?" I laugh.

"Yeah, why not? Have you never ridden around with someone on the back of your bike?"

"No. Have you?"

"My brother and I used to do it all the time when we were younger."

"You must miss him," I say

He pauses for a beat before he answers, "Yeah. Now come on. Get changed and let's go. I'll get changed too and meet you out front." He pushes his seat back and walks out the door. Following his instructions, I changed and loosely braided my hair, as it helps to not have my hair so tight after a migraine. With nimble fingers, I tie my laces and pull on some sunglasses, ready to go.

I find Casey outside, already seated on the bike, waiting for me.

"I checked the tyres and chain, and they're ready, so hop on," he says, holding a hand out to me with a smile on his face. His smile is infectious, and I can't help the happy feeling that bubbles up in me. I kiss him on the cheek before I take his hand and place a foot on the pole at the back. With my weight in his hand, he helps hoist me over the back wheel. Balancing on the poles, I hold on to his shoulders as a nervous energy flows through me.

"You good?" he calls over his shoulder, as Hugh quacks from the porch where he plops himself, ready to wait for our return.

"Yep, I'm ready," I tell him.

He places his feet on the pedals and we're off. I wobble as I figure out how to balance without toppling us over. The wind blows against my face as he travels down the streets in no certain direction. A smile lights my face. Even though my stomach and lower back are throbbing in pain for a minute, I push the pain away to enjoy this moment.

He swerves the bike back and forth, zigzagging down the street, and our laughter fills the air. He ends up riding us down to the beach and along the boardwalk. It's nice to get some fresh air, but soon the pain becomes too much, so I tap his shoulder. He twists his head so his ear is closer for me to talk, so I know he's listening.

"Is it okay if we head back home?"

"Yeah, sure. You okay?"

"Yeah, starting to feel it is all," I tell him, and he looks both ways before crossing the road and gaining speed down the streets to get me home fast. Cold wind whips at me, and I close my eyes for a second to savour it while I hold his shoulders tight. In a few minutes flat, he has the bike turning into my driveway, where we bounce along and come to a stop right outside the door. His hand outstretched to the side waits for me to grab it so I can step off, and then he follows.

"That was so much fun. Thank you," I tell him, as he pushes the bike back to the side of the house where it usually sits.

"You sure you aren't in too much pain?" he asks, as he scans me as if he can locate my pain by looking at me.

"Yeah, I need some more painkillers and rest. It's nothing new," I tell him, as I take a deep breath.

"Well, if you want company, we can watch movies, or I can head off?"

"No, stay for a bit and watch a movie. I don't know how long I'll be able to stay awake, but stay," I tell him.

"Okay. How about you grab your painkillers, and I'll find us a movie?"

"Sounds good," I tell him, as I walk into the house.

"Hugh?" he calls out, and I stop and turn back, but hear a quack coming from around the side of the house, so I don't worry and head inside. I go to the bathroom, bend over the toilet,

164

holding my stomach. My face scrunches at the pain, and I remain there until it settles. I don't want to burden Casey with how bad it is, but at least more painkillers will take the edge off.

I down the pills and head back to the living room to find him on the couch, already flicking through movies. I settle down next to him and rest my head on his shoulder. He threads his arm over me as the movie starts. The stabbing pain in my stomach lessens as the painkillers take full effect, and then my eyes find it hard to stay open.

A bouncing motion has my eyes opening.

"Taking you to your bed. Go back to sleep," Casey whispers, and I realise he's carrying me. He taps my door open with his foot and lowers me to my bed, where I fall back to sleep, but not without feeling his lips touch my forehead in farewell.

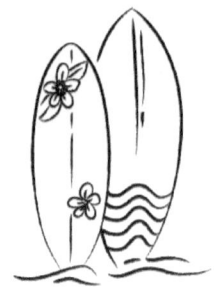

CHAPTER TWENTY-TWO

Dec 30th

Alexis

I've avoided Casey for a few days since he took care of me. I thought the lines were blurring after we fell asleep in his van last week, but now it feels even worse. No one has cared for me in so long, as they are all used to me being in pain, and they know there's not much they can do. But with him being all sweet and taking care of me, my heart forgot I'm supposed to be keeping him at a distance. Now my heart and head feel more tangled together than ever.

Even my surf this morning couldn't settle me, so I know I need to do something. A chat with the girls should help put it into perspective. So that's what I'm doing, lying on my stretch of sand, waiting for them to arrive. I settled here after my surf, not wanting to go home and texting them early to see if they wanted to join me. Both replied that they were free and on their way.

The heat from the sun is still low, and a light breeze flows around me, sending goosebumps down my wet skin while I wait.

Other beachgoers arrive in groups, finding their spots for the day before a shadow blocks my sun. I peek one eye open to find James standing over me with his arms crossed over his chest.

"Hey," I say, as I sit up.

"Hey," he replies, still standing there, not moving. We've hardly talked since he found out about Casey and me. Every attempt I made, he blew off, so I'm surprised he's here now.

"Are you okay?" he asks.

"Yeah, why?" I ask, as my brows pull in together.

He shakes his head and drops his arms before he says, "The other night. I was flippant about your pain, and I'm sorry. It's so normal for us to see you cuddled up in a chair with a migraine or cramps. But just because we are used to it doesn't mean we should ignore it. So, I'm sorry."

"Thanks," I say, accepting his apology.

He nods in reply, and we stare at each other in silence. Neither knows what to say.

He finally builds the courage and breaks it with, "So you and Casey, huh?"

"Yeah, it's nothing serious," I tell him, which only makes his eyes roll.

"Not for you, maybe, Lex, but be careful of him. He seems like he cares," he says, and I drop my eyes to the sand.

"I'm sorry about us. I never meant to hurt you," I confess.

"I know. I guess I cared too much about you, too," he says, before his own eyes drop.

"Hey guys," Kara's voice calls out behind me, and I turn to find her and Ruby walking towards us in their bikinis, beach ready.

"I'm off," James says before he turns and walks away, not even staying to say hi to the girls.

"What's his problem?" Kara asks, and she and Ruby each fling a towel out beside me.

"He's pissed about Casey and me. He didn't say it in so many words, but I can tell he's hurt."

"Well, he has been in love with you for years," Ruby blurts, which has my eyes widening. "Shit," she adds when she sees my face.

"Come on, Lex, you must have known how he felt. He would go all year long, not seeing anyone until you'd come back for the summer, and then he'd be all over you any chance he got. Then he'd repeat it the next year," Kara points out. My head drops back as I close my eyes to the sun and release a sigh.

"I never meant for him to get hurt. I just didn't feel that way about him."

"But you feel that way about Casey?" Ruby asks, as she drops herself on her towel to my left, while Kara drops to my right.

"No!"

"Yes," they both say, which makes them laugh. "We've hardly seen you these last few weeks, Lex. With James, we still saw you every day, but it's different with Casey. You seem, I don't know, happier?" Kara says, which has Ruby nodding in agreement.

"I don't like him like that. I swear."

They both look unconvinced.

"It's okay to let someone in," Ruby says.

"It's not like that. I swear," I say, as I drop my face into my hands.

"You're in denial," Kara says, and again, Ruby nods in agreement.

"Ugh, can we drop it, guys? I don't like him like that. Let's have a fun girls' day on the beach."

"Whatever you say. But Lex, it's okay if you do. It's not the end of the world," Ruby says, as she pats me on the shoulder before she lies down to let the sun heat her body.

"What she said," Kara adds, before she lies back herself. I roll my eyes before I lie back on my towel and let their words filter through my brain. I kept James at a distance and did the friends with benefits thing without getting attached. Why is it different with Casey? I thought I was keeping him at a distance, but he's wiggled his way through my usual defences, and I don't know how to put our boundaries back in place. Some much needed distance is the way to go. Out of sight, out of mind, right?

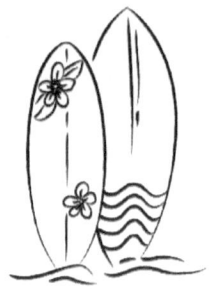

CHAPTER TWENTY-THREE

Dec 31st

Casey

Today's been a long shift. Both Alexis and I were working, along with James and Kara. Corbin said he knew we young ones would party tonight, so he appreciated us coming in today. The beach was full to the brim, and a few saves occurred.

As I'm collecting my bag, I hear Kara and Alexis whispering. It sounds like Alexis is telling Kara not to do something, but I pretend not to hear. I stand up and turn to say goodbye, and find Kara nudging Alexis.

"Have a good night," I say to the pair of them, before I turn to leave.

"Casey, are you doing anything tonight?" Kara rushes out. I turn back around to face them.

"No, I wasn't planning on it."

"Well, they have a New Year's fireworks display down on the pier tonight. People usually come down around seven, and they have a live band playing old cover songs. There are usually vendors there for hot food and drinks, too. You know, if you're free, come down. We'll be down there with Ruby, too," Kara tells me, and my eyes shift to Alexis.

"Yeah, if you aren't doing anything, come."

"Okay, maybe I will," I tell them, before raising my hand in a wave.

My bag hits my back as I fling it over my shoulder and head out the door into the late afternoon sun. The humidity has been unforgiving today and sweat drips down my back as soon as I exit the tower. The van is in the usual spot on the main street, so I walk towards it, finding Hugh nestled down under a tree close by for shade.

"Hugh?" I call, and his head wriggles awake before his wobbly legs waddle him towards me. I pick him up and put him in the passenger seat when I get in the car.

"We're heading to the cove tonight." I'm not sure what it was with Alexis, but it's like she wasn't sure if she wanted to invite me to the fireworks tonight or not. We are spending too much time together, and the lines are blurring. When I thought of friends with benefits, I didn't visualise spending as much time together as we have. We are friends, I guess, and the benefits are few, but weirdly, it doesn't bother me. I should want the physical side more, but I enjoy being around her. Being in her vicinity is enough for me, and that's a problem.

The cove is quiet when I pull up, and I hop out, taking Hugh with me. We sit on the grass, looking down at the beach. There are people down there since it's New Year's Eve. Everyone is ready to go into the new year with big plans and new resolutions. I'm not sure if I'm ready to say goodbye to this year, though.

It's been one heck of a year, and I've lived through things I wish I didn't have to, but I'm still here. If I were going to make a New Year's resolution, I don't even know what it would be.

I break a few blades of grass that are turning brown from too much heat. Releasing them, they drop straight back down with little breeze here today. It doesn't help in cooling me down, as the humidity has been lingering all day.

"Should I go tonight?" I ask Hugh.

"Quack," is his response, and I wish I knew what he meant with that.

My phone vibrates in my pocket, so I pull it out and swipe to open it to see a text from Alexis.

A: *Come tonight and start the year off with a bang.*

That's the sign I was waiting for. I wasn't going to do anything but mope, and fireworks do sound like fun. Instead of texting her back, I push it back into my pocket and think it over instead. I should start living life a bit more and making the most of it. I continue to sit and stare down at the beach below until the sun lowers and reach a decision. It's not like I have anything better to do, so I guess that means I'm going to watch some fireworks tonight.

"Come on, Hugh, let's get moving."

I hang out with Hugh at the cove for a while longer while we watch the sunset and the air cools. Then I drive us back down towards the beach. The main street is full, so I park down a side street and walk to the pier.

It's already bustling with energy as I merge into the crowd. I left Hugh back near the van as I didn't want him getting lost in the crowd, which was a good decision with the volume of people here. It's still early, and already it's hard to walk without bumping into someone.

Kara was right about there being food vendors, so I walked to that side of the pier and grabbed myself some hot chips and a drink for dinner. Somehow, I find an unoccupied seat on a bench and sit there eating the salty food to fend off my hunger.

172

Music and cheers erupt further down the pier, and as I finish my food and pop the rubbish in the trash, my feet lead me towards it. Everyone has pushed in, squishing side by side. The rock song pounds through the speakers, and it's chaos the closer I get.

I decide it's time to live life to the fullest. I push in closer. The heat of nearby bodies makes the air thick with humidity. A light sheen of sweat drips off my forehead, but I ignore it, losing myself in the music. The other bodies around me jump and dance, and a smile tugs my lips at the infectious atmosphere. It's hard not to join in, and I jump along with everyone else.

People around push further in, and the tighter it becomes. My feet stop jumping, but I rock my head back and forth in time with the others' jumps.

"Casey," I hear above the music, and I whip my head to where it came from. Kara, Alexis and Ruby are not too far away, jumping along with the music as well. They all wave at me, showing they have glow in the dark sticks around their wrists and necks, providing a soft, coloured glow in the night. I wave back, but don't make a move to join them. Still feeling uneasy about Alexis not wanting me to come. I don't want to push it.

They don't make a move to come any closer either, until we are a few songs in, and then they surround me.

"Are you having fun, Casey?" Kara's voice shouts.

"Yeah, I am. Are you guys?"

"Yeah," they all yell in unison, as they continue to bop along to the music. My gaze falls to Alexis, and her wide smile encourages me to increase my energy level. I smile back before banging my head along harder to the music.

Distracted by her, I don't see the head in front of me before it's too late, and my nose smashes into the back of the bald skull.

173

"Shit, dude, you, okay?" The guy whose head I whacked asks. My eyes tear up as my nose throbs and my hands cocoon around it, trying to comfort it without touching it. I nod at the guy before I turn away from him. He goes back to his head thrashing as a hand touches my forearm.

"Casey? You, okay?" Alexis asks.

I pull my hands away from my face, and the wide eyes and scrunched up face of Alexis alert me to how bad it is. She grabs my arm and pulls me back through the crowd.

"We'll be back, guys," she yells to Kara and Ruby, who keep dancing to the music. She leads me out of the human cluster of bodies as the warm liquid touches my lips. "Here, I got tissues," she assures me, as she wades through her bag to locate them. She thrusts the yellow packet of tissues into my hands, and I pull one out and hold it up to my tender nose to catch the blood dripping out. "You got him good," she tells me.

"Yeah. I don't think this was the bang you were talking about starting the year off with, though," I joke, which has her laughing.

"Not exactly."

I smile at her even though my nose throbs, and the pain still causes a sting behind my eyes.

"Let's go see if a vendor has some spare ice," she suggests.

I follow behind her with my blood filled tissue pressed to my nostrils. We pass a bin, so I throw it out and replace it with a new one. She heads towards a drinks vendor and talks on my behalf and then hands me a plastic bag filled with ice cubes. I hold it carefully against my battered nose that has already fattened up.

"It's not looking crooked, is it?" I ask, and she removes the ice to get a good look. After inspecting it, she shakes her head.

"No, but it's already bruising under your eyes. I don't think you're gonna be pretty for a bit," she jokes, as she shrugs her shoulders.

"You think I'm pretty?" I tease, which makes her cheeks redden.

"Well, not today, you're not," she teases right back, making me chuckle.

"You can head back to the girls if you like. I'm gonna head back to the van," I tell her, not up to partying anymore with my nose on fire.

"No, it's okay. I can come with you if you want company?"

"You sure? I got the feeling you didn't want me coming tonight," I tell her, and she pushes her lips to the side of her face in thought.

"Come on, let's get out of here and have a talk," she says, as she tugs on my forearm. I follow her through the thinning crowd until we reach the stone wall by the pier, where it's quiet away from everyone.

As we take seats next to each other, she lets out a sigh.

"It's not that I didn't want you to come. It's just that we are supposed to be friends with benefits, but we spend so much time together, it feels more like a couple. I didn't want it getting any more blurred than it already was," she admits.

"Yeah, I get that. We have been spending a lot of time together."

"Right? And friends with benefits are booty calls. We do more couples' stuff sometimes."

"I enjoy your company, but if my being around too much is a problem, then I can pull back, and we can change to just booty calls, if that's what you want."

She drops her head into her hands and lets out a groan before her muffled voice answers, "I don't know what I want. I like hanging out with you, too, but then the girls were asking me all these questions about us and getting into my head. It confused me."

175

"Ahh, I see." Realisation that it's coming from other people and not her settles something inside me. "Why do we have to label it? We enjoy being around one another, and we both know it's only for the summer, so why can't we leave the opinions of others to the side and do what we wanna do?"

"You make it sound so simple," she says with a small smile, as she lifts her head to look at me. I reach forward and tuck a lock of hair behind her ear.

"It is simple. I like you and you like me, right?" She nods in reply. "Then let's do what we want when we want and to hell with everyone else. Deal?" I ask, as I hold out a hand for her to shake. Her palm presses against mine before her warm fingers tighten in a shake.

"Deal." I pull her hand, so she drifts into me with a laugh before I press my lips against her, showing her I don't care what other people think.

"Do you wanna hang around here for the fireworks, or would you like to come with me?" I ask, as I stand by the wall. With my hand outstretched, she thinks over my proposal while her gaze lingers on my fingers before she reaches out and grasps it. Our fingers link, and I pick up my bag of melted ice that I'd dropped, pressing it back against my bruised and battered nose. With her hand in mine, I lead her back to where I parked the van, and we find Hugh hanging around.

She gathers him in her hands and holds him on her lap as I drive back to the cove. There are a few other cars here tonight, people wanting to get a better view of the fireworks.

Reversing the van into a parking spot, I kill the ignition and climb over the console into the back of the van before I open the boot. She follows behind and joins me as we sit in the back, listening to the faded sounds of the band below.

"How's your nose now?" she asks.

"Feels like a punch in the face, but the ice has lessened that a bit."

"We could go get some more ice from my place if you want," she offers.

"No, this is the only place I want to be right now," I tell her, as I look into her eyes. Her eyes soften as her lips pull up, and she leans over to rest her head on my shoulder.

"There's nowhere I'd rather be, either," she whispers, which makes my heart beat faster. After a minute of enjoying the silence, she adds, "Do you have any resolutions for the new year?"

"Not really. I was thinking about it earlier, though, and I want to live my life to the fullest, you know?"

"Yeah, I get that."

"What about you?"

"Hmmm, I want to take more risks this year," she admits.

"That's a good one. You gotta risk it for the biscuit," I joke, making her laugh. She has such a pretty laugh.

"Yeah, something like that."

"Do you have plans for this year?" I ask, wanting to know more about her.

"Finish university and then figure out what I'm going to do for work. I feel like I should already have it all figured out, but I don't."

"It feels like that, but I doubt anyone has it all figured out. I don't know what I'm going to do this year. I'm here for the summer, and then I guess I'll be back on the road to wherever it leads me."

"So, you are gonna leave at the end of summer?"

"Yeah, I never planned to hang around as long as I have already, but I got the lifeguard job and stuff, so I thought, why not?"

177

"Seems weird that you won't be here next summer. I've gotten used to you being around."

"So, I take it you'll be back next summer?"

"Yeah, that's the plan. Finish university, then come back here for the summer before I figure out what I'm going to do or where I'm going to go. Never know, I could end up on a trip driving around Australia, trying to figure out what I'm supposed to be doing."

"You'll be somewhere by the water, I bet," I tell her, before a loud crack sounds in the sky.

"Amazing," she whispers, and I can't help but agree. Another bang sounds as the fireworks explode in the sky, filling the darkness with bright colours. We sit in awe, watching until the last one floats down against the dark backdrop and disappears. In the distance, we hear the faint countdown begin.

"Eight, seven, six, five," we say together as we look at each other. "Four, three, two, one." Faded cheers sound down below us, but they fade away as I stare at the girl in front of me.

"Happy New Year, Alexis," I whisper.

"Happy New Year," she replies, before she reaches forward and kisses me. My hand tangles in her hair and holds her closer. As we lose ourselves in the moment, we both move towards the mattress, and I pull the door of the van closed for more privacy.

Our bodies mould around each other, and we start the new year off with a bang.

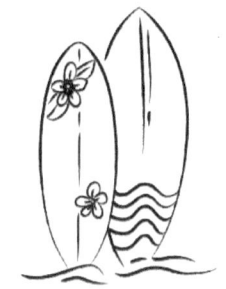

CHAPTER TWENTY-FOUR

Jan 3rd

Alexis

"That was a good session. You're getting better," I praise Casey, as we walk out of the surf, both carrying a board.

"You reckon?"

"Yeah. A few more lessons and then you can take on the big waves," I encourage, as today we spent putting into practice what he had learnt in the whitewash. By the end, he could stand for a couple of seconds before falling. I'm impressed he's picked it up as fast as he has.

"Might have to increase our lessons then if you're able to, as I'm itching to ride the big waves," he says, before he flings his wet hair out of his face.

"Easy tiger, you'll get there. We need to ensure you are ready. Then all this sand and whitewash work will be a distant memory."

We both stick our boards in the sand and grab a towel each to dry off.

"You got plans for the rest of the day?" he asks, as he rubs his blue and white striped towel over his hair.

"I was thinking of getting my belly button pierced. You wanna come?"

"Me? You don't want to go with your girls?"

"Kara is working, and Ruby is busy with her mum."

"Oh, so I'm the consolation prize, am I?" he asks with a raised brow.

"Not at all. I was being nice and asking you, but I can happily go by myself," I say with a straight face.

He lets out a laugh before saying, "Way to make a guy feel special."

"Your ego doesn't need any more inflating. So, do you want to come or not?"

"Fine. I didn't have plans, anyway."

"Let's head back to mine, eat, shower, and then go."

"Cool."

After we scoff our cereal down and shower all the sand and seawater off, we walk the same trail back to the main strip of shops where the tattoo and piercing parlour is.

A guy with blond wavy hair and tattoos down his arms greets us as we walk in, "Welcome, how can we help you guys today?"

"I want to get my belly button pierced. Is anyone available to do it?" I ask as we step to the counter.

"Yeah, sure. Heath will be out in about fifteen minutes. If you fill out your details here, he can sort you when he's free," he says, as he hands over a black clipboard with a page attached to it. Scanning through it, I have a few sections to fill in, so I take a pen and follow Casey to the seats. I write all my details and answer all the questions they have.

"Hey guys, who is getting the piercing?" A deep voice asks, which makes me look up from the paper.

"Me," I say, and he smiles my way.

"Cool. I'm Heath. I'll sanitise the room and then we will be ready to start," he says, before turning his back on us. My knee bounces as I hold the clipboard to my chest.

"Are you nervous?" Casey asks, and I force my knee to stop moving.

"A little. Feels real now," I say, which makes him nod before he reaches out and links my fingers with his and squeezes my hand.

"I'll even hold your hand when he's piercing you if you like," he says, no sarcasm at all.

"Thanks," I whisper.

"You can pick out which jewellery you want," the first guy says, so we stand and walk over to the case with all the different jewellery pieces behind it. "Titanium pieces are quite popular, as most people don't react to them. Sometimes the silver or gold doesn't agree with people and can grow out when the piercing doesn't heal," the guy explains, so I move over to where he points out the titanium pieces. I see a blue and purple plain barbell that I decide on and tell him that's the one.

Heath comes back a few minutes later and takes my completed form. His eyes scan over all my details and questions, and when satisfied, he nods before leading us into the room.

"Lie down for me, Alexis," he instructs, so I hop up onto the black table and lie back. Casey stands beside my head so he can hold my hand. "Now double checking, but you aren't allergic to anything?"

"Not that I know of," I say, as I shake my head.

"You've gotta take care of it. Apply this lotion morning and night so it doesn't get infected. And rotate it around every so often as well. Be a bit more aware that it's there too, as people sometimes get their new piercings stuck on clothes and stuff, and they can get hurt when they get pulled on." He runs through all the home care I'll need and any other things I need to keep in mind about having a new piercing. He applies some numbing cream and continues talking to me while that reaches its maximum effect.

Sweat accumulates where Casey holds my hand, but he doesn't mention it, just continues to let me squeeze his.

"Okay, lie as still as you can. You shouldn't feel too much now since I numbed it. It'll mainly be pressure. You ready?"

"Yeah," I tell Heath, as I squeeze Casey's hand tighter. A dull pinch on the skin above my belly button before he tugs and pulls. It doesn't hurt too much, and I'm thankful he numbed it. I glance at Casey, and his eyes are set off to the side of the room, avoiding what Heath is doing.

A few more tugs and then he's saying, "All done. If you hop up, you can have a look." I swing my legs over the side of the bed after I release Casey's hand and stand up. My smile widens as I step in front of the floor length mirror and examine my new accessory.

"Aww, it's so pretty. Thank you," I gush.

"Not a problem. Come on, we'll head out to reception, and we'll finish the payment and go through home care again." He steps aside for us to leave the room, with Casey close behind me.

Ten minutes later, all paid up and with my lotion in my hand, we leave the shop with one more hole in my skin than when we entered.

"What do you think?" I ask Casey, as we stop a few steps away from the shop, once we've left. My shirt is still rolled up, as I didn't want it rubbing against the piercing.

"It's pretty sexy if I'm being honest," his husky voice says, causing my cheeks to heat and a warmth to flood my body.

"Is that so?"

"Aha," he hums, as his smile widens and he steps towards me, which causes me to step back until I hit the brick wall of another shop, and he invades my space.

"Really sexy," he whispers, as his body pushes against me and his lips drop to mine. My arms wrap around his neck, and for a minute, I forget we are out on the main street of town. It's just Casey and me. He pulls away a few minutes later, smiling at me. Something sparkles in his eyes as his thumb wipes across my bottom lip. We don't speak, but I can't help the warm feeling that spreads throughout me as his fingers link with mine and he holds them the entire way home, not letting go once.

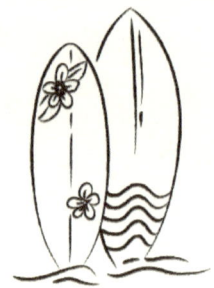

CHAPTER TWENTY-FIVE

Jan 5th

Alexis

"How was your shift today?" I ask Casey, as we sit on the stone wall, watching as people arrive for our bonfire party down on the beach.

"I had another close call with a guy who was drowning today. He'd gotten swept out further and faster than he realised and began panicking. He went under a few times before I got to him, but luckily, we got to him in time," he says as his gaze stares out into the dark ocean before us.

My shoulder rocks against his to gain his attention.

When he looks my way, I say, "Well, if you need the distraction from your thoughts, I'm here. That's what our arrangement was about, after all." His full pink lips pull up in the corner, and my eyes drop to them, and I can't help wanting to taste them. My tongue wets my lips, causing his eyes to drop to them.

SWEET FOR THE SUMMER

"Easy tiger, let's get through the bonfire first, shall we?" he teases, which makes me push my shoulder harder against his as he laughs.

"I…"

"Hey, guys," Kara cuts me off, and we both turn to the sound of her voice. She walks with Ruby, both with a hand on either side of the esky. Casey jumps down from the wall and jogs to them.

"I've got it," he says, as he replaces their hands with his and carries it in front of him.

"Thanks," they say in unison. I jump down myself, and Hugh waddles beside me as we follow them. Kara leads us to where the rest of the group is already sitting. We saw James arrive, but kept our distance as it's already awkward enough, and we don't want to start the night off with tension.

"You guys good?" Marcus greets us, and we nod. Casey places the esky on the sand and then clasps hands with Marcus in a one handed hug. I smile at their friendship because it's nice that Casey has found another friend apart from me.

The girls help me unroll the mat I have with me, then we all sit down and join in on the conversations that are going on around us. Marcus offers a chair to Casey, which he takes, and they fall into easy conversation while Hugh snuggles next to Casey, curling up to sleep.

"Do you want a drink?" Kara asks from beside me, while Ruby sits behind us.

"Yeah, sure. I don't have plans for tomorrow, so I'll have a beer," I tell her.

"Yes, let's drink the night away," she squeals, and Ruby and I join in laughing with her. She hands me a cold beer from the esky, and we clink our cans together after I pull back the tab. The cool liquid slides down my throat, and I lay my legs out in front of me, ready to relax for the night.

"This summer feels like it's going fast," Ruby says, and I nod in agreement.

"Yeah, it does," I murmur, as my eyes roam over Casey as he talks to Marcus.

"We need to make the most of what's left. It always speeds up faster the closer it gets to the end. Especially when it's nearly time for you to leave, Lex," Kara adds.

"I wish you lived here all year round," Ruby mumbles.

"Yeah, me too. Who knows, maybe at the end of the year that will be a possibility. Or I'll end up travelling or something. I will probably end up working a boring job, though," I ramble, before the can hits my lips again for another drink.

"Well, we will be here whatever you end up doing," Kara says.

"I'll definitely be back next summer, anyway," I tell them, and I catch Casey's eyes as he looks my way and smiles.

One drink turns into two, then three and four, and before I know it, my vision is blurring and I'm laughing louder with the girls about stories from the past. Our group has formed somewhat of a circle, and everyone adds stories and memories, and we all join in with snippets of what we remember. It's a nostalgic vibe, and we all radiate with it.

Casey isn't drinking. He sips on his cola can, watching and laughing at our stories. His eyes linger on me longer, and I wish we were alone, but I stay where I am for fear I may jump into his lap if I move.

A few more drinks and stories later and Kara declares she needs to pee.

"I'm coming."

"Me too," Ruby and I declare, so we push up to stand, our giggles following us as we wander down the beach to the toilets.

"Hey, wait up," Casey calls, and we stumble around to look at him.

"You come to be our bodyguard?" Kara asks, which only serves to increase our laughter.

"Something like that," he mumbles, as his eyes linger on me. "Come on, let's keep going," he adds, and we turn our attention back to our destination.

After a lot of stumbling and laughing, we make it to the toilets, and Casey waits outside for us to come out.

On our way back to the others, he grabs my hand and pulls me into his side. We stop and look into each other's eyes, and the world drifts away; only the sound of the waves hitting the shore surrounds us.

"You guys coming?" one of the girls yells, but I can't make out who.

"You guys go ahead. We'll catch up," I call back, and their laughter and words grow more distant the further they get. Casey and I stand in the dark, the bonfire further down the beach, where we are in a world of our own.

"You having fun?"

"Yeah. Are you?" I ask.

"Yeah, I am. I don't know, I missed you or something," he says as he stares into my eyes.

"I'm right there," I say, as I squint an eye at him, trying to focus.

"I know, but you feel a million miles away," his soft voice says, as he pulls me closer, holding me loosely around the waist.

"You doing okay?"

"Yeah," he says, but in a distant part of my brain, I suspect it's a lie. My finger reaches up and pushes against his cheek to make him smile.

"Why don't you look happy, then?"

187

"Stuff on my mind," he admits, as he drops his forehead to mine.

"You wanna talk about it?" I ask as my feet stumble, trying to hold myself steady.

"Not tonight. Let's have fun," he says.

"You wanna look at the stars?"

"Huh?"

"The stars? I usually look at them more when I'm here because it's a lot clearer than in the city. Come," I say, as I tug on his hand and pull him as I stumble to a dry patch of sand. I drop and pull him with me, and we laugh as we fall. He tucks his arm under my head, and I wrap my arm around his waist as we gaze up at the dark sky with the millions of bright stars above.

"It's so pretty out here," I mumble.

"Yeah, it is," he whispers back, as he delivers a kiss to my temple.

We lie in silence, lost in our thoughts, but comfortable. My head spins from the alcohol, and the stars blur as I fight to keep my eyes open.

"Wish we didn't have to part," I mumble, as my eyes struggle to stay open.

Casey's voice fades, but I hear, "Me too." With his arms around me, the warmth from him fills me, and I drift away.

The sounds of voices pull me from wherever I drifted to as I bounce around, disoriented.

"I got you. I'm taking you home. It's okay," Casey's voice reaches my ear, as Kara and Ruby's laughs surround me.

"Thanks for walking us home, Casey. And take care of Lexi. Bye, Lexi," Kara says as her hand squeezes mine.

"Bye, guys," I murmur, which makes them giggle.

"Bye," Casey says as he lifts me higher in his arms, and then I'm bouncing again as he walks away from them.

"You walked them home?"

"You fell asleep, and I suggested that I walk them home. So that's what we did. Now I'm carrying you home."

"Thank you," I whisper.

"It's not a problem. Gotta get you guys home safe," he says.

"We are here," he adds, and I must have drifted off again while he walked us home. He places me on my feet outside the front door to my dad's.

"You wanna sleep on the couch?" I ask, as he holds me up, but he shakes his head.

"Nah, I'll sleep in the van," he says, as his eyes flick to his van in my driveway.

"How about I sleep with you? I don't wanna go inside."

"That's not a good idea. Your dad might see us," he says.

"I'll sneak into the house later. Please?" I ask, as I try to bat my lashes at him, but with the way he chuckles, I'm not sure I pull it off.

"Come on, then," he whispers as he helps me stumble down to his van. He opens the boot, and we climb in before he shuts it behind us, trying not to make noise. I crawl over the bed and go to kick my shoes off when I realise they are missing.

"Where are my shoes?"

"On the porch. I carried them as you took them off at the beach," he says, as he crawls up beside me. I turn to face him as our bodies wrap around each other, and he pulls his blanket over us.

"I wish this summer could last forever," I whisper, and his finger wipes my hair away from my face.

"Maybe fate will bring us back together one day," he says.

"Maybe," I say, as my heavy eyes close.

"Sleep, Alexis." His soft lips touch my forehead, and that's the last thing I remember.

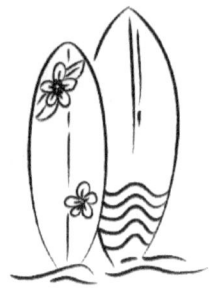

CHAPTER TWENTY-SIX

<u>Jan 7th</u>

Casey

Darkness surrounds me. I can't see. My heavy feet trudge through mud as if they are sinking. Step after lethargic step. Where am I going? I'm unsure of my destination. All I know is I must keep going.

Keep pushing.

When I get there, I'll know.

I can feel it.

It's just out of reach.

With every step I take, it feels as if the destination moves further out of reach.

As I crawl through the thick mud, my body curls over itself. My tired body pushes on. My heart urges me to keep going. I must keep going.

"Why?" I scream.

No answer.

My body senses that I must continue, though.

I can't stop now.

I'm so close.

My tired breaths surround me in the pitch black as I crawl through the sludge. Fatigue weighs me down, but I can't stop. There's something out there I need.

Something I'm searching for.

My movements slow as my body gives up, while my heart continues to wail at me to keep going.

But I can't.

As my body drains of its last bolt of energy, my hand slips, my head falls and then…

"Ahhh," my body flings upright as my laboured breaths fill the van. I'm safe. I'm in the van. It was a dream.

Sweat drips into my eyes, so I wipe it away with the back of my hand. My shaking fingers thread through my hair, pushing it away from my sticky skin.

My chest heaves as my heart pumps in my chest. Adrenaline floods through me. Hugh sleeps next to me, undisturbed. It's still dark outside in the cove, the world around unaware of the turmoil racing through my veins.

My head drops into my hands, and I take a deep breath, holding it for a count of three before exhaling. Working to slow my heart rate back down. I repeat the process, over and over. In and out. In and out. Until my breaths quieten.

My head flops back onto my pillow, and I fling the drenched blanket off. My body needs to cool down.

I grab my phone, the light illuminating my face as I read the time. 1.13 am. Still too early to be awake. I'm not sure if I'll get back to sleep, though. Not after that. I thought I had them under control, but I guess not. Everything is temporary. Nothing is forever.

191

I drop my hand, and my phone falls face down on my mattress. My eyes flutter shut, and I force myself to think of sleep. Trying to force myself under. Sleep. If only it were that simple to fall asleep when you wanted to. Then wouldn't life be so much easier?

My body tosses and turns, but sleep doesn't come.

"Beep, beep, beep." The sound of my alarm arrives, but I'm already awake. I've been awake since the nightmare, not able to drift back to sleep. Rolling my neck from side to side, I stretch out the stress. It's going to be a long day, and I'm going to need a caffeine hit before I meet Alexis and the others, so I'd better get moving.

The blankets hit the side of the van with a thwack as I fling them off and change my clothes. Then I open the boot of the van, let Hugh out, brush my teeth and double check my backpack for all I need.

Back in the van, I drive to Alexis's house, where we are all meeting. The van bumps down the rocky driveway until I park and see Alexis on the porch, gathering a couple of surfboards and her stuff. Her head raises as I hop out of the van and greet her.

"Good morning," she says, as her excitement wafts off her. I push the lingering effects of the nightmare away and absorb some of her energy, letting that flow over me instead.

"Good morning, you," I whisper, as I wrap my arms around her waist and taste her lips before I can stop myself. Luckily, the other night I woke her before her dad so she could sneak back into the house without him realising she spent it with me.

The sound of another car travelling over the gravel of her driveway is the only thing that pulls me away. I step out of her space before they see us. We are still friends with benefits, but it seems the lines have blurred completely. I often wonder if we were ever that from the beginning. It always seemed like more, even when neither of us would admit it.

I don't know how it happened. One day she's asking me for the arrangement, and the same night I stay on her couch, and we go from one to a hundred. I don't regret it, but if she hadn't proposed the arrangement in the first place, then I doubt either of us would have taken a second glance at the other person. Neither of us was looking for a relationship.

"Hey, you two. You ready?" Marcus greets us as he steps out of his Ute.

"Yeah, can you fit these boards in the back?" Alexis asks, as another car comes down the drive, parking behind Marcus.

"Yeah, I got them. Chuck your bags and stuff into the back, too. Then we can sort out who is going in which car when we've all arrived."

"Feel it's gonna be a great day," Kara calls, as she and Ruby walk up from their car.

"Yeah, it does, doesn't it?" Alexis calls back. I help load up the boards for Alexis in the back of Marcus's truck, and Marcus grabs the big esky. Alexis also has bags with snacks, so I put those in the back of his truck, along with my backpack. A few more cars arrive down the driveway before more people join us. James is one of them, and I avoid his irritated gaze.

"Is that everyone?" Marcus calls, and everyone gathers in front of him as he's somehow become the designated leader of this trip. Well, he is the reason for this trip.

"Okay, I'm taking my truck. Kara has her car. James, are you taking your car, too?" Marcus asks.

"Yeah. I got Riley and Grotto coming with me," he responds.

"Alexis, Cascy, you guys can jump in with me or with Kara and Ruby if you like? Courtney should be here in a minute too, and she's coming with me," Marcus informs us. I glance at Alexis, and she nods at Marcus, so I'm not sure who she wants to go with, but I assume it will be with Kara and Ruby. "Everyone can follow me, but if you get split from the group, we can always pull over along the way for someone to catch up. We need to get a move on, though, as we gotta be there by 8 am to sign up for the competition."

Excitement sweeps through the air at the day trip we are taking up the coast. Everyone moves around, heading to the cars they are riding in.

"You wanna go with the girls?" I ask Alexis as I step closer to her.

"Yeah, you wanna come or are you gonna go with Marcus?"

"I'll ride with you if that's cool?"

"Yeah, we can ride in the back. I'm gonna say bye to Dad and remind him that Hugh is around. I'll be back."

I step over to where Hugh grazes near the van and bend to pick him up.

"Hey, bud, I gotta go for the day. But I'll be back tonight. Corbin will take care of you," I tell my feathered friend, as I stroke his soft feathers before placing him back on the grass.

"Quack," he replies, before he wobbly wanders away from me.

"Okay, kids, have a pleasant trip. Drive safely there and enjoy yourselves. Good luck, Marcus," Corbin yells out, so everyone can hear him.

"Thanks, Corbin," Marcus says. Corbin raises his hand in farewell before Alexis delivers a kiss to his cheek. He smiles at her before she rushes off to Kara's car.

"Thanks for watching Hugh for me," I say, as I pass him.

"Not a problem. Have fun and I'll see you later," he says, before I make my way around to the other side of Kara's car and jump in the back with Alexis. A girl with black hair comes running past as I close the door, and she sits in the passenger seat of Marcus's Ute.

"That's Courtney. Lucky, we didn't go with them because it's likely they will end up fighting," Alexis tells me, which makes her, Kara, and Ruby burst out laughing.

All the cars reverse one after the other, and then we follow each other down the roads until we reach the highway going north.

"Have you been up this way on your travels, Casey?" Ruby turns as she speaks to me.

"No, I haven't."

"You'll love it. Wattle Downs is nice, but the beach we are going to is a lot clearer. They always start the skim competition over the summer there, and Marcus and Alexis usually compete, so our group always goes if we can," she informs me.

"Are you nervous?" I ask Alexis.

"A little. This is my third year doing it now, so I'm used to it as I know what to expect."

"I'm sure you'll be great," I say, as I wink at her, which makes her smile. I slide my palm face up across the back seat, and her gaze drops to it. She links our fingers, and we rest them together as we look out our opposite windows. My head falls to the glass, and I watch as the trees along the highway pass us by. The girls sing along to some old songs from the early 2000s that they know all the words to, and I let their happiness wash over me. My eyes drift shut, and I finally get the much needed sleep I was after.

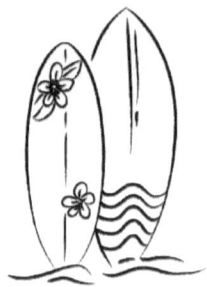

CHAPTER TWENTY-SEVEN

<u>Jan 7th</u>

Casey

"Hey, Casey, we're here," Alexis's soothing voice drags me from my sleep as she shakes my shoulder. The bright sun hits my eyes as I squint when opening them.

"Hey, did I sleep the whole way?" I ask, as it's just the two of us in the car. Kara and Ruby are missing.

"Yeah," she laughs. "Our fabulous singing must have been a lullaby to you." I laugh at her joke.

"Where are the others?"

"Everyone found car parks close together, so they all hopped out to find a place to set up for the day. You, okay?" she asks, as her head tilts to the side and her eyes flicker back and forth, as if in search of something.

"Yeah, I didn't sleep well last night. Think it was the excitement of seeing you guys compete that kept me awake," I lie, but her smile widens. It doesn't completely reach her eyes, though, so I'm unsure if she bought it or not.

"I know we agreed to avoid deep talks, but our boundaries seem skewed. We're friends, so if you need to talk, I'm here to listen, okay?"

"Thanks, Alexis," I say, as I click my seatbelt and remove it, then lean over the chair and press my lips to hers. I tuck her hair behind her ear as we stare into each other's eyes. "I bet you are going to be amazing today."

"Fingers crossed. I wouldn't mind winning the prize of a thousand bucks. So, let's go meet the others."

We exit the car and walk away from the car park and find our group setting up close to where the action will be for the day. There are marquees set up for the people hosting the event, and we aren't far from them. The guys are setting up beach bungalows to keep us shaded. Meanwhile, the girls are laying out a big picnic mat for everyone to sit on.

"What do you guys need help with?" I ask, as we reach them.

"Hey, sleepyhead. There's a shop across the road if you guys wanna grab some ice?" Kara suggests.

"On it." Alexis follows me. We duck into the shop and grab four bags of ice. She stands and watches as I throw them on the footpath to break them up. Then we carry them to the eskies and fill them up.

"Alexis? We gotta go sign up," Marcus calls to her, so she turns and heads off with him to the marquees, and the rest of us find a spot to sit for the day. She and Marcus return about fifteen minutes later, smiling, and I can feel the excitement coming from her.

She drops beside me, and Ruby rolls over from her spot on a towel to talk to her. My eyes gaze out at the clear water in front of me. The others were right; it is a pretty beach. Even clearer blue waters than Wattle Downs. Thoughts wash over me as I stare out at the horizon, and I let them wander.

"Hey, you good?" The nudge of Alexis's elbow against my arm brings me back to the present.

"Yeah, just admiring the beach. It's nice here," I say, trying not to expose myself and that my mind is a million miles away.

"Yeah, it is. Dad and I used to travel a lot over the summers up and down the coast, and this beach is one of my favourites," she admits. She sits close enough that I lean back on my hands, stretch my legs out in front of me and wriggle my fingertips to touch hers. The soft touch of her finger sliding back and forth across my hand sends a flood of warmth through me. My smile drifts out to sea, not wanting to look at her as the others are all close by. So, we stay in our little bubble, hoping the others don't notice us.

"Let's go, Lexi," Marcus calls about an hour later.

"Wish me luck," she says, as she stands.

"Good luck," I reply, as the others all yell out their own words of encouragement at the duo. They grab their boards, which are smaller than the regular surfing boards, and head over to the other competitors.

We watch and cheer as everyone competing takes turns running out and skimming along the sand into the small waves. Marcus heads out, and the cheers from our group are so loud that they block out what the commentators say. He looks effortless out there, and we aren't the only ones who roar for him.

Alexis is a few people later, and I'm mesmerised as she runs and glides as if she were born to the sea. Her board whips back and forth, and she rides the small wave and comes out on her feet, instead of getting bowled over like many of the others.

The day passes, and the competition ends by lunchtime. Marcus took out the whole thing with Alexis, lasting until the top four. She dries herself off and sits beside me, a big smile on her face.

"You did amazing," I whisper.

"Thanks. It was so much fun."

"My shout for lunch, everyone," Marcus yells to our group, as he waves his envelope with his winnings in it. Our cheers erupt, and with everyone in high spirits, we make our way down to the burger joint that isn't too far down the beach.

We all place our orders, and Marcus pays. We eat, laugh and talk, and as I sit there, I can't help but feel how nice this is. I've never had a close knit group of friends growing up. Not ones who cared about me as a person. So, glancing around at everyone joking and smiling, I let it wash over me. Contentment. If I could stay here forever, I would, but it's not in the cards for me.

After lunch, we head back to our spot, and everyone lies out on towels to soak up the sun or heads into the surf for a swim. I follow the swimmers, wanting to get into the water. I drift off from the group and swim back and forth, completing some laps and working off some of the tension that has filled my body since this morning. My head usually feels lighter after a swim, so I push myself until I'm drained.

Once I'm done, I head back to the sand where the girls lie out on their towels.

"You look amazing out there, man. You compete?" Marcus asks, as we both dry off.

"Yeah, I used to. Not anymore," I tell him, and he nods in understanding. We both drop to rest and grab a drink each. I spend the next hour talking with him about swimming and surfing, and I enjoy his company. It's been a while since I've made a genuine friend apart from Alexis, so I savour it.

The afternoon turns into evening, and we pack up and head back to our cars to head back to Wattle Downs. Everyone piles into the cars they came in, and I find myself in the back seat with

Alexis again. She keeps holding her stomach the further we get from the beach, so I ask if she's okay.

"Yeah, cramps. Nothing I can't handle," she whispers back, and it pinches at my heart. She's always so strong. Even when she's in pain. I tug on her hand and wriggle my legs over as I pull her head down to rest on my lap.

"Try to rest," I whisper, as I run my fingers through her hair. She curls up on her side, the best she can, with her seatbelt across her. One arm wrapped around her stomach. Her eyes close, and I continue stroking her hair until her soft breaths even out and she sleeps. I rest my head backwards and let the long day pull me under, too.

I wake up as we are pulling into the driveway of Alexis's place, so I give her a light shake to wake her. We all get out and say our goodbyes as the girls reverse out. The others all headed straight home, so it leaves Alexis and me on her driveway alone.

"Sleep on the couch tonight?" she asks, and I nod. She takes my hand to pull me to the door of her house, but I halt her and press her against the side of the house. It's dark out, and the sun has already set. My fingers thread through her hair as I wrap my other arm around her. Our lips connect, and I deepen the kiss. The feel of her in my arms has me squeezing her tighter as we continue the kiss until we are both out of breath.

"I've wanted to do that all day," I admit, as my forehead rests on hers. Her eyes lift before she presses her lips once more against mine, before she finds my hand again and pulls me through the door this time.

The couch is ready to go. Corbin is hoping I will stay. Hugh is nowhere in sight, but Alexis tells Corbin we are home safe, and when she comes back, she tells me where Hugh is.

"He's cuddled up by Dad's head," she giggles, and I can't help how my smile lights up.

"Guess those two are best buddies now," I joke. "Thanks for today. I had fun."

"Yeah, it was a good day. I'm gonna take some pain meds then crash out. I'm exhausted. You gonna be okay?"

"Yeah. Goodnight, Alexis."

"Goodnight," she says, as she turns and walks to her room. When she reaches her door, she raises her hand in a small wave, and I do the same before she steps into her room and disappears. I lie down, and it isn't long before my exhaustion washes over me, too.

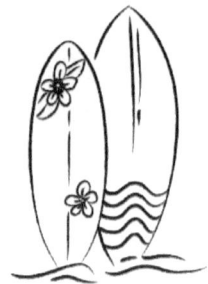

CHAPTER TWENTY-EIGHT

Jan 11th

Alexis

I'm not sure how to explain it, but Casey is pulling away. He seems physically here, but mentally, he's distant. I often catch him staring off into space, lost in his thoughts. Every time I ask if he's okay, he says he is, but I can't help but wonder if he is. I know we set the boundaries about no deep conversations, but sometimes I wish I hadn't. He still feels like a stranger. We may know the other's body, but lately I've been craving to dive deeper with him. I don't know when it happened, but I don't want him to feel like a stranger anymore. I've finally found someone I want to let down my guard with.

Since we arrived back from the skim contest, I haven't seen him. We worked the same shift a few days ago, but with different partners. He left right after, so I didn't get to talk to him.

Today I have a day off, so I'm sitting down on my spot at the beach. The girls were both busy, and I texted Casey to come hang out with me, but he never replied, so I didn't push it. I wish I knew what was bugging him.

The heat from the sun warms my skin as I lie on my towel, head covered with my hat and let my thoughts float around in my head. I still don't know what I will do after this final year of university. I should worry about that, but I guess it can wait until the summer is over. For now, it's in the future, and I don't need that stress weighing me down.

The presence of a body sitting next to me causes me to pull my hat off my face, squinting against the sun to see who invaded my space. Casey's naked torso faces the water, with sunnies covering his eyes as he sits next to me, not saying a word.

"You came," I say. His gaze remains on the sea, and I wish I could pull him out of wherever it is he's gone. Silence. It stretches between us before he releases a sigh and lies down next to me.

"Sorry. Just have a lot on my mind," he utters.

"You can talk to me if you wanna unload?" I offer. His head turns my way, and we stare at each other. I can't see behind his dark lenses, though, so I am without a clue what his thoughts may be.

"Can we lie here without talking? I'm not up to company, but I didn't want you to be alone since you asked me to come," he says, and I nod.

"Yeah, we don't have to talk," I tell him, as I lie down beside him and cover my face with my hat again. Forcing myself to focus on my breathing to settle the frantic beat in my chest, I pretend he's not here. If silence is what he needs, then silence is what he'll get. My body warms back up from the sun's heat while the sounds of children playing and family and friends laughing invade my ears. I focus on their summer sounds instead.

Roughly twenty minutes into our silence, his hand slides into mine and links our fingers. I squeeze him tight, hoping he can feel what I want to say, but don't.

We remain like that for the rest of the day. We turn over but find each other's hands again. I apply sunscreen, and so does he, but our hands reconnect after. He goes for a swim to cool down, then lies back down and again finds my hand waiting for his.

We spend the day like that. Not talking at all. And when the sun sets, he finally loosens his grip on my fingers. He grabs his backpack and towel and stands. I pack up my stuff, and we end up staring at each other, waiting.

"Thanks for today, Alexis. I'll see you later," his hoarse voice says, before he leans into me and kisses my cheek, before he walks away from me. And I watch him leave. How do I reach someone who seems so far away?

CHAPTER TWENTY-NINE

Jan 13th

Alexis

Over the last few days, I've been thinking about doing something nice for Casey. There's something about him I can't quite put my finger on, but I often sense a dark cloud hovering over him. I've become more aware of it because I spend so much time with him, and we've developed a kind of connection.

A few loose pebbles under my thongs dig in through the leather, so I slide my foot back and forth to move them when I hear it. The loud hum of his Crombie van as it comes down the street, a few seconds before Casey drives it down the bumpy driveway of ours.

My smile stretches wide as I step to the side for him to pull up next to me.

"How are we this morning?" I ask, as I fling the passenger door open and hoist myself inside.

"Half asleep. Why did we have to leave at the ass crack of dawn?" he grumbles.

"You got the boards?" I ignore his comment with my question.

"Yes, they are in the back, where we stowed them last night. I worried they were gonna fall on me all night." His sullen mood continues.

"Well, you know very well you could have slept on the couch, and it wouldn't have been an issue," I remind him.

"We already talked about this. I don't want the lines blurring." He releases a heavy sigh.

"I already told you they weren't blurring on my end," I lie, and by the way he raises a brow at me, I know he knows I'm lying. I ignore his look and change the subject. "You'll cheer up when we get there," I say. His straight face tells me he's not impressed as he looks at me while reversing.

"Where is this magical place, anyway?" He questions, as a yawn takes over his face, and he goes along with the change of subject. He waits until his yawn is over before he backs onto the road and drives.

"Head towards the highway, and I'll direct you from there. We had to leave early so we could get there early enough for the surf."

"We should have left last night," he tells me.

"Well, I thought you would have been too tired after your shift," I explain. He shrugs his shoulders and follows my instructions and heads to the highway. I turn the knob on the radio to play some light music. Nothing too crazy for three in the morning. The humidity is suffocating in the van, so I lower my window.

"Where's Hugh?" I ask, craning my neck to the side to get a glimpse of him.

"He's still sleeping down the back. He's not silly enough to wake up at this hour if he doesn't have to."

"You should be a morning person with all the morning swims you've been fitting in."

"I am, but not this early. And I had trouble falling asleep last night," he admits.

"Maybe you needed some stress relief. You should have texted," I tell him as I keep my eyes out the window.

He ignores my comment, and we ride in silence for most of the two hour journey. Casey, I've noticed, isn't the biggest talker and is content to sit in silence if you allow it. I usually like to talk. But being around him, I've learnt to enjoy the silence more or else I just enjoy being around his silence. Something about it is soothing. Comforting even.

"Turn off here," I instruct, pointing to the off ramp up ahead. I continue directing him until we hit the main road to our destination. Welcome to Tempest Cove, the sign reads as I tell him to find a parking spot. He pulls into an empty one and cuts the engine.

I open my door and jump out, and he follows. The sun is already beginning to rise, and there are only a few surfers out catching the high waves that the ocean is producing this morning.

The strong wind that rustles past us offers a pleasant breeze and a break from the constant humidity we've had to endure this summer so far.

"You ready to surf?" I ask. My feet are already taking me to the back of the van to grab my board.

"Ready as I'll ever be. The waves look a lot bigger than I've tried, though," he says as he watches the other surfers who are already out there.

"You'll be fine. You can't grow in your comfort zone," I tell him, with a smile on my face.

"Oh, you're all wise this morning, are you?" he jokes as he pulls the boards out for us. He helps Hugh down as well before closing the boot of the van.

"I'm always wise." My remark has him rolling his eyes like he doesn't believe me.

"Stay here, Hugh. We'll be back." He instructs his duck, which earns him a big quack, before we walk down the grassy bank towards the sand.

Once we reach the sand, I wax my board up, then hand over the bar to him and watch him do the same to his board. We attach our leg straps to the boards and then head into the sea. I place my board on the water and slide on, using my arms to stroke through the coolness to propel me forward.

Casey keeps a little distance between us, so our boards don't hit, but he keeps pace with me. The waves are rougher than what we get at Wattle Downs, so it'll be a challenge that sends a thrill through me. I only get to surf during the summer at Wattle Downs, and I'll rarely take a weekend trip somewhere in the year while at my mum's to get a surf in. The beaches I find can be hit or miss, so it's always nice to get challenged with bigger waves, as it's a rare occurrence.

As the waves push forward, we hang onto our boards to navigate past them without toppling off. Casey impresses me as he wrangles his like he's been surfing for a lot longer than the couple of weeks I've been teaching him.

It helps that he's spent as much, if not more, time in water than I have with his swimming. We paddle through some waves to reach the break. There, other surfers sit on their boards, waiting for the waves they want to ride. I sit on mine with my feet hanging over either side of the board. Casey copies me and flings his hair back out of his face with one hand. I can't help but stare. It's strange that someone I didn't think was anything special at first sight now makes butterflies swirl in my stomach. I just wish he didn't.

I push the thought away and distract myself by focusing on the incoming waves instead. Peace washes over me as we wait. The lull of the waves as the anticipation builds has become a feeling I crave. It's the moment right when you see a wave coming and it hits you in the gut that it's going to be a good one, and you react. Your arms work in overdrive, pushing you to get to the exact spot you need to catch it and ride it as far as you can.

Then it hits me, the feeling in the gut when I see the next wave. Casey always asks me how I choose my waves, but I find it hard to explain to him. I just know. Straight down on the board, I go as my arms work to pull me forward, and as the wave builds under me, I push to my feet and I'm there. Riding the wave. Feet planted and weight distributed keep me on my board as I weave through it. I follow it down until it barrels over, and I come off the board.

An enormous smile crosses my face that I don't think could get wiped off even if I tried. I catch my breath and then paddle back out to where Casey still sits in wait.

"That was amazing," I beam at him.

Finally, the lightness I've been missing reaches his eyes as he replies, "Yeah, you looked pretty amazing out there."

"Think that's one of the biggest waves I've ever ridden."

"Well, you rode it like a pro."

"You gonna grab the next one?" I ask.

"I thought I was supposed to feel it in my gut and not just take whatever came along?" he questions, as his brows furrow.

"Well, you might end up sitting out here all day if you don't take one."

"It's a chance I might have to take to wait for the right one," he says, with a cheeky grin on his face. I shake my head while I settle my eyes back on the horizon and wait.

It's a few hours later when we head in from the surf, both with wide smiles on our faces.

"See? It wasn't too bad to get up early, was it?" I tease.

"Sure. I'd love to wake up early again to drive all this way to wipe out several times," Casey's sarcasm is evident, which has me chuckling.

"You're still learning. You'll get there. This is only my first time on these big waves, and I wiped out a couple times, too, remember?"

"Yeah, I guess."

"Now, how about we put the boards in the van, rinse off and find something to eat?"

"Sounds like a plan," he says, and side by side, we walk back to where we parked. Loading the boards in, we grab a towel each and walk back towards the outdoor shower to wash the salt water off our skin. There are two available, so I place my towel on the stone wall. Then, I hit the button with my fist to start the water.

Cold water hits me as I rub my hands up and down my face to remove the salt that will leave my skin feeling tight if I don't remove it now. My heavy hair hangs down my back, and I untie it to wash it the best I can without having products with me. My hair spends most of the summer in the sea, so I'm used to it now.

It has the rest of the year to be sparkling clean. I rub my hands over my body, removing any sand still hanging on, and when the water stops, I step away and grab my towel to dry myself. Casey is doing the same, and once we finish, we wrap our towels around our waists and head down the main street.

Tempest Cove resembles Wattle Downs in the fact it has shops on the main road. It's a few takeaway bars and cafes as they are the most logical to have around a beach, but there's also the odd clothing store filled with beachwear.

It's also a lot smaller than Wattle Downs, but I like it. It feels cosier. A couple of cafes are open, so we walk to the nearest one and order some big breakfast meals with a coffee each. We get the number seven on a small pole and take a seat to wait for our order.

"I know we said no deep conversations, but is everything alright? You seem down the last few days," I blurt, as we have a moment with nothing to do. Why I thought this was a good time to bring it up, I don't know.

His fingertip runs a circle pattern on the wooden table while he watches his movements. The silence stretches so long that I'm not sure if he's going to acknowledge my question or not.

"It's my birthday tomorrow," he says, as his finger halts its movements and he lifts his eyes to mine.

"What? How did I not know this?" My wide eyes and raised brows stare at him.

"Probably cos I didn't tell you. I don't even know when your birthday is."

"June 29th, now you know," I say, as I give him a fake smile, which only makes him roll his eyes.

"You know what I mean. We don't do personal, Alexis," he states, and I let out a heavy sigh as I lean my head on my hand.

"Yeah, I know, but can I ask why you're looking sad over your birthday?" I ask, as our coffees arrive and get placed in front of us.

"Missing home, I guess." He shakes out two sugar packets before he rips them open and empties them into his mug before stirring it.

"Have you got plans to head back anytime soon?" I ask, as I blow on my coffee before taking a small sip.

"I'm thinking I will at the end of the summer." And my heart sinks. It's the first time I'm reminded that this thing between us is only temporary. I still have my last year of university ahead of me to get through, and he has a life outside of Wattle Downs waiting for him. Even though he doesn't talk about it, you can sense that it's part of the reason he withdraws.

"End of summer," I whisper more to myself than him, but he hears it anyway, and his fingers reach out to grasp mine that lie on the table.

"Still a good chunk of time before the end of summer. We'll make the most of it." His fingers squeeze mine as I offer him a tight smile. I don't know why I thought I could go through life having friends with benefit arrangements. It was always going to bite me on the butt, eventually. I shake the thoughts away as a new one takes root.

"That's a good point, and I know the perfect place we can visit today. We can call it a little birthday adventure," I tell him.

"Is this little trip out here not a birthday surprise?" he asks.

"Well, I didn't know it was your birthday, but we can add this other activity in. Trust me, it'll be fun." He opens his mouth to argue, but our food arrives, and then we are both busy enjoying the meal to talk.

CHAPTER THIRTY

<u>Jan 13th</u>

Casey

By the time Alexis is leading me to this unknown location, it's already midmorning. There's a light breeze around the cove now, but it's nice. I follow the winding road as we go up and around a mountain to wherever she's taking me.

I can't help but glance at her beautiful face with her hair blowing around her. She usually has it tied back in her plait, but I like it when it's wild and free like this. It makes her look more carefree. Eyes back on the road, I steer us into one of the parking spots she directs me to. No other cars are up here, so it must be only us. It's way too much of a hike for someone to walk up here.

Without a word, she unbuckles, hops in the back of the van and strips out of her clothes.

"Alexis?"

"Come on. It'll relax us before the next part," she informs me, as she stares at me from her knees, naked in the back of my van. I can't help but move towards her. Lightning quick, my clothes come off too, and then I'm on top of her. Her gorgeous smile focuses on me, and I can't help the feeling it swirls in my gut. If only it were a different time or place, I tell myself before my selfishness consumes me and my lips drop to hers.

"Condom?" I ask, between kisses.

"Front pocket of my bag," she informs me, so I stop to grab one. I lay it beside us as our hands explore each other's bodies. Hugh quacks from the front seat, but we ignore him, too lost in the hunger for release. I sheath myself before I line up and enter her. We both moan, a smile lighting my face. It isn't long until I find a rhythm, but she moans for me to go faster. Increasing my pace, sweat drips from both our bodies as we slide against each other.

"I'm close," she admits. I lift one of her legs over my shoulder and find a deeper angle and chase my release. As her moans take over as she orgasms, I pound faster as she pulses around me. I keep pace until I drop my face to her neck, but she grabs my face and kisses me to swallow my moans as I jerk inside her. The kisses turn softer as we both drift down from the high, and I roll off her. I kick my blanket up from the base of the mattress and cover us.

She wriggles into my side, and I lift my arm for her to cuddle closer.

"How about a little nap?" she suggests, as she lets out a yawn.

"Sounds perfect," I admit, with my eyes already closed. As I catch my breath and they even out, I fall asleep in no time.

"Come on, we can't sleep all day," Alexis's small hands push against my side, waking me.

"I was comfy though," I whine, not wanting to get up yet.

"You can sleep later," she says, as she grabs her swimsuit and pulls it back on. I pull my board shorts on and follow her out of the van. There's still no one else around, so I'm not sure what we are doing here. I let Hugh out for a breather and lock it up.

"Put the keys on the front wheel," she says, and I raise a brow. "Trust me, okay?"

I do as she says and tell Hugh I'll be back. Alexis grabs my hand and pulls me along a hidden path. A giddy energy wafts off her, and I'm weary of what she has in store.

I'm right to worry as we walk out onto a cliffside with a perfect view ahead of us. There's also a perfect drop below us, which makes my heart sink to my feet.

"Cliff diving?" I squeak as I take a step back, releasing her hand.

"Yep." Her giddiness increases with the look on my face.

"How is this a birthday present?"

"You'll feel invincible afterwards."

"Have you done it before?" I ask, as I take a small, tentative step forward to peek at the drop. It's high from up here, but it's a clear blue sea below. No rocks lay hidden, as we can see through the surface. There's a secluded beach off to the side as well that you can only see from up here.

215

"Yeah, Dad brought me here a few times over the years," she admits.

"How do we get back to the car?" I ask, worried it'll take us forever.

"There's a path from the beach which doesn't take as long as you'd think. You game?" she asks, as her whole face beams at me.

I stand there for a beat, not moving until she holds out her hand.

"We can even do it together on the count of three," she suggests. Her fingers wriggle at me, and I can't help the pull she has over me as I step towards her and link our hands tightly.

"Alright. On three," I tell her, as my heart beats a million miles a minute.

"Step back here. We'll get a runup. Are you ready?"

"As ready as I'll ever be," I admit.

She leans forward and delivers a soft kiss to my lips. She moves to pull away, but my hand slides into her hair to deepen the kiss, and she smiles against my skin. If I'm going to plummet to my death, I want my last moment to be a good one. Neither of us pulls away, and we lose minutes in the moment, savouring it. It isn't until she pulls away a final time that I let her.

"Your distraction won't work. We are still jumping," she jokes, and I laugh before I kiss her forehead and take her hand back in mine. Standing side by side, she counts us down.

"One, two, three," she screams, and we take off hand in hand, racing to the end. Our hands squeeze the other as our feet leave the cliff, and we are flying for what feels like forever before we are plummeting. Our screams surround us, and a second later, our feet hit the surface, and we sink with a sting. I hold my breath and release her hand so I can use my hands to swim upwards. We went further down than anticipated, and my lungs burn. When I reach the surface, I'm gasping for air.

Glancing around, there's no sign of Alexis, and my heart jumps from the rapid thought of her hurt until it settles when her head pops up and her radiant smile looks at me.

"Best birthday ever, right?" she pants between breaths, as she swims my way. When she's in reach, I grab her and pull her towards me. She wraps around me before I answer.

"Yes, best birthday ever," I agree, as my feet paddle under us, keeping us afloat in the deep water. Her hand pushes my hair off my forehead before she takes my lips again in hers. We stay like that for a while as the adrenaline floods through our veins until we are both ready to swim out and make the small trek back to the van.

It doesn't take us as long as I thought to reach the van, and we dry off before changing and lying down to relax on the mattress.

Cuddled up into my side again, my eyes close.

"We still have one more thing to do before we finish here," she tells me, which has my eyes opening as I tilt my head towards her.

"What? There's still more?"

"You didn't think we drove all this way for the surf, did you?"

"Yeah, actually I did," I admit.

"Well, I saved the best for last. We can nap again because it's gotta be dark for the last part. Then we can either drive back late or crash here for the night and drive back in the morning."

"I'm not rostered on tomorrow, so if you're keen to stay, we can stay the night and drive back tomorrow after another surf?"

"Sounds perfect," she says, as her eyes close again, and I follow suit as the adrenaline leaving my body has left me drained.

We wake when dusk is settling in, and Alexis stretches her arms above her head with a yawn.

"That was the best nap I've had in ages," she comments, and I reply with a hmm. "Come on, let's go. I'll show you the way," she says as she climbs through the van to the passenger seat. Hugh settles back to sleep on the mattress while I hop over and start the car, following where she leads.

"Back at the beach?" I ask, when she tells me to park, pretty much in the same spot we parked this morning.

"You'll see," she says with a tilt of her head.

"Come on out for a bit, Hugh," I say over my shoulder, and he waddles forward so I can pick him up. I carry him out of the van and place him on a grassy patch to explore. The beach is empty and I'm sceptical of what this mysterious surprise is. "It's not skinny dipping, is it?" I yell out as she's running on the sand towards the sea. The outline of her body disappears the closer she gets to the water.

"Happy birthday, Casey," she yells, as I lose sight of her. I close my eyes and release a heavy sigh, drawing a deep breath into my lungs.

"Happy birthday," I repeat, as I hear the splash of water and open my eyes, and I stick to the spot at the sight. One beat, two beats, three. And then I'm off running.

"What kind of voodoo is this?" I yell, and her laughter floats to my ears.

218

"I told you it was an amazing surprise," she yells back. A few more steps, and then the cold water hits my feet, but I don't stop. I run full force into the dark, in the direction I now see her. The fluorescent blue hue splashes up as her hands wave back and forth through the water, and I'm mesmerised.

"This is so cool," I admit, as I run towards her, watching the blue light up behind me with the movement.

"It's this bioluminescent alga that sometimes comes to this spot, and it's a chemical reaction that causes the sea to light up with movement," she explains. We continue playing in it for what feels like hours, running back and forth and splashing around with our hands, making circles.

The smile etched into my face feels like it will be a permanent fixture from this day on, and it's all thanks to this wonderful girl. I stare at her, amazed that she planned this trip for me in hopes it would cheer me up. As she passes me, continuing to run around with unlimited energy, I grab her by the waist and pull her towards me. Her hands hold on to the bottom of my shirt as I wrap my arms around her shoulders.

"Thank you for this. This is the best present," I admit, and I'm sure if I could see her clearly, her cheeks would blush.

"You're welcome," she replies. She stretches on tiptoes to press her lips to mine in a quick peck, and then I pull her close as we both wrap our arms around each other, holding on tight.

"Let's sleep in the van tonight and head back tomorrow," I breathe, and she agrees with a nod against my chest.

"Sounds perfect," she says, as her head tilts back and looks at me as I gaze down at her.

"Yeah, it does," I agree. I close the distance, and with all that I'm feeling, I push my emotions into the kiss and hope she can feel it. When we pull apart, I grab her hand and lead her back to the van. I snatch Hugh up from where he sat on the grass and deposit him in the passenger seat as I lie down with Alexis.

This time, we'll take it slow. Unlike before, when things were rushed, we savour every moment. I relish in the feel of her curves and commit all her sounds to memory, not wanting the moment to end. Then we fall asleep in each other's arms. And like I said, we wake early for a morning surf before heading back to Wattle Downs, leaving our perfect little cove behind.

CHAPTER THIRTY-ONE

Jan 16th

Alexis

"Lexi, pair up with Casey today," Dad calls, as we stand in a circle around him for our meeting before shift starts.

Casey stands across the circle from me, and at the mention of his name, my eyes move to him. He raises his head, and my face heats at the minuscule tilt of his lips.

I nod as my dad continues talking for fear my voice will come out with a croak and have the crew giving me weird looks.

"Let's have a great day, everyone," Dad says, before we split off into our pairs.

Casey already has our supplies ready to go before I even think of grabbing the backpack.

"You're organised this morning?" I tease, as we make our way down the ramp and head towards the side of the beach that has the skatepark.

"Just excited to be on shift with you," Casey says, and I know my face must be bright red as it burns under his watchful gaze.

We don't talk as we walk along the sand, keeping our eyes out for anything that may need our attention. The radio is silent too; nothing noticeable is going on. It isn't long before that changes, though.

"Shark!" The scream carries over the wind, and the frantic people running out of the water have Casey and me racing towards them.

"Looks like there might be a shark in the surf down by us. Can you see?" I radioed to Dad.

"I see the commotion, checking it out. Get everyone out of the water, now." Dad's rushed words crackle back over to us, and we gain ground.

"Out of the water. Everyone, out!" Casey calls as we reach the spot where people are already running out of the waves. I run into the surf to help a mother get her two young kids out to safety while Casey helps an older couple.

The shark alarm goes off over the intercom, alerting everyone on the beach that there's a shark in the water. Everyone races out from the surf further down the beach, and I know all the lifeguards are evacuating the water further down, too.

"Lexi, there's someone further out in the surf who isn't coming in. Down by you guys," Dad says, and Casey comes to my side as we scan the surf.

"There they are," Casey points to the left of us, and you can see their brown hair bob up and down in the water.

"Hey. Get out of the water," I yell with my hands cupped around my mouth, but they are too far out to hear me.

"I'll go get them," Casey says, but I grab his forearm to stop him.

"No," I tell him. "Dad, can we get someone to bring the boat out to get them? They can't hear us," I ask over the radio.

"Okay. Sending Cheese your way now," he replies.

222

"You gotta assess things first. I know you want to get them to safety, but in this instance, your safety comes first because of the shark. So, we wait for the boat to come out to get them," I explain, and he nods. It isn't long before Cheese arrives, and Casey jumps on the boat to head out with him. I keep watch from the sand to make sure no one enters the water. Five minutes later, they came back with the swimmer on board.

With everyone out of the water, Dad comes down to the beach along with the rest of the lifeguards.

"Keep everyone out of the surf. It's best we close the beach today. I've contacted the local authorities, so they'll be here soon to get the shark to move on, if possible," Dad informs us.

We nod along as he talks.

"Should we tell people it's closed?" Cheese asks.

"Yeah, let's do that. Better safe than sorry," Dad says, so we split off and start informing people of the closure.

The hum of a helicopter overhead grabs my attention, and I raise my eyes to the sky. The TV news logo in big green letters is visible from the beach.

"Reporters will be down here soon," I tell Casey, as we move from group to group. Most are already packing up and heading home, as sharks in the water can be unpredictable, and I guess most don't want to hang around.

"Really? Do they always show up when there's a shark?"

"Yeah. More if there's an attack, but we are lucky today. We got everyone out in time."

Once everyone's informed from our side of the beach, we head back to meet Dad, who stands guard where the shark was seen. A reporter and her camera crew are setting up to report as we greet Dad.

"Can you two patrol the boardwalk and let anyone who is coming along the main strip know the beach is closing for now, please?"

"Sure, let's go," Casey rushes out, as he tugs on my hand to pull me away.

"Hey, what's with you? What's the rush?"

"I don't want to get interviewed by the reporters," Casey says, as he continues to tug on my hand.

"Camera shy, are we?" I tease, while he looks over his shoulder at me. He smiles, but it doesn't reach his eyes.

"Something like that. Come on, it looks like people over there are gonna come down to the beach," he changes the subject.

We spend the next few hours patrolling the beach and letting people know they can't swim. Most people have gone, but a few remain, content to soak up the sun from the sand.

Dad calls it an hour before finishing time, letting us know we can head off for the day. The local authorities get the shark to move on, and hopefully, it won't be back. The helicopter and news crew packed up a while ago once they got their story for the day, too, which I noticed had Casey relaxing once they were gone.

"I feel like a burger," his voice breaks through my thoughts, and my smile shines at him.

"That sounds like a good idea. Let's go," I tell him, as I hold out my hand, and he takes it. Squeezing my fingers, we head to the local burger joint across the road and the chaos of the day is forgotten as we enjoy our delicious food.

CHAPTER THIRTY-TWO

<u>Jan 22nd</u>

Alexis

The days are passing faster than I realised, and it's almost the end of January. I can't believe how fast the summer is slipping by. My days now consist of seeing Casey, and I can't complain about that, as I love spending time with him.

Even though we have the friends with benefits arrangement, it doesn't stop my heart from wanting more. The thick walls around my heart help protect me, but they feel shaky now. One look or smile from Casey could make them tumble down.

I've never felt this way about anyone, not even James. There's something about Casey that I can't quite put my finger on, but he's somehow gotten under my skin. Now I'm scared of what will happen when summer ends. I know we're just a summer fling, but my heart hasn't gotten the message yet.

I can't help but wonder if his feelings for me go any deeper than physical. When we're together, the chemistry is amazing. There's no care in the world. Still, something nudges my mind. I can't quite figure it out. Maybe it's the fear of falling for someone. Who knows? I'll keep enjoying my time with him for as long as the summer lasts.

CHAPTER THIRTY-THREE

<u>Jan 24th</u>

Casey

"Come back. Come back. Come back." My voice fades into the darkness, along with the figure that walks away from me. My outstretched hand tries to reach for them, but they blend in with the dark, so my efforts are futile. Laboured breaths sound around me.

Warm air engulfs me.

My chest rises and falls.

Rise and fall.

Until the pace picks up.

Panic sets in, and my fingers claw at my neck, needing a breath.

Sharp scratches sting my skin to break through.

Air.

I need air.

Tears burn my eyes as my throat strangles me from the inside out.

And I'm out of breath.

Falling into oblivion.

"Aaahhhh," my screams fill the van, as I'm flung upright from my nightmare. Sweat drips into my eyes as my loud inhales surround me.

"Quack," Hugh calls beside me.

"It's okay, Hugh. I'm okay," I reassure him, my breathing slowing. I throw off the blanket and bury my face in my hands, my fingers tangling in my hair, as I try to cool down.

I unlock the boot and step out into the cool air, needing it to calm me and my fevered skin. The dewy grass slides under my feet as I step towards the bench seat in the cove. With a heaviness in my bones, I drop to the seat, and the loud thrashing of the waves sounds over the beating of my heart.

Focusing on the waves, my mind and body settle, but I continue sitting out there, not wanting to return to the van. Worried if I try to sleep, it'll pull me back to the nightmare I woke from.

So, when the first rays of the sun hit the sky, I drag my feet finally back to the van and get myself changed to start the day.

CHAPTER THIRTY-FOUR

<u>Feb 11th</u>

Casey

The last few nights, Alexis and I have walked hand in hand along the beach at night. It's peaceful and makes me want to live by the beach forever. The smell of the salty air to wake up to and the sounds of waves crashing on the shore feel good for my soul. I'm glad I stopped in Wattle Downs.

"I can't believe the summer is nearly over," Alexis says.

"I know. It's flown by."

"Have you got plans for when summer is over?"

"No, nothing yet. I guess I'll travel around some more and see where Hugh and I end up," I tell her, but the thought of being without her pulls at my heart. I'm about to tell her I want an actual relationship, even after the summer ends, but the potential for rejection has me stopping myself. James' words about Alexis not getting attached have me wavering along with the conversation with Marcus. I'd forgotten that she had broken James' heart, and it all comes back to the fact that she doesn't do serious relationships. Caught up in the excitement of it all, it keeps slipping my mind that this is temporary.

"Have you ever been skinny dipping?"

"What? No. Have you?" I stop in my tracks and turn to her. My mind is now distracted by thinking of her naked.

"No, but there's no one around and it's dark," she whispers, as her gaze looks back and forth down the deserted beach.

"Let's go," I say, as I tug her hand. Her giggles follow as our feet pad through the sand towards the sea. We come to a stop, and I pull my shirt off as she does the same, pulling her red sundress over her head. Before I can change my mind, I strip my shorts and jocks off, cupping myself to hide the goods, in case there are prying eyes. I take off running into the water.

"Your butt is so white," she calls after me, and I hear the laughter in her voice.

I splash through the surf before diving under the dark, warm water to cover myself. Alexis' splashing has me shaking my head to clear the water from my eyes, but she dives under the water before I get a glance at her. Her wet hair emerges in front of me, and I pull her into my arms. Her sweet smile has me forgetting my worries, and instead, I come back to the moment.

Her arms and legs wrap around me as I spin us around in the quiet water.

"This is nice," I confide, and my heart can't help but fall harder for her with the way she smiles at me.

"Yeah, it is."

My hand skims along her back before I sweep a strand of wet hair from her face. The tension cackles in the air as we gaze at each other, committing the memory. Our smiles fade as we gaze at the others' lips. My hand tightens its hold around her head, and I can't restrain myself anymore, so I pull her closer. Her salty lips touch mine, and sparks ignite. We don't rush. Our lips and tongues are taking, savouring the moment, and all it does is make Alexis burrow deeper into my heart.

I'm aware of Alexis' hands as they move across my head, but my brain doesn't connect the dots until she's pushing my head underwater. Her limbs release me, and I come up coughing after taking a mouthful of water to hear her laughter surrounding me.

"You think that's funny, do you?" I taunt, as I move towards her.

"Yes, very," she taunts back, which has my smile growing.

I dive into the water after her, and her squeals ignite. I reach out to grab her and dunk her as well. We end up splashing each other and swirling around in our little cocoon of happiness.

We remain like that, playing and laughing until wrinkles appear on our fingers, and then we head to shore. Double checking the coast is clear, we make a mad dash to our scattered clothes and pull them on fast. They cling to our wet skin as our wide smiles shine at each other.

We both hold our hands out for the other and, without uttering a word, take them. We head back to my van, where Hugh is waiting, and I drive us to the cove where we spend the rest of the night content in each other's arms.

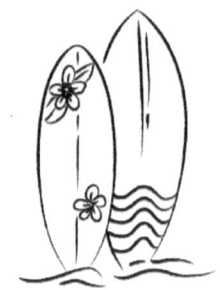

CHAPTER THIRTY-FIVE

Feb 17th

Casey

"Do you want to come to James' tonight? He's having a party for his birthday," Alexis asks, as we walk side by side up the porch and into her house. We worked together with Kara. It was almost a relaxing shift. There were no people to save in the surf. The only excitement came from a pickpocket who stole phones and wallets while swimmers enjoyed the water. He got caught, though, and that seemed to be the most excitement we had for the day.

"Yeah, I guess so. You don't think he'll mind us turning up? He hasn't been very welcoming since he found out about us."

"Well, he's the one who invited us. He texted me today, so he must be okay now," she informs me. Something stirs in my stomach, though, making me feel uneasy.

"Sure, let's go, then," I answer, with reluctance.

She smiles at me as I sit at the kitchen table, and she fixes some sandwiches for us. She promised me something to eat after the shift if I drove her home, so that's what we are doing.

After showering and changing, I drive us down to the main strip to the liquor store. We both don't have work tomorrow, so Alexis decided she felt like drinking. We walk the small aisles as she weighs up what to buy before finally deciding on apple ciders.

I drive us back to her place and park my van in the driveway, which has become a natural part of my life now. We say goodbye to Corbin, who arrived home while we were out, and then we walk to James' house.

One good thing about living in a small town like Wattle Downs is that everyone lives close. You can walk from one side of town to the other in thirty minutes. So, it doesn't take us long at all to make our way to James'.

Loud music comes from the lit up house, and people mingle out in the front yard when we arrive. Alexis waves to a few of them before she grabs my hand and drags me into the house.

"Kara and Ruby texted and said they were already here, so let's find them," she tells me.

I follow behind her as we squish through people. It's packed for a small town party. The other parties we have been to over the summer didn't have as many people. This feels as though everyone from the town is here.

We wade through the crowds, and Alexis finally spots Kara against a wall in the living room, talking to Marcus, so we make a beeline straight for them. Music pumps through the house that we must yell over.

Kara's face transforms into a smile as she sees Alexis, who has Marcus turning our way.

"Hey, man," he says, as he holds out a hand for me to shake and then leans in for a one armed hug.

"Let's dance," Kara's voice rises above the music, as she grabs Alexis' hand and pulls her away from me.

I stand, talking with Marcus, as I watch the girls sway back and forth. I place the box of Alexis' cans by my feet as she holds and sips one.

Marcus seems happy enough to chat with me, so as I keep watch over Alexis, he keeps me company. She comes back every so often, as one can empties, to grab another.

A few hours pass, and more people arrive, and the girls continue to dance. Ruby joined them a while ago, and the more Alexis drinks, the more she sways.

After her fifth can, the girls stagger towards us, and I grab Alexis as she stumbles into me. Her arms wrap around my waist as she gazes up at me, and it makes my heart thunder in my chest. With my palm, I push the hair off her face and tuck it behind her ear. Looking at her now, all I see is her, and it makes me realise I can see a future with her.

"Look, it's the birthday boy. I've been wondering where you were," Marcus calls.

James is staggering himself as he heads our way. His eyes lock on mine before they flicker to Alexis, where she's wrapped around me. His face drops for a split second before he focuses back on me, and his face transforms with twisted malice.

"So, Colin, how are you enjoying Wattle Downs?" his snark lashes out, and my back straightens.

"Who are you talking to, man?" Marcus laughs at his friend.

"I'm talking to Colin. You guys don't know Colin?" he says, as his eyes lock on mine, and I hold my breath.

"What are you on about?"

"Oh, that's right. You don't know him as Colin. Well, I'll let you in on a little secret. You know the celebrity couple, The Carlisles? The woman, Regina, is the soap actress from Wild at Heart, and her husband, Graham, is the host of the morning news on Channel Eight. Well, they had two sons. One died a year ago, but the other one has been right under our noses the whole summer," he explains, as I release the breath I was holding.

"How much have you had to drink, James? You aren't making sense," Kara says.

"Let me spell it out for you, then. Isn't that right, Colin? You're the famous Colin Carlisle, and you've been pretending to be your dead brother, Casey, this entire summer?"

As everyone's gazes whip around to me, the world silences. I'm frozen in place. James's sinister face stares at me as the others all look at me with wide eyes and open mouths. It's the feel of Alexis' grip around me loosening that pulls me from my panic.

"Casey? What's he talking about?" Her small voice shakes as her arms flop to her sides.

Sweat drips down the back of my neck as I reach my fingers out to grab her, but she takes a step back out of reach.

"I can explain," I mumble, as my feet move towards her.

She retreats, her backwards footsteps speeding up before she turns and runs from the room.

I'm hot on her tail, following her as best I can. I knew my lies would catch up with me someday, but I didn't think I'd ever care what anyone thought. Now I care too much about Alexis, and I have to make this right.

CHAPTER THIRTY-SIX

Feb 17th

Alexis

"Alexis, wait," his faint calls follow me, as my feet propel me further away. The couple of cans of cider I had were making me tipsy, but now that has completely worn off with the revelation. Casey isn't Casey. He's Colin. How can that be?

My muddled brain won't stop working in overdrive as my sneakers smack against the pavement in the dead of night.

"Please, would you stop and listen to me?" he says, as his fingers wrap around my forearm and I spin. His wide eyes stare at me as we both draw big breaths in. "Please, can we talk?"

As I stare at his pleading face, I can't help as rage fills my blood, and my words lash at him like barbed wire.

"Who is it that wants to talk? Casey or Colin?" My hurt exposes me as my voice shakes and eyes burn.

His own eyes close as his head drops, but his grip on my arm remains strong. It's as if he knows the moment he lets go, I'll be back to running away from him.

"Can we go somewhere and talk?"

"Why? So, you can manipulate me some more?"

"It wasn't like that. You know it wasn't."

"I know nothing. I don't even know your first name, apparently," I fume at him.

"You know me. I may have lied about my name, but that was it. Everything else was all me. Please, will you just let me explain?"

"I can't right now. We should cut our losses. We were only an arrangement for the summer, so why don't we call it quits now and go our separate ways like we were going to do soon, anyway?" As the words leave my mouth, my heart splinters.

"Is that what you want?" his shaking voice asks, and as the first tear falls, my walls go back up.

"It's for the best," I lie as the salty truth betrays me as it slips down my cheek.

His grip on my arm softens as he releases me, along with a sigh.

"I didn't take you for a coward," his whispered jab hits my ears.

"What was that?"

"You're a coward."

"And you're a liar," I scream.

"And so are you," he snaps back.

"What's that supposed to mean? I've never lied to you."

"You're lying to yourself. As soon as you see an out, you're taking it. James was right. You were never gonna let down your walls far enough to let me in. I was stupid to think that we could have a future," he says.

"A future? And what would I call you in the future? Casey or Colin?" I mock.

"I may have lied about my name, but you won't even let me explain. But at least I'm not standing here now, lying about how I feel. I love you, Alexis, and I want a future with you, not just the summer. Can you honestly tell me you don't want any more? That you can let me walk away from your life so easily?"

My head spins at his words, but still my walls remain in place, adding another layer of protection.

"I'm tired and I can't think clearly. I'm gonna go," I tell him.

His eyes scrunch shut. The moment they close, I turn and race away. Only my footsteps sound this time, and I make it home within a matter of minutes. I pound up the porch, and the door slams shut behind me.

"Love bug?" Dad's concern comes from the kitchen.

"I'm fine," I state, as I storm down the hall and slam my bedroom door shut behind me. I flop onto my bed face down, and only then do the tears release as my face lies hidden against my pillow. All my pain escapes, and with every tear that drops, another brick adds to the wall surrounding my heart.

CHAPTER THIRTY-SEVEN

<u>Feb 18th</u>

Colin

After the fight with Alexis, it didn't feel right staying in her driveway in the van, so I hopped in it as soon as I followed her home and drove to the cove. I've texted her so many messages, asking her to let me explain, but they all get left on read.

My phone calls ring and go unanswered. So, I find myself today holed up in the back of my van, in my cove. My sanctuary of sorts. I'm hoping that if I ignore the outside world that the next time I dive into it, it will all have been a bad dream.

Grey clouds hang overhead, causing the humidity in the air to cling to my skin and make me sweat. It's hard enough to sleep in my van with my head racing, but the dense air makes it worse.

The shrill ringtone of my phone has me lunging at it and answering without checking the caller ID.

"Alexis?"

"Son?" My dad's voice sounds through the earpiece, and my heart drops as I let out a sigh. "You finally answered. It's so good to hear your voice. Are you okay?" he rambles on, and his voice brings back a tirade of memories I was forcing myself to forget.

"Hey, Dad, ah, now isn't a good time."

"Please, Colin. We haven't heard from you in months. Please talk to us. We can't help you if we don't know what's going on." My fist clenches around the phone as my eyes close.

"You can't help me," I release with a sigh.

"How many times do we have to tell you it wasn't your fault?"

"It was my fault. I should have been with him and stopped him," I yell into the confined space, as my eyes fling open.

"Son, you were not your brother's keeper. Please come home. We worry about you. It's as if we lost two sons."

"I'm sorry for worrying you. I know you're both hurting, too, but I'm fine."

"You're not, though. You haven't been fine since Casey died. Please come home. Even if it's for a short while. So, we can see with our own eyes that you are okay. I'm begging you. For your mother's sake," he rushes out.

My empty hand runs across my face, wanting to rub away the bone deep tiredness.

"She's not doing too well, son. Please come and see her."

My loud exhale echoes in the van as thoughts overpower me, causing me to lose my resolve.

"Okay. I'll be back as soon as I can," I tell him, and I pick up the sigh of relief he releases.

"Thank you, Colin. We'll see you soon. Come home safe, son."

"I will. See you," I say, before my hand drops and I hang up the phone. My head drops as I run my hands over my face, then scratch at my scalp. And repeat. Maybe if I press and scratch hard enough, I can force the unwanted thoughts out of my brain. Time passes, and I don't know how long I will stay in that position. Unsure of what to do. I finally picked my phone up again to check if I'd missed any messages, but still, there were no notifications. I type out another text to Alexis and press send, but I don't expect a reply.

My head flops back onto my pillow, eyes scrunched close, and I lie there and fight the thoughts flying through my mind. If I continue fighting, then sleep will eventually come, and at least then I'll get some peace.

CHAPTER THIRTY-EIGHT

<u>Feb 24th</u>

Colin

It's been a week since I've seen or heard from Alexis. I've shut myself away at my cove, too chicken to venture down to the beach in case I run into someone else. All I want is to speak to Alexis and sort through this mess, and explain to her. Every day, I've tried to call and text her, but it all goes ignored. I've had to cancel my lifeguard shifts and lied to Corbin, telling him I was sick.

It's all a lie, though. I can't bring myself to tell him I lied to him and Alexis when they have been nothing but kind to me. I don't know how I will explain to everyone about my name, but all that matters right now is getting Alexis to listen to me. She's the most important person to me right now, and I need her to hear me out.

As I sit on the bench seat at the cove, I gaze out over the beach below. It's crowded as the sun shines high in the sky without a trace of a cloud. Hugh nestles up beside the leg of the seat, content to sleep. With the heat beaming down on me, I close my eyes. I'm heading back home. With things the way they are here, it feels hopeless to stay. And the pull to see how Mum is doing with my own eyes tugs at my heart. She had fallen into a deep depression before I left. The pain of losing her son was too great. I was so busy trying to keep my head above water that I couldn't even factor her into it. And that's why I ended up running away. Too scared to stay there and confront my pain.

The shrill ring of my phone sounds from my pocket, causing my heart to pound in my chest. As I see the caller ID, I release a breath before answering.

"Hey, I was wondering if we could meet and talk?"

I release a sigh before I say, "Yeah, sure, okay. Where?"

"I'm at home. I'll see you soon."

I hang up the phone before taking one last glance over the beach. With a forceful exhale, I stand and pick up Hugh. Once loaded into the van, I drive us the familiar route and slow down as I travel down the bumpy gravel driveway. I let Hugh out into the familiar yard before I knock on the door.

"Come in," Corbin calls, and as I open the door, he sits on the couch, waiting for me. "Thanks for coming," he says, as he looks me up and down.

"I'm guessing you heard," I reply as I step into the room.

He pats the couch beside him, so I take a seat.

"Yeah, I did, but I wanted to hear your side of the story. You're a good kid, so I wanted to see what was going on and if you are okay," he tells me.

My eyes flick up to his worried gaze, and it's the concern etched on his face that has me crumbling, and I burst into tears.

"Shit," he cusses, as I drop my head into my hands. His hand pats me on the back as he moves closer. "Let it out. It's better out than in," he comforts, as the pain I've kept inside for so long releases.

We stay like that for a long time. My cries fill the air until I've run out of tears, and my body and mind calm down. Tear soaked eyes find Corbin's, and he sits waiting for me to speak. It's another few minutes before my courage builds up, and then I tell him my story.

"I'm sorry you had to go through all that, Colin, and I'm sure once you talk to Alexis, things will work themselves out," he consoles me.

"I don't know. She was pretty mad and isn't answering my calls or texts."

"She went with the girls up the coast to clear her head, but she will be back in a few days," he tells me.

My phone rings, halting our conversation, so I pull it out to see my dad calling again. I answer it this time, and his rushed words hit me in the chest.

"Colin? Thank God you answered. Can you come home, son? Your mum is in the hospital."

"What? Is she okay?" I stammer as I stand, ready to run to her.

"I'm not sure. The doctors are doing tests. She collapsed this morning at the house, but she hasn't been eating properly lately. Can you come home?" he pleads.

"I'll leave today," I tell him, knowing I need to go to my mum.

"Thanks, son. I'll see you soon." I hang up the phone, and Corbin's worried gaze finds me.

"My mum is in the hospital. I need to go," I tell him, and he nods.

"I hope everything is okay. Keep trying with Alexis, she'll come around," he encourages.

"Thanks for everything, Corbin. I appreciate everything you have done for me this summer," I tell him, as I lean in for a hug.

"You're welcome. And you take care of yourself, yeah? Come back anytime. You are always welcome here."

"Thanks," I reply, as I release his embrace. I turn and open the door, and he follows me out.

"Bye, Hugh. Take care of him, will you?" he yells to Hugh, as I pick my feathered friend up from the ground.

"Quack." His reply has a smile lighting up Corbin's face before he waves and stands on the porch. I deposit Hugh onto the chair and then reverse down the driveway. Corbin waving from his spot on the porch is the last thing I see before I turn onto the road and say goodbye to Wattle Downs, determined to head home to my mum.

CHAPTER THIRTY-NINE

<u>Feb 25th</u>

Alexis

Time spent away from Wattle Downs is what I needed. Especially time with Kara and Ruby. I've hardly seen them this summer, so it was nice to have girl time away and forget my problems. I felt bad about leaving Dad in a tough spot. He was short two lifeguards, with both Kara and me gone. Plus, I don't think Casey, I mean Colin, had been in to work recently either. But Dad said he could handle it, and it was fine for me to go.

The girls drop me off at home, and I lug my bag up the stairs and into the house, but Dad isn't around. He's probably down at the beach working. I dragged my luggage straight to the laundry and threw all my dirty clothes into the machine, as we didn't have time to do laundry over the last few days.

We spent our time up the coast surfing, lying on the beach, or getting drunk. It was what I needed to chase my blues away. After setting the machine to start, I head into my room and place my now empty bag in its spot in the closet. Exhaustion calls me, so I flop onto my back on my bed and close my eyes. That only lasts a few minutes until I turn over and curl into a ball.

My eyes flicker open, and there on my bedside table sits a white envelope with my name scrawled across it in black marker. With shaky fingers, I grab it and roll onto my back as I open it and pull the few pages of paper out.

Dear Alexis,

I'm sorry I've had to write this all in a letter. I wanted to talk to you face to face and explain, but my mum is in the hospital, so I've had to leave. Please know that I only left because of that. Otherwise, I would have stayed.

I don't know where to start, as it all seems like one big mess to me, but let me start at the beginning.

My name is Colin Carlisle. I wish I could go back in time and tell you that truth from the start, but then I doubt we would have met. You see, Casey, my brother, was the outgoing one. He loved to party and socialise, but all I cared about was swimming. I've never had many friends, as I spent all my time in the pool trying to reach a goal that was always going to be out of my reach, no matter how hard I tried. I realised too late and after too many wasted years that hard work and wanting it were never going to be enough.

Anyway, I'm getting a little off track. You see, even though Casey was the social one, it also caused him to associate with the wrong people. And being born into a high profile life, we both used what we had at our disposal to avoid it. I used swimming, whereas Casey used partying, drugs, and alcohol.

Over the years, Casey's addiction got worse, and every time he left the house, I'd get anxious and end up finding him and dragging him home. Until I'd had enough. I thought, why is this my life, and why do I have to devote it to keeping him alive? Shouldn't he want to live himself? The one night I didn't follow him, as I was sick of doing it, was the night he ended up overdosing and dying.

I keep thinking that if I'd found him like I always did, he'd still be alive today. But deep down, I know that's not true. He was headed to an early death, with or without me following him. I just can't accept the fact that he's gone.

When I turned up at Wattle Downs, I had the stupid thought that if I pretended to be someone else, then I could harness their energy and, like them, I could make friends, too. So that's why I let people believe I was Casey.

It's funny, though. I couldn't party like him or attract people like he did. He was like a bright light people couldn't help but flock to, and that isn't who I am, no matter how hard I pretended. I couldn't be him.

So, I may have used his name, but everything else was purely me. All that I lied about was my name. And the birthday we celebrated was his birthday. My first one without him. I care about you, Alexis. That was all true. Even though it started with a fake name, the rest was all real.

I know you're hurt, and you may never forgive me, but I love you. I'm sorry, Alexis. My wish is for you to have the best in life, and I hope you find happiness. And if we ever cross paths again, I hope we can start again, but on the right foot.

With all my heart,

Colin and Hugh xx

Tears stream down my face. He left? I never gave him a chance to explain. Now my stomach aches with regret. Hot tears slip down my face, and I swipe them away as fast as they come. I take a few minutes to calm myself before I pull my phone out and dial my dad's number.

"Hey, love bug," he answers, after several rings.

"When did he leave?" My defeated voice shakes through the phone.

"Aww, Lexi. He left while you were away. He said that you weren't answering his calls, and I thought you might have needed the space. But then his mum got admitted to the hospital, so he had to go. He left, but then ended up driving back and giving me the letter to give to you. I take it, you read it?"

"Yeah," is all I can reply.

"How about I grab us some takeout on my way home and you have a movie night with your old man?"

"I don't know if I'll be great company," I sniffle into the phone.

"You know, sometimes in life, things happen for a reason. Maybe Colin was only supposed to come into your life for the summer. I know it hurts right now, love bug, but who knows what the future holds? Maybe the timing isn't right."

"I'll see you later, Dad," I sniffle again, before I hang up. The fresh tears fall, and I tug my knees into my chest. Dad's right about one thing. It hurts. It hurts for what Colin's been through, and that I never let him explain. And it's with that train of thought that I realise my walls were never as strong as I made myself believe, because Colin came in and knocked them down with ease. My heart didn't see him coming. But did we have it right all along, and was it only meant to be sweet for the summer?

CHAPTER FORTY

Feb 26th

Alexis

The days ended up melting into one another. I spend my time with the girls on the beach. Dad found another lifeguard to replace Colin and me, so he said I could enjoy the last days of my holiday without worrying about work.

Ruby and I are lying on the soft sand with the warm wind swirling around us.

"Hey, Lexi, could I talk to you for a minute?" James's voice has my eyes popping open as he stares down at me with his hands in his pockets. His toe kicks at the sand while he avoids my eyes.

"Make it quick," I say, as I stand and walk away from Ruby. I head over to the brick wall that Colin would sit on, waiting for me, and it makes my heart drop that I won't see him again. I'm too chicken to text him, too. What would I even say? He was right. I am a liar, and I'm too scared to take a chance when my walls have been built back in place, the longer Colin is out of my vicinity. I guess out of sight, out of mind, is a real thing.

"Lex, I'm sorry." James stares at the sand as his words hit my ears, breaking through my thoughts of Colin.

"Why did you do it?" I demand, with my hands resting on my waist. His head tilts to the side as his eyes finally meet mine.

Releasing a sigh, he says, "I was jealous."

"I thought we were friends."

"Come on, Alexis, you can't be that oblivious. You gotta know how I feel about you. I've been waiting for you to feel something for me after all these years. Then you start up a friend with benefits with him, a stranger, and suddenly, you are falling for him. How is that fair?" his voice rises, the longer he talks.

"I'm sorry I never felt that way about you, James, but I can't help who I fall in love with," I whisper.

"You're in love with him? Even after he lied to you about who he is? What the heck, Lexi?" he roars.

Staring at James' red face, it hits me. I love Colin, but because of my stubbornness, we will never be together. Dad was right about more than one thing. It was the wrong timing, and we weren't meant to be in the grand scheme of things.

"You know what? I am, but it's over now. Plus, it's none of your business," I yell back at him.

"It is when I'm your friend."

"Friends don't treat friends how you treated me, James. So, for now, we aren't. I might forgive you someday, but what you did was awful. Right now, I can't be around you," I say, then turn my back and walk away.

"Lexi, come on, don't leave like this," he calls after me, but with another brick adding to the layers around my heart, I make my way back to Ruby.

"You okay?" she asks, as I lie down beside her in the spot I vacated.

"I will be," I whisper, and her fingers intertwine with mine as we lie under the sun. We stay like that with her hand, offering me strength without words. Like an actual friend.

CHAPTER FORTY-ONE

<u>Feb 27th</u>

Alexis

"You'll be back next summer, right?" Dad whispers in my ear as his arms wrap around me.

"You bet. Nothing can keep me away," I say, as his arms squeeze me harder.

"Enjoy your last year of university, love bug. Make lots of memories and don't stress too much about what you want to do next year. It'll all work out in the end. I'm sure."

"Thanks, Dad. Make sure you look after yourself and call me every week," I tell him, as I stare up into his glassy eyes. "Come on, Dad, don't start or you'll set me off."

"What? This? It's my allergies playing up," he jokes.

"You don't have allergies, Dad."

"Yeah. Okay, you guys better get a wriggle on to get home before dark," he says, as he wraps an arm around my mum and delivers a kiss to her temple.

"Take care, Corbin," she says, and Dad grabs my suitcase and puts it into the boot of the car.

"You too, Darce. Message me so I know you guys got home safe," he adds, before I give him another hug goodbye.

"I will," Mum says.

"Lexi," Ruby and Kara holler as they come running down the driveway at top speed.

"What are you guys doing? We already said goodbye this morning," I remind them.

"Yeah, but we both needed one more group hug before you go," Kara says, as tears form on all our faces. We pull each other in. The three of us cling to each other as our sniffles begin.

"I'll miss you guys," I tell them for the hundredth time today.

"We'll miss you too," Ruby adds. We continue to hug each other for a few more minutes before we finally pull away. Wiping the tears from our eyes, I can't help but feel grateful for having these two as my best friends in life.

"The year will race by, and I'll be back before you know it," I say, trying to sound happier than I am. They nod and step back, so I make my way to the car. As Mum and I hop in and she reverses out of the driveway, I wind down the window. I can't believe the summer is over, and I'm headed back home. It's always bittersweet when I leave, but this time it's a lot more painful than usual.

It feels like I'm leaving a summer behind that was once in a lifetime and that I'll never get back. That's all because of Colin and falling in love with him. It was a summer of living in the moment and letting down my guard, but also building those walls back up. A summer that I'll never forget.

I raise my hand and wave as I leave behind my happy place, and they wave back as they grow distant, and then we are on the road.

"Did you have a wonderful summer, honey?"

"Yeah, I did."

"I'm glad."

As we drive along, we come to the bright blue and green sign that says, 'You're leaving Wattle Downs. Thanks for visiting.'

I pull out my phone and force myself not to think too much as I type out the text.

A: *Thank you for the summer. I hope one day we meet again and can start on the right foot x*

I let my guard down for a moment, hit send, and put my phone away. With my head against the window, I close my eyes, trying to sleep since we have a long drive ahead. But then my phone buzzes, catching my attention, and I open the text with my heart pounding in my chest.

C: *Until that day, I'll be thinking of you xx*

As a smile creeps across my face, I close my phone and let the happy memories of the summer wash over me. I've held my walls around me for so long, maybe it's time I finally did something about them so that I can let someone in.

CHAPTER FORTY-TWO

Ten months later

Alexis

My sore eyes peered open to the darkness of my room. It's been a few weeks since my mum left to head back home. I've nearly called her several times to see if she would come back and get me. I don't know if I can stay the entire summer here this time, when all I'm surrounded by are reminders and memories of him.

I rub my eyes with the pads of my fingers, not wanting to hurt them. They're already sore from crying myself to sleep once again. I thought I would be okay. I've had ten months without him, and I kept telling myself that if it was meant to be, it would happen. That's how we left it. Up to fate or the gods or whatever power in the universe that I stupidly thought would bring us back together. Maybe the summer we shared wasn't as great as I remember it? They say that sometimes our memories become distorted, and over time, we remember things in a certain light that sometimes aren't close to reality. That may be what's happened to me. His memories and my memories are both distorted, and all we will have is a memory of something that isn't even close to the reality that it was.

I admit I've searched online for hints about him. A few articles talked about his mom's depression after losing Casey. Both she and her husband stepped back from the spotlight. They were focusing on healing as a family. That article made me leave things to fate. I felt Colin needed time with his family. If we crossed paths again, then it was destiny.

I sit up and rest my head backward to stretch my neck muscles. The pull on my jaw is much needed. I've spent most of the last few days out on my surfboard on the water. Needing time alone to think and be. My friends have left me to wallow. They knew how things between Colin and me had ended, so they thought that was the end. They didn't think I would be this heartbroken. I didn't even think I would be this heartbroken.

It is what it is, I tell myself. We were never meant to be, I guess. I release another breath before I straighten my spine and throw the blanket off my lap. My feet trudge to the bathroom, and I relieve myself and brush my teeth. Back in my room, I pull on a swimsuit and zip up a wetsuit over the top. Leaving the house, I hear Dad's gentle snores from his room. The sun is only now creeping up above the horizon as I grab my board from the side of the house.

Making the trek down the familiar streets, I take the same route I always do to the beach. My bare feet pad against the cool concrete. At least that's one good thing about going for a surf this early in the morning. I don't need to worry about my feet burning to death.

The light chirps from the birds in the nearby trees keep me company as I continue my path. Comfortable in my decision to take one last moment on the water to think of Colin and then finally let him go for good. I reach the wooden planks, covered by the sand, that lead down to the spot that I always surf at. I walk across it until the wood turns into sand, and my steps slow with the resistance. The streak of the sun on the horizon rising shines at me, so I avert my gaze for a moment so as not to get blinded when the full effect of the sunrise occurs. The sounds of the waves crashing on the shore promise a fulfilling surf ahead.

With my head down, I concentrate on my feet, pushing through the dry sand until I reach where it's wet and my feet don't sink as much. Finally, reaching the spot I've always called my own, I push the tip of my board into the soft sand to take a glance at the rising sun. I draw in a breath and feel a mix of emotions. I'm sad, yet I can still see the surrounding beauty. Resolute in my decision, I turn to pull my board out of the sand.

"Quack." The sound has me on alert as the familiar duck with the wonky leg waddles in front of me and nestles himself into the sand like he belongs there. In a trance, I stare at him before a shadow creeps across the sand.

A lone figure steps up beside my board, pushing his board into the sand on the other side of him. My breath catches. His eyes remain focused on the sun rising. I can't pull my eyes away from the beautiful sight in front of me, though. He's clad in his wetsuit, ready to take on the surf like I am.

It's as if time stops, but I know that's not possible as the dawn moves and lights the sky, clearing the darkness away. His eyes still don't acknowledge me, so I break the silence, not able to contain myself any longer.

"You came back?" I stutter, but still his eyes remain on the ocean before him.

"Did you know ducks can find their way home?" he says, as his soothing voice eases the ache in my soul.

"What?" I ask, my brows furrowed in confusion.

"Ducks. Well, birds. They know their way home. Wherever they are in the world, they can make their way home. I don't know if it's a built in radar or if they navigate by minute details only they know, but they find their way home regardless," he explains.

"No, I didn't know that. And I don't understand," I confess. His eyes finally turn to me, and he holds my gaze as the sun reaches higher in the sky, lighting his features. His full lips pull up in the smallest smile, making my heart flutter.

"You could set me free every day, for the rest of forever, but this bird knows its way home, Alexis. You are my home. If you'll have me, that is?"

I draw a few deep breaths into my lungs before I answer.

"I'll have you," I tell him, reaching out a shaky hand for him to take.

He grasps it and shakes it, "I'm Colin, by the way. It's nice to meet you." A smile forms on my lips.

I say, "It's nice to meet you, Colin." Then he pulls me close. Our lips meet, sharing all the love we held inside for ten months. As we pull apart, he takes my hand back in his and uses his other hand to grab his board. I do the same, and we run hand in hand with our boards under our arms towards the ocean that brought us together.

"Is your mum doing okay now?" I ask with concern.

"She's doing much better. Both my parents are. I'm sorry I didn't come sooner. I needed time to sort things out. My family had to learn how to live without Casey. But not a day went by without me thinking of you," he explains.

"I understand. I didn't go a day without thinking of you either."

"Well, here's to starting on the right foot," he says, as his smile spreads wider across his face.

"I like the sound of that," I admit. My smile shines back at him. As our feet carry us to the water, the sun on the horizon, I can't help but feel this summer's going to be better than the last.

THE END.

ALSO BY THIS AUTHOR

TNT Trilogy

Who do you turn to when your whole world falls apart?

Tamsyn's world is struck by tragedy. She doesn't know how to cope so she falls deep into a darkness she so desperately wants out of. Everyone around her is unaware of her struggle until the new boy in town arrives and sees a part of her no one else does: pain.

Tate makes it his mission to help Tamsyn while keeping a secret of his own.

Follow Tate and Tamsyn's journey as they fight to overcome their struggles. These two fragile hearts have only two options: shatter or become unbreakable.

This young adult romance features mental health themes and the beauty of true friendship.

A boy, a girl, a boatload of nineties crazes, mayhem ensues, and you end up with an unforgettable tale.

You know those moments in your life, the ones you know are going to change your life in some way? Well the day I met Lacey was one of those moments for me. I knew deep in my bones my life had been changed forever.

Life is a journey not a destination and meeting Lacey was definitely an experience. It was the start of an epic journey full of love, laughter, tears, sadness and all life has to offer.

Inside these pages is our love story. It may not always be pretty and at times the moments may seem inconsequential, but they shaped us and the world around us. A series of defining moments (that don't always follow a traditional timeline) both great and small intertwined to make up the story of our lives.

Come share our journey with us while you reminisce about the good old days or are introduced to some of the crazes we enjoyed in the nineties when we were younger. It may not always be smooth sailing, but I can promise you it will be worth it. Enjoy.

Chance x

This is a young adult standalone romance.

A secret meet cute, enemies to lovers, grumpy hero, second chance romance.

Four magical words to solve almost any relationship problem.

Let me give you some worthwhile advice.

Pissed off a girl?

Reduced a girl to tears?

Made the most colossal mistake of your life?

Make it right with flowers. Sunflowers to be exact. According to the girl of my dreams, they are a surefire way to make sure she knows you're thinking of her, and they scream effort and thought, not like roses. Roses are out boys, sunflowers are in.

Four little words are all you need to know. SAY IT WITH SUNFLOWERS.

You miss a date? Buy her sunflowers.

You forget to buy takeout on your way home? Buy her sunflowers…. the dirtier the better.

Get your minds out of the gutter. I'm talking about the flowers. The dirtier they are the more important she must be to you or something along those lines. You get the gist.

I won't make the same mistake I did the first time around, so I'll make sure I say it with sunflowers. Go big or go home, right? I just hope my big plan isn't too crazy.

Sully x

This is a NA standalone novel containing some domestic violence scenes.

All Of My Sundays

How long would you wait for the woman you love?

Sophia Philips has one goal in life. She wants to finish school and get as far away from her controlling parents as possible. Unfortunately, people who live to control others rarely want to relinquish their power.

Lorenzo Moretti is moved to a new school to get away from the wrong crowd. His gramps wants what's best for him and apparently, a school with a bunch of snotty rich kids is the best answer. Lorenzo's leather jacket and motorcycle catch the eye of every girl in school but only one girl catches his.

While destiny seems determined to keep them apart, Lorenzo is determined to grab the bull by the horns and fight for what he wants, no matter the cost.

Could a deal with the devil or a marriage pact be the answer he is looking for?